W9-CXN-681

A PLEDGE—AND A PROMISE

I, SEAN O'GRADY, and I, JD ROBERTS, do solemnly swear to do anything—and *everything*—in our power to right past wrongs and reunite our children, Linc and JoAnna. And we're not above some harmless trickery to get our way, either. We take full responsibility for foolishly allowing our bullheadedness and stubborn pride to wedge the young lovers apart. But since we have officially ended our feud, the time has come to knock some sense into our headstrong children and get them to rekindle those fiery sparks of theirs. After all, we have a hankering for grandkids, and we certainly ain't getting any younger....

Signed,

Sean O'Grady
_____

JD Roberts
_____

ΛΛΛΛΛΛΛΛΛΛΛΛΛΛ

⌐FAMILY⌐

ΛΛΛΛΛΛΛ

~ F A M I L Y ~

Myrna TEMTE

Powder River Reunion

Make me a Match

Silhouette Books

Published by Silhouette Books
America's Publisher of Contemporary Romance

If you purchased this book without a cover you should be aware that this book is stolen property. It was reported as "unsold and destroyed" to the publisher, and neither the author nor the publisher has received any payment for this "stripped book."

SILHOUETTE BOOKS
300 East 42nd St.,
New York, N.Y. 10017

ISBN 0-373-82183-2

POWDER RIVER REUNION

Copyright © 1990 by Myrna Temte

All rights reserved. Except for use in any review, the reproduction or utilization of this work in whole or in part in any form by any electronic, mechanical or other means, now known or hereafter invented, including xerography, photocopying and recording, or in any information storage or retrieval system, is forbidden without the written permission of the editorial office, Silhouette Books, 300 East 42nd Street, New York, NY 10017 U.S.A.

All characters in this book have no existence outside the imagination of the author and have no relation whatsoever to anyone bearing the same name or names. They are not even distantly inspired by any individual known or unknown to the author, and all incidents are pure invention.

This edition published by arrangement with Harlequin Books S.A.

® and TM are trademarks of Harlequin Books S.A., used under license. Trademarks indicated with ® are registered in the United States Patent and Trademark Office, the Canadian Trade Marks Office and in other countries.

Visit us at www.romance.net

Printed in U.S.A.

Dear Reader,

Welcome to one of my favorite stories,
Powder River Reunion. While there isn't a real town
named Powder River, Montana, there are many small
communities in the southeastern corner of the state that
could serve as the setting just as well. Ranching, oil
production and tourism keep these little towns alive
economically.

This is dry, rough country, the transition between
America's Great Plains and the Rocky Mountains farther
west. Survival for the early homesteaders took strength,
determination and a willingness to share the work with
neighbors. A large, extended family one could count on
for help was an incredible asset.

Some of the families who now live in this area can look
back on three or four generations who have fought this
land for a living and won. Relationships within and
between these families provide a constant source of
entertainment for those who know their local history—
the really good stuff you hear over ten o'clock coffee at
the bakery, the café, the bowling alley or wherever folks
gather to "visit."

When it comes to matters of the heart, sometimes these
families are more hindrance than help. Take JoAnna Roberts
and Linc O'Grady for instance....

Happy reading,

Myrna Temte

Please address questions and book requests to:
Silhouette Reader Service
U.S.: 3010 Walden Ave., P.O. Box 1325, Buffalo, NY 14269
Canadian: P.O. Box 609, Fort Erie, Ont. L2A 5X3

My thanks to Pat and Vic Phillippi for their endless patience in answering my questions about ranching in Powder River County. And to many, many others who made our years there so memorable—especially, Darlene and Les Thompson, Pat and Dave Gardner, Laura Lee and Vic Ullrich, Wendy and Vic Vallejo, Dick and Bernice Rolfson, and Judy and Jay Mellor.

This book is dedicated to my dear parents, Ben and Lela Gum, who always told me I could accomplish anything I wanted to, and then gave me the tools to do it. Thanks.

Prologue

Cursing the late spring snowstorm under his breath, Sean O'Grady shouldered his way into the Silver Dollar Bar and kicked the door shut behind him with the heel of his boot. He paused in the doorway, whacking his Stetson against his leg to get the snow off while his eyes adjusted to the dim light. A second later, he saw a hand wave from a table at the back of the tavern and he set off across the room with long, angry strides.

When he reached his destination, he unzipped his down-filled vest, pulled a check out of his shirt pocket and slapped it on the table. Glaring at the man he'd driven seventy miles to meet, he said, "Here it is, Roberts. The last payment."

JD Roberts looked at Sean from impassive gray eyes for a moment. He reached across the scarred tabletop, picked up the bank draft and tucked it into the pocket of his plaid flannel shirt. He took a leisurely sip of Scotch from the glass in front of him. Then he lifted his Stetson, combed back his iron-gray hair with one hand before settling the hat on his head again and drawled, "Well, it sure as hell took ya long enough, O'Grady."

Sean's blue eyes bulged out of their sockets, practically shooting sparks and emphasizing the deep lines carved around them from years spent working outdoors. He slammed the palms of his hands on the table. "Why you son of a—"

"Aw, simmer down, Sean. Your Irish is showing."

JD crooked a finger at the bartender, ordering his one-time friend, long-time nemesis, a drink. When he looked back at the lanky Irishman and found him still standing there glaring down at him, JD let out a disgusted sigh and said, "For God's sake, sit down. Now that you've paid back the loan, we've got other things to talk about."

"We got *nothing* to talk about, Roberts."

JD rose out of his chair and leaned forward until he was nose to nose with Sean. His ears turned red with the effort to control his legendary temper as he spat out one word, "Please."

Sean glared for another second, then grudgingly subsided. "Make it quick. I've got calves droppin' in snowdrifts. Why the hell we had to meet in Miles City is beyond me."

He accepted the drink the bartender had carried over and tossed his hat onto an empty chair. When the bartender was out of earshot, he ran a hand over his salt-and-pepper crew cut, adding, "And it wasn't a loan. More like blackmail."

After settling back in his chair, JD rubbed his knuckles as if the damp March air had made his arthritis flare up. "Saved your miserable excuse for a ranch, didn't it?" he pointed out.

"Damn you, JD. That loan cost me my son."

"Yeah, well, your damn son cost me my daughter," JD shot back. "I'd say that makes us even."

Sean held JD's fierce gaze for a moment, then looked away and knocked back the rest of his drink. JD followed suit and signaled the bartender for another round. Neither spoke until the fresh drinks had been delivered.

"I asked you to drive up here so we could have a little privacy," JD said when they'd both taken a sip. "This damn feud we've been carrying on for thirty-five years is what really cost us our kids, Sean. Hell, we've been at it so long, I barely remember what it was all about in the first place. Don'tcha think it's time we ended it?"

"Bull, you don't remember," Sean scoffed. "But since you're gettin' so senile, I'll refresh your memory. We've fought about a lot of things over the years, but the feud started over

Katherine. Lord knows why she chose you instead of me, but even after I married Mary Ellen and Linc was born, our feud was always over Katherine.'' He raised his glass in a toast. ''God rest her soul.''

JD returned the salute and sighed. ''Yeah, she was one hell of a good woman, but she's been gone five years now, Sean. And Mary Ellen's been gone for eight. Can't we be friends again? They both wanted that.''

''You still want that land down by the pond?'' Sean asked. Suspicion glinted in his eyes when he warned, ''I still ain't gonna sell it to ya.''

JD snorted. ''What would I want it for now? Jodie'll just sell off the ranch when I croak.''

Sean relaxed at that and leaned back in his chair. ''I heard she was back east somewhere.''

''Yeah. Says she's too busy with her business to think about gettin' married. I think she's turned into one of them yuppies ya see on TV all the time.''

''She comin' home for the big reunion this summer?'' Sean asked.

JD shrugged. ''Who knows? She might. Linc comin'?''

Sean's mouth stretched into a wide grin. ''Yup. First time since you ran him off. Jodie ever forgive you for doin' that?''

JD shook his head. ''Nope. We've been a little closer since her mother died, but I doubt she'll ever come home to Montana.'' He fell silent for a moment, then asked, ''How about Linc? Still on the rodeo circuit?''

Sean nodded. ''He's gettin' a little old for it, but it don't look like he's ever gonna settle down, either. Get this, he's started modeling.''

''Modeling what?''

''Jeans, boots, underwear.''

JD's bushy eyebrows shot up. ''Underwear! What the hell kind of a thing is that for a man to do?''

''If you'd ever read magazines, JD, you'd know all kinds of guys like baseball players have done it. Make damn good money at it, too.''

''Well, if Linc's makin' so much money, why didn't he help you pay off the loan? The whole mess was his fault anyway.''

"I wouldn't let him help, that's why," Sean retorted. "And as I recall, your sweet little girl wasn't so innocent, either."

"She was only seventeen."

"Linc was only eighteen. And that mess was our fault if it was anybody's. Hell, if we'd had any brains, we'd have known the worst thing we could do was tell two teenagers they couldn't see each other."

"Could be you're right about that," JD answered, rubbing his chin thoughtfully. A moment later he grinned and said, "But I hated your guts too much to care back then."

"No more than I hated yours," Sean replied with an answering grin. Then his grin faded and he let out a disgruntled sigh. "But now they've both grown up and made their own lives. They don't need either one of us."

JD grunted his agreement and leaned forward to rest a beefy forearm on the table. "Yeah. But dammit, O'Grady, we need them. Or at least some grandkids. I haven't worked my butt off on that ranch for thirty-five years to have it end up belonging to strangers and neither have you."

Sean nodded and gulped the rest of his drink. Then scowling at JD, he said, "Well, that's tough, pal. They're gone, and there's not a damn thing we can do about it."

JD drummed his fingers while he pondered the situation. Suddenly his fingers stilled. He looked at Sean and gave him a slow, cunning smile. "Ya wanna bet?"

Chapter One

"And now, folks, we've got a special treat. You all know it's dang near impossible to keep a secret in this town. But, in honor of our fifty-year celebration for Powder River County High School, I believe we've finally done it!"

JoAnna Roberts tuned out the gabby rodeo announcer for a moment while she scanned the crowd. Despite the blistering July heat, the dust and the hard wooden bleachers, everyone appeared to be having a great time. Her father sat beside her, studying the mimeographed program. When he suddenly jerked his head toward the announcer and stiffened, JoAnna straightened up and started listening again as well.

"Our next rider is one of our graduates. In fact, he was a valedictorian. He hasn't been home in twelve years now, but we can't blame him for that. He's been out makin' quite a name for himself."

JoAnna's breath caught in her chest. *No. It couldn't be...* She leaned forward for a better view of the center chute. A cowboy straddled the wooden cage, his feet balanced on the side rails, while an enormous Brahma bull shifted restlessly beneath him.

The announcer's voice droned on. "This young fella's been

the national champion in bull riding for the last five years and the national all-around champ in the Professional Rodeo Cowboys' Association twice."

The cowboy gingerly settled himself onto the animal's broad back, and the bull thrashed in the chute in response. JoAnna winced when she saw the top rails shake with the force of the impact. Bringing the audience to a fever pitch, the announcer finished his introduction.

"Folks, please join me in welcoming back our very own Irish cowboy, ridin' that infamous Brahma, Old Number K6, Linc O'Grady!"

JoAnna's heart climbed right up into her throat when the gate opened. Then Linc and K6 exploded from the chute amid a cloud of dust, wild cheers from the audience and the clanking bell attached to the rigging Linc gripped with his right hand.

The bull bucked with all the power of his huge body, plunging first to the right, then to the left. Linc's hat flew off, but he remained seated, his left arm raised in the classic position. K6 added some whirlwind spinning to his efforts.

Linc stayed aboard the infuriated animal the full eight seconds. He jumped free at the buzzer, landing on his feet to a standing ovation. While the clowns distracted the bull, Linc retrieved his hat and waved to the crowd. His eyes moved back and forth across the bleachers, halting when they reached JoAnna and JD. Flashing a cocky grin, he tipped his hat, then turned and sauntered from the arena.

JoAnna sat down with a hard thump, breathing deeply through her nose in an attempt to still her racing heartbeat. Why on earth had Linc come back to Powder River after all these years? she wondered. And why had he tipped his hat at her like that? Darn him. She could already feel the eyes of the community zeroing in on her and hear the whispers buzzing through the crowd, reviving the old scandal she had worked so hard to live down.

Nudging her father in the ribs, she whispered fiercely, "Why didn't you *tell* me Linc was coming?"

"I didn't know," JD whispered back.

She raised an eyebrow at him. "You're the chairman of the reunion committee."

JD shrugged. "I'm just the coordinator, honey. Sean O'Grady

was in charge of the rodeo committee. You know damn well he'd love to pull a stunt like this without telling me."

Still eyeing her father doubtfully, JoAnna asked, "Has Sean finished paying off the loan then?"

"Yeah."

"You could have at least told me that, Dad. For heaven's sake, it only stands to reason Linc would come back for a visit."

"What difference does it make?" JD countered, his eyebrows drawing into a dark scowl. "You got over him a long time ago. Didn't you?"

JoAnna answered, "Of course I did," and looked away.

JD gave a noncommittal grunt and turned his attention back to the arena. JoAnna copied him, feigning intense interest in each contestant to hide the growing uneasiness she felt. But no matter how hard she tried, she couldn't push Linc's image out of her mind.

After crossing and then uncrossing her legs, she silently assured herself it didn't make one darn bit of difference if Linc was here. It was only the surprise of seeing him again so unexpectedly that had unnerved her. She would undoubtedly run into him during the weekend, but so what?

She certainly wasn't interested in him anymore. And Linc O'Grady, rodeo champion, model and celebrated playboy wouldn't be interested in her anymore, either. After all these years, he was just another old classmate, and she would treat him as such. Right? Right!

With that piece of logic settled firmly in her mind, it was easy to smile when JD put his arm around her and gave her a quick hug.

"You all right, honey?" he asked quietly.

"Fine. I'm a big girl now. Remember?"

JD scowled at her. "You may be twenty-nine years old, Jodie, but you'll always be my little girl."

"D-a-a-d," JoAnna drawled, provoking the expected sheepish grin from her father.

JD rolled his eyes while he dug into his jeans pocket and pulled out a five-dollar bill. He handed it to his daughter. "Excuse *me*, JoAnna. I'm so dry I can't hardly spit. Go get us a beer, will ya?"

Chuckling, JoAnna accepted the money and left. JD watched

her slowly make her way through the crowd. When she reached the steps leading down to the grass outside the arena, he looked over to his right, caught Sean's eye, and wiggled the brim of his hat twice. Sean's hat wiggled in response, and a moment later, JD saw Linc heading for the exit. He pulled his hat back down to shade his eyes, stretched out his long legs and sat back to enjoy the calf roping.

JoAnna smiled as she passed the 4-H refreshment stand, remembering all the years she had worked behind that counter at Fourth of July rodeos. It felt good to stand up and get away from the arena's dust for a few minutes. She got in line at the Jaycee's beer stand and raised one hand to lift her heavy dark hair away from her neck for a moment. Then a deep, familiar voice from the past rumbled in her ear, sending shivers of unwanted anticipation and unexpected pleasure up her spine.

"It's been a long time, Jodie."

Unreasoning panic gripped her for a second, but she sternly reminded herself that she'd gotten over her affair with Linc O'Grady at least a decade ago. Then JoAnna dropped her hand, plastered on the smile she reserved for prospective clients and turned to face him.

"Hello, Linc."

Her normally unflappable poise flapped when she looked up into his face. The ground beneath her feet seemed to rock slightly, and her pulse revved up as her eyes took an immediate inventory of his features.

His chin was a bit more angular than she remembered; his lips were curved into an engaging smile. There were well defined crow's feet etched around his eyes now; his eyes were still that same, heart-melting blue that darkened whenever his emotions were aroused. His eyebrows were more distinctive; his dark hair was still too unruly to remain confined beneath his straw hat.

He was a good six inches taller than her five-feet-eight-inch height; the contours of his body were more solidly muscled than in his youth. He wore the same basic uniform of western shirt, jeans and boots he'd always worn; now his belt buckle proclaimed his prowess as a rodeo champion.

There were signs of the rough life he'd led on the circuit—a new bump along the bridge of his nose, a white scar above his right eyebrow, a different, more leathery texture to his skin than she remembered. The good-looking boy she'd loved when she was seventeen had become a virile, devastatingly attractive man. Her feelings for him at the moment were anything but platonic. And darn it all, she hadn't expected—didn't *want* to feel this way!

JoAnna swallowed hard. Then, realizing she must be staring up at him, she blurted out the first thing that came to mind. "Uh, how are you?" *Oh, that was really original, Roberts*, she chided herself.

Linc's gaze traveled slowly over her face, then his eyes made a quick, thorough inspection of her sleeveless pink blouse and tight jeans, which brought a smile of masculine appreciation to his mouth before he drawled a response.

"I'm fine. You're sure lookin' good."

JoAnna's resolve to treat him as an old classmate hardened when she saw that smile. He was looking at her like...like a wolf licking his chops when he sighted dinner on the hoof! Putting a touch of aloofness into her voice, she said, "Thank you. That was quite a performance you put on for us."

"I'm glad you enjoyed it, Jodie," Linc replied, giving her an aw-shucks-it-was-nothing shrug.

"I go by JoAnna now."

His smile broadened, as if he found the information as amusing as JD did. But he didn't tease her as the old Linc would have done. "I'll try to remember that," he said. "So, uh, what are you doing these days? Teaching school like you planned?"

JoAnna shook her head and resisted the urge to wipe her suddenly sweaty hands on her jeans. "I own an employment agency in Wisconsin."

Linc's eyebrows shot up, and he put his hands on his hips. "Well, I'll be damned," he muttered, shaking his head in amazement. "How in the world did you wind up there?"

She shrugged, as if leaving Powder River hadn't been the most heartrending decision she'd ever made. "I went to college in Madison and liked the area so much I decided to stay."

The line at the beer concession moved on. JoAnna turned away from Linc and placed her order, relieved to have an excuse to break eye contact. Cursing herself for feeling so damnably attracted to him, she inhaled a deep, hopefully unobtrusive breath while Slim Erickson counted out her change. When she couldn't stall another second, she crammed the money into her pocket, accepted the cans of Budweiser from Slim and turned back to face Linc.

Flashing him a friendly, yet dismissive smile, she held up one of the beer cans. "I'd better get this back to JD before it gets warm. Nice seeing you again, Linc."

She started moving away, feeling better with each step she put between them. So she'd felt attracted to him. Big deal. She'd handled the encounter and hadn't betrayed her reaction to him. That was all that mattered. Then his big, callused hand closed around her bare arm, stopping her dead in her tracks.

"Jodie..."

Trying to ignore the surge of heat rushing through her at his touch, JoAnna looked up at him and immediately wished she hadn't. His eyes were almost navy blue as they bored into hers, and she felt naked and vulnerable. She masked her emotions behind a polite smile. "Yes, Linc?"

"I want to talk to you," he answered in a soft tone he might use to soothe a skittish mare.

JoAnna stiffened at that tone. She'd heard it before—every time he'd made love to her. She shut her eyes against the memories threatening to break loose, and his grip on her arm eased. His thumb swept across her skin, leaving gooseflesh in its wake. The scent of leather and horses and an undefinable masculine essence assailed her as he stepped alarmingly close.

She opened her eyes, but didn't look at him. "What about?"

He swept his thumb across her arm again and said bluntly, "About what happened between us twelve years ago."

JoAnna raised her eyes to his and suddenly felt as if she were standing on the edge of a high cliff with a bad case of vertigo. Once she'd been so close to this man, she would have done anything he asked and damned the consequences. But she wasn't seventeen anymore. She'd learned to be more cautious, especially when dealing with men. Appalled to realize she was actually tempted to listen to what he had to say, she pulled out of his grasp with a nervous chuckle.

"Oh, that. I forgot the whole thing years ago, Linc. Don't give it another thought."

Linc's lips tightened, his nostrils flared and his eyes narrowed.

He opened his mouth, but before he could say anything, two giggling teenage girls sashayed up, looking at him with hero-worshipping eyes. One of them asked breathlessly, "Can we have your autograph, Mr. O'Grady?"

An eager army of females ranging in age from thirteen to thirty-six immediately joined the girls. JoAnna moved away while Linc was dealing with the dog-eared rodeo programs and pens thrust at him, chuckling again as an expression of pure consternation crossed his handsome face. Unable to resist, she wiggled her fingers at him around a beer can and said, "Bye, Linc."

"We'll talk later," he called after her before turning to the women clamoring for his attention.

JoAnna muttered, "Don't count on it, Buster," and headed back toward the bleachers. She didn't want to talk to him again—not later, not ever. She couldn't imagine why he'd want to talk about their affair after all these years, and she didn't much care.

She'd wasted a whole miserable year of her life after Linc O'Grady left Powder River. And when she found out about JD's role in Linc's sudden departure, she had lost another man she'd loved dearly—her father. It had been a hard blow for "Daddy's girl" to take.

But her relationship with JD had improved recently. Though it wasn't the same as it had been before her affair with Linc and probably never would be the same again, she loved the old curmudgeon. She had finally convinced him to stop interfering in her life, but the way he despised Sean O'Grady, she doubted JD would continue to do so if he got the slightest inkling she was getting involved with Linc again.

She'd be a lot better off if she avoided him for the rest of the weekend. When the reunion was over, Linc would go back to the rodeo circuit and she'd probably never see him again. But JD was her only living relative. She glanced back over her shoulder for one last look at Linc but could only see part of his hat above the crowd surrounding him.

It was just too darn bad he hadn't gone bald and grown a paunch.

* * *

Linc automatically scrawled autographs and watched JoAnna from the corner of his eye until she disappeared into the grandstand. He'd come back to Powder River for two reasons. One was to see his dad and all the improvements he'd made on the Shamrock ranch. The other, more important reason, was to see Jodie Roberts again. Well, now he'd seen her.

It was too bad she hadn't gotten dumpy and married, he thought. He'd been hoping to find her with scraggly hair, a boring husband with bad breath, and three or four snot-nosed kids clinging to her legs. Then he could have wiped her out of his memory for good the way his friend Marty Taylor wiped out a bad take with the computer in his recording studio—one push of a button and poof, she'd be gone.

But damn it all, she was gorgeous. With her black hair cut shorter so that it brushed her shoulders before curling under, her big brown eyes that still did funny things to his stomach and her figure more curved with maturity but still slender, she was even more beautiful than he'd remembered.

He hadn't wasted his time mooning over her or lived as a monk since he'd left Powder River. The fight they'd had the last time he'd seen her had convinced him that his dad was right— Jodie Roberts was nothing but a spoiled brat who wasn't worth breaking his heart over. Unfortunately he'd never been able to forget her, though God knew he'd tried.

The constant travel and excitement of the rodeo circuit had made him famous and restored his battered ego after his affair with Jodie. The modeling he'd started out doing for kicks and his partnership with Marty Taylor had made him financially independent. On the surface, at least, he had everything a man could want.

But over the last couple of years, he'd felt increasingly dissatisfied with his life. Lately he'd been giving some thought to settling down. Unfortunately, whenever he started getting serious about a woman, his memories of Jodie would kick in and he'd know deep in his gut that this woman, no matter how beautiful or sweet or loving, was not the one he would marry. If she wasn't Jodie, she wasn't the right woman. It was as simple and as complicated as that.

Knowing that he was comparing every woman he met to Jodie had frustrated him, infuriated him, damn near driven him crazy.

He'd come to the reunion determined to put an end to the hold she had on him. After that lousy crack she'd made about forgetting the whole thing years ago—as if what they'd shared had been so much garbage—he was even more determined to do so. It shouldn't be all that hard to accomplish.

He hadn't seen even a hint of the girl he'd once loved in the cool, sophisticated woman he'd just talked to. Compared to his memories of Jodie, JoAnna Roberts had shown about as much genuine emotion as a Barbie doll. He didn't like to admit he was still attracted to her at all, but he was—on a purely physical level, of course. Maybe that attraction was the answer to his problem.

Linc's lips curved into a cynical smile as he wrote his name across the front of a well-endowed young woman's T-shirt in red Magic Marker. He tolerated the kiss she insisted on giving him, then ignored the come-hither look in her eyes as he reached for the next program and turned his mind back to JoAnna.

Yeah, maybe his attraction to her was the answer. No matter what she'd said, he *knew* she wasn't completely indifferent to him. It might take a little doing, but he figured he could get her into bed before the reunion was over. He'd have a roll in the hay with her for old time's sake, get her out of his system and make damn sure her old man found out about it.

For twelve years, he'd dreamed of getting back at JD Roberts for all the humiliation and pain he'd caused him. He'd missed his own mother's funeral because of that stinking loan JD had forced on his dad. What better way to get revenge than to show the old bastard Linc O'Grady could still have his precious daughter if he wanted. *And what if Jodie gets hurt?* his conscience asked. *And what if you're not satisfied with that one roll in the hay?*

Linc pushed those uneasy thoughts aside and continued signing autographs. After the brush-off she'd given him, he doubted JoAnna would be hurt. As for the other, well, he'd worry about that if and when it happened.

As soon as there was a break in the crowd of autograph hounds, Linc bought a couple of beers and went back to the arena. Sean accepted the can Linc offered him with a grumpy complaint.

"A man could die of thirst waitin' for you, Linc. What took ya so long?"

Linc tipped the brim of his hat forward to get the sun out of his eyes. "I signed a few autographs. And I ran into Jodie Roberts."

"Oh for God's sake," Sean muttered, popping the top on his beer can before turning to glare at his son.

"What's the matter with you?" Linc asked his father. "You didn't think I'd go the whole weekend without seeing her, did you?"

Sean took a long gulp of his beer, then shook an admonishing finger under Linc's nose. "That gal is nothing but trouble, and you know it. Her old man won't like it if he thinks you're sniffin' around her again, so stay the hell away from her, will ya?"

Linc's jaw hardened, and anger flashed from his eyes like lightning from a thunderhead. "I don't give a damn about JD Roberts."

"Now listen, boy, I just got the old SOB paid off, and I don't want any more trouble with him. Is that too much to ask?"

"Yeah, Dad. It is," Linc answered with quiet determination. "The deal's off since you paid off that loan. I aim to see a lot of Jodie before I leave. And if JD doesn't like it, he can stuff it."

Linc turned and faced the arena floor then, his expression indicating that as far as he was concerned, the conversation was over. Sean swallowed another gulp of beer, stretched his legs out as far as he could in the cramped bleachers, then reached up with his left hand and wiggled the brim of his hat twice.

Over in the center section of seats, JD Roberts smiled.

Chapter Two

"And that concludes our rodeo program this morning. Hope you enjoyed it as much as I did," the announcer said. "I've been asked by the reunion committee to direct you all across the road to the city park for the picnic. Each table is arranged to hold two graduating classes, so be sure and find the right one before you sit down. Have a nice afternoon, folks."

By the time JoAnna and JD joined the ragged line snaking across the park to the buffet tables, the air was filled with the aroma of barbecued beef and the laughter and chatter of old friends catching up with each other after years, and in some cases, decades of separation. JoAnna raised one hand to shade her eyes from the sun's harsh rays and nearly jumped right out of her boots when two small strong arms unexpectedly wrapped around her waist from behind.

"Guess who," a giggly little voice commanded.

Instantly recognizing the voice, JoAnna smiled and said, "Pee-Wee Herman."

"Nope."

"Joe Montana."

"Nope."

"Superman."

"Nope."

"Well, then," she said slowly, shifting her feet for a quick pivot and reaching down to scoop the little boy up into her arms. "It must be that handsome devil, Timmy Scott!"

Timmy shrieked with laughter at JoAnna's sudden move, flailing his hands in a futile attempt to prevent her from planting kisses all over his red hair and freckled face. They grinned at each other for a moment before JoAnna set him back on his feet with a theatrical moan.

"Oof! You're getting awfully big, Tim. Better stop that growing or you'll turn into a giant."

"Aw, you're just teasin' me," Timmy replied.

"Where's your mom?"

He pointed toward a line of picnic tables covered with white paper on the other side of the park. JoAnna's gaze followed his outstretched finger and she chuckled with delight when she located the petite woman who had been her best friend since first grade. Timmy started hollering and waving his arms, and a second later, the blonde looked up. When she recognized JoAnna, Gaye Scott waved, hurriedly finished her task of setting out decorations and ran across the grass.

JoAnna ran to meet her. The two women hugged each other like long-lost sisters. "Oh, it's so good to see you!" Gaye said in her usual machine-gun delivery. "You were supposed to call me when you got in. And when you didn't, I was afraid you decided not to come at the last minute."

Linking her arm through Gaye's, JoAnna walked her over to Timmy, explaining, "My flight into Billings was late. I didn't get in until after midnight."

Timmy took off to play with his friends while Gaye and JD greeted each other. Once JD had gone back to his conversation with another rancher, Gaye pulled JoAnna aside. Though she lowered her voice, she couldn't keep the excitement she felt out of it. "Have you seen him yet?"

JoAnna sighed inwardly and told herself she should have expected this. Gaye was an incurable romantic despite her ex-husband Brady's sudden allergy to responsibility, which had resulted in his leaving to "find himself" three years ago. Ever since high school, she had insisted that JoAnna and Linc were star-crossed lovers, a modern-day Romeo and Juliet, who would one day be reunited if there was any justice in this world.

"Have I seen who?" JoAnna asked, nodding and smiling at one of her former teachers who walked by.

"Linc, *idjit*," Gaye replied, shaking her head in disgust. "Who else?"

JoAnna shrugged. "I talked to him for a few minutes at the beer stand."

"And?" Gaye prodded impatiently.

"And what?" JoAnna replied, impatience creeping into her voice as well. "I talked to him. We were friendly and polite, but it was no big deal. How's business at the store?"

Gaye's face fell so abruptly JoAnna nearly laughed out loud. But then her friend's green eyes took on a calculating gleam, and JoAnna felt a twinge of uneasiness. "Never mind the store, and stop being such a liar," Gaye said, grinning. "I've seen Linc, too, JoAnna. And like the old song says, he could park his boots under my bed anytime."

JoAnna sighed—audibly this time—then laughed at herself for even thinking about trying to keep anything from Gaye. "All right. I'll admit he's attractive. But so what, Gaye? We're strangers now."

"You could get to know him again."

JoAnna shook her head at her friend's eternal optimism. "I don't want to," she said firmly. "Now let's talk about something else. Okay?"

Gaye tipped her head to one side and thought for a moment before asking softly, "Are you scared of him?"

JoAnna glanced away while she considered the question, then looked her friend in the eye. "Yes, I guess I am," she admitted. "After what happened last time, wouldn't you be?"

Nodding her agreement, Gaye put an arm around JoAnna's waist and nudged her toward the gap that had formed in the line while they talked. "Yeah, I guess I would. My worst nightmare is that one of these days Brady will show up with some perfectly reasonable explanation for abandoning Timmy and me and ask me to take him back."

"Oh, Gaye, you wouldn't—"

"I don't know if I would or not. Sometimes I hate him enough to kill him. But there are other times..." Gaye gave a sad little shrug that tore at JoAnna's heart, then looked up, wrinkled her nose and chuckled. "Lord, would you listen to us? We're supposed to have fun at this shindig."

While they waited to reach the food-laden tables, Gaye filled JoAnna in on the latest developments at the clothing store she owned and then launched into a hilarious description of several of their former classmates JoAnna hadn't seen yet. When they finally filled plates for themselves and one for Timmy, a disturbing thought struck JoAnna. "Which class is our year sitting with? The one ahead of us or the one behind?"

Her eyes sparkling with amused understanding, Gaye said, "The class ahead of us."

JoAnna rolled her eyes toward the bright blue sky before muttering, "Somebody up there hates me."

Gaye chuckled sympathetically. "Come on, it won't be that bad. I doubt if anyone else will even remember—"

"Hah! In *this* town? You've got to be kidding."

Drawing herself up to her full five-feet, three-inch, height, Gaye solemnly promised, "Don't worry, JoAnna. I'll protect you. Now come on."

Calling to Timmy to come and eat, she took off across the grass. JoAnna followed reluctantly, wondering if Gaye planned to protect her from Linc or from the cattier members of their class.

Powder River, Montana, population 967, didn't have a health spa, a frozen yogurt shop or a Kmart store. It didn't have a McDonald's, Burger King or Pizza Hut. It didn't have a hospital, a TV station or a shopping mall. But it had a grapevine second to none.

With the exception of a few disgruntled souls, the gossips were not intentionally vicious; boredom with the daily routine of a small rural community and too few outside distractions provided ample motivation to take an active interest in one's neighbors and their affairs. To be fair about it, JoAnna had to admit the community was extremely democratic about choosing its subjects for discussion; anybody who did *anything* out of the ordinary—from getting your hair frosted to shooting your spouse—was considered fair game.

The problem was that if you'd entertained the home folks with an escapade once, you were more likely to draw their attention again. JoAnna suspected that many people were hoping something exciting would happen at this reunion—something they could hash over while waiting in line at the bank, at the post office for the daily mail pickup and over ten o'clock cups of coffee at the bowling alley.

But darn it, she didn't want to be that "something" this time. Her reputation had been dragged through manure once because of Linc O'Grady. Once was enough.

Linc had already drawn attention to her this morning at the arena when he tipped his hat. By talking to him at the beer stand, she might've already set a few tongues wagging. If he approached her in public again, even just to talk to her, everyone would assume something was going on between them. The whispers would start, and then JD would blow his stack and *really* give them all something to talk about.

Ah, the joys of coming home, she thought, wry amusement tugging up the corners of her mouth. Realistically there was nothing she could do about the gossip in Powder River. If people wanted to talk about her, they would. But if she treated Linc exactly the same way she treated everyone else, maybe the gossips would find them too boring and turn their attention elsewhere.

"Yeah, and one of these days Arnie Zwiffelhoffer's sow will fly to Miles City," she muttered under her breath.

Gaye found a spot wide enough for three on the west side of the table, and JoAnna sat down between Timmy and Marilyn Watson's ten-year-old son Kevin. There was no sign of Linc, but at least he couldn't sit beside her when he did show up, she thought with a smug smile. Unfortunately Kevin was in a rush to get back to playing with his friends and visiting cousins. He practically inhaled his food and left the table before anyone else started eating.

JoAnna watched the uncouth little varmint run toward the baseball diamond with a sinking sensation in the pit of her stomach. Nevertheless, she joined in the conversation, ignoring the empty seat on her left as best she could. Sandy Barber, a compulsive talker with an irritating tendency to whine, extolled the virtues of her four marvelously gifted children for what seemed like a solid hour. After that, it was almost a relief when a dark shadow blossomed on the white paper beside her plate and everyone on the other side of the table suddenly stopped talking.

Heads whipped around. Elbows nudged. Whispers and quiet snickers started at the ends of the table and traveled toward the center. Eyes flashed expectantly from the shadow's owner to JoAnna and back again.

"Mind if I sit down?" Linc's deep voice drawled above her.

JoAnna schooled her features into a nonchalant smile and looked up at him. "Of course not."

Linc set his plate down and climbed over the wooden bench, greeting everyone around him with a smile and a handshake. Gradually the others at the table began asking him about the rodeo circuit, and those who couldn't hear his answers went back to their own conversations. JoAnna buttered Timmy's roll for him and asked him about his pets, grateful for the distraction his happy chatter provided—not that it provided much.

The seating at the table was cramped for everyone. Linc's shoulders were so broad, his right arm brushed against her left one every time he raised his fork to his mouth. Despite her best efforts to block him out, she found herself listening to him talk and enjoying the familiar cadence of his speech. He laughed at a story the former class clown, Todd Hanson, told him, and the sound brought back heart-wrenching memories of times when he had laughed with her.

Sitting so closely beside him, JoAnna couldn't avoid seeing his hands move in smooth, confident gestures, and she remembered those hands touching her with both tenderness and passion. Her mouth went dry, her throat felt tight, and sweat broke out at her hairline that had nothing to do with the ninety-degree heat. She inhaled a deep breath to steady her nerves, and inadvertently filled her head with the musky scent of his warm body.

She had just decided to make an excuse—any excuse—to leave the table, when Cathy Williams, a former cheerleader who must have gained at least fifty pounds since graduation, batted her eyelashes at Linc and said in a voice that easily carried to both ends of the table, "I can't believe a handsome man like you hasn't gotten married yet, Linc."

"You finally gettin' tired of poor old Dan, Cath?" Todd Hanson asked with a broad grin.

Cathy reached over and gave her husband's knee a reassuring

pat while sending Todd a withering look. "Oh, hush, Todd. I'm just curious like everybody else. I mean, it seems kinda funny that Linc and Jodie were such a hot couple when we were in school, and now they're still the only ones who've never been married."

"I know why JoAnna's never been married," Timmy piped up, smiling proudly when he suddenly received undivided attention from so many adults.

"Why's that, Timmy?" Todd asked.

Timmy puffed out his chest and informed the group, "She's waitin' for me to grow up so I can marry her."

Everyone laughed, and JoAnna leaned down to kiss the top of the little boy's head. "That's right," she said. "I know a quality man when I see one."

Cathy waited until the answering laughter had died down. Then she gave JoAnna a malicious smile before turning her attention back to Linc. "I'll bet Jodie's forgiven you for dumping her by now, and you still make a nice-looking couple. Maybe you could take pity on her and keep her from turning into an old maid."

JoAnna inhaled a sharp breath. She'd known since the minute Linc sat down beside her that somebody would probably make a remark about their past affair, but she hadn't expected such a frontal assault. She shot a glance at Linc, but looked away before he could see the mortification that must be showing in her eyes.

Gaye jumped into the conversation before Linc could respond to Cathy. "I swear, some things in Powder River never change. You had the meanest mouth in the class twelve years ago and you still do, Cathy. Maybe we ought to give you a reward for that." She gave the hefty woman a smile sweet enough to give her cavities.

Though she was grateful for Gaye's interference, JoAnna had had enough. "Much as I'm enjoying this conversation," she said calmly, picking up her paper plate and plastic silverware, "I have to go take some pictures for JD. Enjoy yourselves." She climbed off the picnic bench with as much grace as she could muster and left, her head held high and her stride unhurried.

"Yeah, some things never change," Cathy remarked in a snide tone. "Jodie was stuck-up back then, and she's stuck-up now."

"And you were jealous of her because she was so smart and Linc liked her instead of you!" Gaye answered.

"Oh come off it, Gaye. It's easy to get good grades when all you do is study. Jodie was our valedictorian because she didn't have one date during our senior year—not even for the prom. And Linc didn't think she was so great after he got what he wanted or he wouldn't have walked out on her."

"Oh gir-ruls," Todd interrupted.

Gaye and Cathy turned on him and snarled in unison, "What?"

"I hate to spoil your fun," he informed them with a devilish grin, "but Linc and Jodie are gone."

The two women gaped at him for an instant, then turned in time to see Linc's broad shoulders moving down the aisle between the crowded tables in the same direction JoAnna had taken.

Disturbed by the scene that had just taken place at the table, Linc hurried after JoAnna. On the one hand, he'd have liked to wring Cathy Williams's pudgy neck for being so cruel; on the other hand, maybe Cathy had done him a favor. For an instant there when her vicious remark about JoAnna had registered and dead silence had fallen over the table, he'd seen a glimpse of his old Jodie.

JoAnna had recovered quickly and made a dignified exit she could be proud of, but she hadn't fooled him. Somewhere in the back of his mind, he had questioned her hard veneer of sophistication when he'd noticed the warm relationship she shared with Gaye's son. But that one flash of vulnerability in JoAnna's eyes when Cathy attacked her was enough to really make him wonder if his first impression of JoAnna this morning hadn't been a false one.

Maybe she'd been nervous and uncomfortable about seeing him again. He could understand that; he'd been pretty uncomfortable himself. If that were the case, maybe her aloofness had been an act.

Then again, he might be seeing softness and vulnerability in her because he wanted to see it; the Jodie Roberts he'd known and loved was a warm, generous human being, and he hated to think that person no longer existed. But maybe she just had a soft spot for that one little boy. Maybe she'd simply been surprised by Cathy's barbed remarks. Maybe she *was* as cold and hard as he'd thought she was.

That left him with a pile of ifs and maybes. The only thing he knew for certain was that he needed to spend more time with her before making any judgments.

Linc slowed down when he saw JoAnna stop beside a red GMC pickup with the Double R brand stenciled on the side. She yanked open the passenger door, grabbed a purse and camera bag off the floor and dropped them none too gently onto the seat, and he couldn't help smiling when he realized at least one thing about Jodie Roberts hadn't changed. She still had her old man's temper.

He moved forward again when she dug a brush out of the purse and winced when he saw her start jerking it through her windblown hair in long, punishing strokes. Approaching the truck silently, he didn't have to wonder who she meant when he heard her muttering, "Damn him. Damn him. Damn him," with each stroke of the brush. He'd always thought she was adorable when she was madder than hell.

Crossing his arms over his chest, Linc leaned one hip against the side of the pickup and struggled to keep the amusement he felt out of his voice. "Might go bald if you keep that up."

Whirling to face him, JoAnna pointed her brush at him. "Get the hell away from me, Linc O'Grady."

"You plan to shoot me with that brush if I don't?" he asked.

JoAnna glared at him, gulped, then whirled back around and shoved the brush into her purse. He could feel her struggling for control and guessed she was probably counting to ten. His amusement waned when he heard her take in a deep, shuddering breath. He put his hand on her shoulder and said, "Listen, Jodie, I know you're upset—"

Turning to face him again, JoAnna slapped his hand away. "No, *you* listen," she told him in a low, furious whisper, "I don't want *anything* to do with you. Don't touch me. Don't talk to me. Don't even come near me again."

"For cryin' out loud," Linc protested. "I'm sorry you were embarrassed back there, but you can't let a witch like Cathy Williams get to you."

"Oh yeah? Well maybe if you'd stuck around a little longer last time, Linc, I might be interested in hearing what you have to say. But you took off before all the cow pies hit the fan, and I was stuck here another whole year. What you heard back there at the table was just a small sample of the crud I had to take, so don't tell me how I should feel. Now will you *please* just go away and leave me alone?"

It was Linc's turn to gulp as he looked into her eyes and saw her hurt and humiliation laid bare. One part of him wanted to cheer; though she'd just raked him over some pretty hot coals, his Jodie was suddenly standing right in front of him. Another part of him ached inside for her, and a familiar stab of guilt pierced his conscience. He wanted to pull her into his arms and comfort her as he would have done years ago, but he knew she wouldn't stand for it.

Instead, he answered bluntly, "No. I can't do that. We have some unfinished business to settle."

"After twelve years?" she jeered. "Give me a break."

"After twelve years." He widened his stance and put his hands on his hips. "I won't take no for an answer."

She glared at him for a long moment. Then she looked away, her shoulders slumped as if the fight had suddenly gone out of her, and she asked, "Why are you doing this to me?"

"Doing what, Jodie? I'm only trying to talk to you."

She looked back at him, livid with anger again. "Don't call me Jodie," she snapped, her voice pitched so low he had to strain to hear her. "And you know damn well what you're doing. Every gossip in this county is over there in the park, practically falling off a picnic bench trying to see what we're doing."

"So what? What do you care what they think?"

"JD's not getting any younger. One of these days I plan to come back and help him run the ranch. And when I do, I'd like to be able to live in peace."

Looking down at the toes of his boots, Linc slowly shook his head and blew out a gusty sigh. "I understand what you're saying, and I don't want to make things hard for you." Then he lifted his head and looked her squarely in the eye. "But you were the best friend I ever had in this town, and I've never felt

good about the way we parted. I want to talk to you about it.
What's wrong with that?''

"Linc, there's no point in—"

"There doesn't have to be a point. Come to the dance with
me tomorrow night," he suggested impulsively, liking the idea
even more once it had popped out of his mouth.

"Are you loco? JD would have a fit, and so would your dad."

"Let 'em. We're not kids they can boss around anymore. Do
you realize I've made love with you but I've never danced with
you? And if we're right out in plain sight where everyone can
see us, what'll they have to talk about? Come on, JoAnna, it'll
be fun."

Silence stretched out between them as she looked up into his
eyes. A ghost of a smile played at the corners of her mouth, and
he could see she was tempted, at least a little bit. Yeah, his Jodie
was in there all right. And by golly, he was going to coax her
out.

But then she blinked and shook her head, and the cool, indifferent mask that had irked him so much this morning reap-
peared. Turning away, she reached into the truck and picked up
her purse and camera case.

"Come to the dance with me, JoAnna," he repeated when
she turned back to face him again.

"No." She slammed the pickup door shut. "I'm not into nostalgia. Nice seeing you again, Linc."

Linc bit back a curse as she walked away. Damn the infernal
woman. He'd felt close to her there for a minute, as if a small
window in time had opened up and the resulting breeze had
blown away the bitterness and... Oh, hell, maybe he *was* loco.

Well, even so, he wasn't done with JoAnna Roberts. Not by
a long shot.

JoAnna felt the touch of his gaze burning into her spine every
step of the way back to the park and wondered if *she* wasn't
crazy. Because for a moment there, a part of her had wanted to
stay and hear what Linc had to say. Part of her wanted to thumb
her nose at the busybodies and their feuding fathers and go to
the dance with him, because darn it, it *would* be fun.

Though they hadn't been allowed to date the way the other

kids had, JoAnna had always had fun with Linc. Their stolen hours together had been spent riding horses, swimming in the pond and sitting in the shade of a big old tree sharing their most private thoughts and dreams. She had dated dozens of other men over the years, but she'd never experienced with anyone else that deep level of intimacy she'd known with Linc. Lord, how they'd talked and laughed and kissed....

Shaking her head as if to clear it, JoAnna chided herself for indulging in nostalgia after all. The heat must be getting to her. She was not, absolutely *not*, going to give in to that impulsive, reckless part of herself that had gotten her into so much trouble in the first place. Oh, damn the man for being so attractive.

For the next hour, JoAnna moved through the crowd snapping pictures with her Nikon. She sat through the speeches with the class of 1945 and got several good shots of Powder River's mayor and the governor of Montana at the podium. When the governor finally finished his speech, JD took over the microphone.

"I hope you folks have enjoyed the reunion so far." He paused while the crowd whistled and clapped in response. "The reunion committee has decided to ask all the valedictorians to meet at the gym tomorrow night before the dance and have a group picture taken. We'll hang it in the high school lobby in honor of this celebration. That'll be at seven o'clock, and the dance will start at eight on the town square."

The audience applauded again, and JD held up his hands for quiet. "Just one last quick announcement," he promised. "I need to see the members of the reunion committee right here for a short meeting before you leave. See you all tomorrow night."

Confusion reigned over the park while people packed up belongings and collected their children, and the cleanup committee broke down the extra tables that had come from the schools and local churches. JoAnna finished off her last roll of film, walked over to one of the park's permanent picnic tables and sat down to wait for JD, trying without much success to put Linc O'Grady out of her mind.

Linc shoved the end of the last table into the back of Todd Hanson's pickup, slammed the tailgate shut and waved as Todd drove away. Brushing off his hands on the seat of his pants, he walked back to the park to see if his dad was ready to leave. Since the reunion committee was still meeting over by the podium, he looked around for a place to sit and spotted JoAnna heading for a table under the shade of an old cottonwood tree.

He'd cooled off since their confrontation by the pickup and had already scrapped his cynical plan to seduce JoAnna and get back at JD. Although he'd still find a way to teach the old SOB a lesson if he could, he knew that he couldn't consciously do anything to hurt the woman Jodie Roberts had become. But did he really want to approach her again?

Her refusal to talk to him was damned irritating. On the other hand, he could understand her reluctance. In a bigger town few people would have given a second thought to a couple of teenagers who'd gotten caught making love, but in Powder River... Well, he could imagine what she'd gone through after he left.

But did she ever remember the good times they'd spent together? Had that wacky sense of humor he'd enjoyed so much survived? Damn it, he wanted to know at least that much about her before the reunion ended.

He set off across the park, angling his route to prevent her from seeing him before he wanted her to. After their last encounter, she was liable to be as jumpy as a rabbit with a hawk circling overhead where he was concerned. He braced one shoulder against the tree, crossed one foot over the other and watched her pack away her camera. In fact, he'd been watching her all afternoon.

Lord, she was gorgeous, even with her raven hair mussed again from the breeze and her sweet mouth bare of lipstick. She zipped up the camera case and turned around on the bench, giving him a clear view of her profile. His lungs forgot how to breathe when she leaned back with both elbows on the table behind her, pushing her full breasts into sharp relief. Maybe JoAnna wasn't into nostalgia, he thought with a wry smile, but his body sure was.

She might have heard his quiet gasp when his lungs started working again. She might have simply sensed his presence. Whatever the reason, she slowly turned her head and looked at him.

Their eyes met and held, and his heart lurched when he saw a flash of emotion, perhaps sadness or regret or longing—it was too quick for him to be certain—cross her face. Then she dropped her arms to her sides, her expression hardened, and in a tone she might use to greet an obnoxious magazine salesman or a drug pusher, she said, "Oh. It's you again."

Linc chuckled. He couldn't help it when he could see how hard she was trying to look snooty. He pushed himself away from the tree, shoved his hands into his pockets and ambled over to sit beside her on the bench.

"Yeah, it's me," he drawled, scooting closer to her until she moved away, eyeing him warily.

He smiled at her, and she snapped her head around to face forward like a buck private ordered to attention. He sighed with resignation when he saw the mulish set to her chin. "Nice weather we're havin' for the reunion," he said.

No response. Linc leaned back, stretched out his legs and added, "Looks like just about everybody came home for it."

No response.

"You still write poetry, Jodie? I mean, uh, JoAnna," he corrected himself while he moved closer to her again. "I still write a poem or two every now and then."

She scooted away again without acknowledging his presence. Damn, but she could be an obstinate critter.

"I saw old Mr. Blake about twenty minutes ago," he told her, continuing his ridiculous pursuit across the picnic bench. He figured they'd be lucky if one of them didn't get a splinter in the butt, but he was willing to risk it. "Remember the time Todd mooned him from the bus window?"

One side of her mouth twitched, but she stared straight ahead and didn't speak as she retreated.

"You ever see one of my underwear ads?" he asked, relentlessly inching closer.

A sudden blush tinted her cheeks, and she shot him a guilty, sideways look that told him more plainly than words that she had, and better yet, she'd liked what she'd seen.

"Ya know," he drawled, risking his buns again, "they paid me a lot of money for that job, but I felt like a damn fool standing there in those fancy drawers while everybody else had all their clothes on. Takes a lot of people to do a shoot like that."

An odd, strangled sound leaked out the side of her pursed lips. She looked at him and the message in her eyes was as plain as if she'd spoken it out loud. *"Stop. Please stop or I'll laugh. And damn you, I don't want to."*

If they got much closer to the end of the bench it would probably tip over, but he smiled wickedly and moved closer anyway. "You might as well talk to me and get it over with, honey. 'Cause if you don't, I'm gonna act like a bad case of acne all weekend."

Her eyes widened at his playful tone, and her voice wavered as she took the bait. "Acne?"

He leaned down until their noses nearly touched. She started to scoot over again, but stopped when the bench creaked in warning. "Yup," he answered. "I'll just keep poppin' up wherever you least want to see me, and I won't go away till I'm damn good and ready."

Her eyes slammed shut, and she shook her head, desperately mashing her lips together. Linc tipped his head to one side and waited, thinking, *Go on, JoAnna. I dare you not to laugh.* She sucked in a ragged breath and held it for a least half a minute. Then she sputtered, "Linc, that's terrible!" and surrendered to the laughter he'd worked so hard to pry out of her.

He closed his eyes for a second, savoring that sound the way a connoisseur would savor a glass of a rare vintage wine. It was a genuine, melodious laugh that came from deep inside her chest, not the high-pitched titter some women had that set a man's teeth on edge. Lord, he'd missed that sound over the years and hadn't even realized it until now.

When he felt her inhale another shaky breath, he looked at her, their eyes met, and she started laughing again. He found himself joining in and slid his arm around her.

Gasping for air, she unconsciously relaxed into the curve of his arm. She sighed, then murmured, "Only *you* would say something like that."

"Made ya laugh, didn't it?"

"You always did."

She smiled sincerely at him for the first time, her dark eyes shining with pleasure. A lump the size of a saddle horn lodged in his throat as he realized that small window in time had swung open again. *This* was how it used to be between them. *This* was why he'd never been able to forget her.

He raised his hand and gently touched her cheekbone with his fingertips. He would have kissed her then, and he thought she would have let him, but a raspy male voice shattered the moment.

"Jodie! Time to go home."

JoAnna stiffened at the sound of her father's voice. She glanced at JD, then shut her eyes for a moment and muttered, "Oh, Lord. Here we go again."

Slowly lowering his hand from JoAnna's cheek, Linc turned and looked at the only man he'd ever honestly hated. JD Roberts hadn't changed much. His hair was a little whiter, his face a little more weathered, but he looked damn intimidating when he loomed over you, glaring down at you with his cold gray eyes.

Linc glared right back. Taking his time about it, he stood up, determined to make JD be the first one to look away. After a moment, JD nodded and said, "O'Grady."

Linc's nod was equally slight, his tone equally curt. "Roberts."

Sean O'Grady approached the group. Taking one look at his son and JD squared off, he said, "Let's go, Linc."

Linc glanced at his father and nodded before giving JD another long, hard stare. Then he turned his back on both older men and offered JoAnna his hand. She gave her father a defiant look and hesitated only a second before putting her hand in Linc's, allowing him to help her to her feet.

JoAnna's hand was icy, and Linc could feel tension radiating from her body as she stood beside him, but she smiled easily and turned to Sean. "Hello, Mr. O'Grady. Your committee put on a wonderful rodeo this morning."

Sean returned her smile and answered gruffly, "Thanks, Jodie. Good to see you again." He cleared his throat and tipped his hat back on his head before clapping Linc on his right shoulder. "Well, come on, son. We've got things to do."

Linc shrugged off his father's hand. "In a minute, Dad." Ignoring JD he turned to face JoAnna. Still holding her hand and smiling down at her, he asked, "Sure you don't want to come to the dance with me?"

She glanced toward JD and Sean and sighed at the tense, expectant expressions on both their faces. Then, softening her refusal with a wry smile, she shook her head. "No thanks, Linc."

Gently sqeezing her hand in understanding, Linc replied, "All right. But don't forget the acne."

Linc and JoAnna turned and started off toward the last two pickups in the parking area. "Don't forget the acne?" JD muttered to Sean. "Now that sounds real romantic. I think your boy's a little teched, Sean."

Sean winked at JD. "They both are," he whispered. "Ain't love grand?"

Chapter Three

JD reached for the bowl of potato salad in the center of the round oak kitchen table. "Jodie, be reasonable," he demanded. "You really oughta have a date for the dance, and I know Hank Simpson'd be more than happy to take you."

"I'm sure he would," JoAnna replied as she passed the rolls to JD's housekeeper, Sally Metzger. "But I don't want to go with him."

Sally, an attractive redhead who had recently celebrated her fortieth birthday, winked at JoAnna. "I don't blame you. Hank's a nice guy, but he's not much of a talker. Might as well go to the dance with a fence post."

JD glared at Sally. Giving him an unconcerned smile, she passed him the platter of roasted ears of corn. He plunked one onto his plate before turning his attention back to his daughter. "All right, forget Hank. What about Jordan Collins? He just got a divorce and—"

"Dad," JoAnna protested. "I don't need a date."

"Well, I think you do," JD argued. "Folks have been looking forward to this reunion for a long time, and they're bound to get rowdy. If you don't have a date, you'll have every buck in the county pesterin' you and who knows what'll happen?''

JoAnna snorted in exasperation and looked to Sally for support. The older woman's blue eyes danced with amusement. ''I don't have a date for the dance, but that's not gonna stop me from going.''

''That's different,'' he grumbled.

''How is it different?'' JoAnna asked.

''Sal can take care of herself. But you're my daughter, and I don't want...''

When JD's voice trailed off and he looked away, JoAnna prodded, ''Don't want what?''

Scowling at her, he answered, ''I don't want you getting involved with O'Grady again. All right?''

''For heaven's sake, Dad—''

''I saw the way you two were lookin' at each other at the park.''

''So what?'' JoAnna asked. ''If I choose to get involved with Linc, there's nothing you can do about it.''

JD smacked the table with his fist. ''Damn, I knew it! The minute I saw him come out of that chute this morning I knew you'd get all hot and bothered over him again. Didn't you learn anything the last time?''

''Didn't you?'' JoAnna shot back.

A vein stood out on JD's forehead, and his face flushed a dark red. ''What the hell do you mean by that?''

JoAnna took a deep breath. ''When I was in high school,'' she said quietly, ''I resented having you give me orders, especially where my friends were concerned. That's one of the reasons I was so determined to sneak around and be with Linc. And I still resent it, probably even more now than I did back then.''

JD sighed and rubbed his eyes with the thumb and forefinger of his right hand. ''I just don't want to see you get hurt again, honey,'' he said gruffly.

''I know that. I've always known that,'' JoAnna answered with a wry smile. ''But sooner or later, you're going to have to admit that I'm an adult. I've made some mistakes, but they've been *my* mistakes and I've learned how to live with the consequences. Can't you trust me to look after myself?''

He looked away for a second before slowly nodding his head. "I'll try." Then his eyes narrowed. "But you'd know just how hard it is to let your kids make mistakes if you'd ever settle down and have any."

Rolling her eyes, Sally said quickly, "Oh please, don't get into that one now. The food's already cold enough."

JoAnna chuckled and dug into the fried chicken Sally had prepared for their supper. JD followed suit, and a comfortable silence settled over the table.

"Who are you taking to the dance, Dad?" JoAnna asked when they were almost finished eating.

JD set down the ear of corn he'd just finished and wiped his buttery fingers on a napkin. "I don't have a date," he answered with a sheepish grin.

"Nobody'd put up with you for one evening?" JoAnna teased, knowing full well that that was hardly the case.

"Lord, you're a sassy kid. I oughta take you out to the woodshed. I'll have you know, at least four gals have asked me to take 'em to the dance."

Sally abruptly stood up to clear the table. Joanna handed Sally her plate before asking, "So why didn't you accept?"

"There ain't many good-lookin' bachelors like me around these day," JD answered, puffing out his chest and leaning back in his chair. "I figured I'd do all the single women a favor and sorta spread myself around tomorrow night."

A loud clatter of pots and pans erupted from the area by the sink. JoAnna and JD both jumped at the sudden noise. "Take it easy, Sal," JD called. "We can wait a little for dessert."

Then he turned to JoAnna with a devilish grin. "Who knows? Maybe I'll meet a pretty little filly who'll jump start my battery."

Another loud clatter came from the sink. Though Sally had her back to them, JoAnna noted that her spine was ramrod straight and she was staring out the kitchen window as if Tom Selleck might start doing a striptease in the backyard any minute. Then Sally wiped her hands on a towel and brought the coffeepot over to the table.

Sally refilled JoAnna's cup, and when she moved around the table to fill JD's, JoAnna was startled to see her shoot him an angry, almost hurt look he failed to notice. Puzzled, JoAnna watched Sally return to the work island, cut up a freshly baked rhubarb pie and scoop ice cream onto the pieces, which she served with quick, jerky movements that seemed out of character for the normally easygoing woman.

She was about to ask what was wrong, when the housekeeper plunked down a piece of pie in front of her and another in front of JD. One look at the fiercely controlled expression on Sally's face told JoAnna this was not the time for questions.

JD's eyes lit up when he saw his favorite dessert. He started to compliment Sally, but she waved the words of praise aside. "Will there be anything else, boss?" she asked.

He raised an eyebrow at her stilted tone, then frowned when he realized she had only served two pieces of pie. "Aren't you gonna have some with us, Sal? Looks too good to pass up."

"Not tonight. I'm going for a walk. I'll finish the dishes when I get back," she answered abruptly.

She started to turn away, but JD put out a hand and touched her arm. "Is something wrong?"

Sally swung around to look at him, her expression cool and detached. "Not a thing, boss," she replied dryly. "Enjoy your pie."

JD shook his head as he watched her walk away. When the screen door on the back porch slammed a moment later, he turned to JoAnna, frowning in bewilderment. "Well, now, what do you suppose is gravelin' her drawers?"

Though she was beginning to get an idea, JoAnna shrugged and cut into her pie. "I don't know, Dad."

"She's been awful moody lately," he said thoughtfully. "She's a little young for it, but do ya think she might be goin' through the change or havin' some kinda female trouble?"

JoAnna nearly choked on a bite of rich rhubarb filling and sputtered, "Dad! What a thing to say!"

JD had the grace to flush, but he quickly defended himself. "Shoot, Jodie. I was married to your mother for thirty years, and I've been nursemaidin' cows for longer than that, so I do know a thing or two about females. I like Sal, and I'm concerned about her. What's wrong with that?"

Tempted to inform her father that what he knew about women could fit into a thimble with plenty of room to spare, JoAnna restrained herself with difficulty. "Nothing's wrong with it," she replied.

The phone rang as JD was finishing his dessert. He glanced at the clock and jumped to his feet. "That's probably Bud Eldridge calling about that bull he wants to buy. I'll get it in the den."

Shaking her head, JoAnna watched him stride away, then got up and cleaned the kitchen for Sally. When she'd finished, she grabbed a couple of carrots from the refrigerator and walked out to the pasture behind the corral to visit the horses. She paused when she spotted the housekeeper sitting on the top rail of the corral fence, her shoulders hunched forward in dejection.

Spook, a gelding named for his tendency to shy at the slightest provocation, caught JoAnna's scent on the warm summer breeze and trotted over to the fence. Sally turned to see who was coming and waved as JoAnna closed the distance between them.

After climbing onto the fence beside Sally, JoAnna scratched Spook behind the ears and fed him a carrot. "Feel like talking about it?" she asked.

Sally let out a disgruntled sigh before answering. "I can't say that I really want to, but I guess I'd better."

A bay mare named Blaze came over to investigate what was happening at the fence. JoAnna patted her neck and fed her the other carrot while she waited for Sally to begin.

The redhead sighed again. "I'm going to start looking for another job."

Stunned by the blunt statement, JoAnna felt as if her heart had dropped right down to the toes of her boots. Sally Metzger had become a cherished friend since moving in to help take care of JoAnna's mother shortly after Katherine first became ill. It would be like losing a sister if the redhead left the Double R.

JoAnna shooed both horses away. "Why, Sally? If JD's done something to upset you, I'll be glad to talk to him for you."

"No, please don't do that. It doesn't have anything to do with him." When JoAnna shot her a skeptical glance, Sally smiled wryly. "All right, it does have something to do with him, but he didn't do anything. The problem's mine, not his."

JoAnna studied Sally intently for a moment while her friend blushed. "Are you in love with him?"

Sally blanched and turned her head away so fast, she nearly

fell off the fence. Realizing she'd scored a direct hit, JoAnna grinned with delight. Now that she thought about it, Sally would make a good match for her cantankerous father. She wasn't intimidated by JD's temper or overly impressed by his wealth, and she'd taken such excellent care of him over the last seven years, he'd be lost without her.

While JoAnna was still smiling over her discovery, Sally darted a glance at her and asked indignantly, "Well, what's so funny about it if I am? He's only eighteen years older than me."

JoAnna scooted closer and put her arm around the redhead for a quick hug. "Nothing's funny about it. I was just thinking you'd be good for him. That is, if you're sure you love him. He's not an easy man."

Sally chuckled. "Now *there's* an understatement if I ever heard one."

"But..." JoAnna prompted when Sally started staring off into space with a wistful smile on her lips.

"But I love the old jughead," Sally replied. She looked at JoAnna again before admitting, "I don't mean to sound disloyal to your mother's memory. She was a wonderful lady, and I admired her a lot, but I think I started loving JD about a month after I came to work here."

"Don't worry on my account," JoAnna said quietly. "My mother's been dead a long time. She used to worry about Dad being left alone, and I know she thought a lot of you. Now tell me what's been going on."

Sally gave her a grateful look. "You know, when I came to the Double R, I'd just gotten my divorce. My ex-husband used to knock me around some, and I was scared of your dad at first, especially when he got mad. But it wasn't long before I noticed that even though he bellered a lot, he could be real gentle. He was so patient and tender with your mother. He's a hard man in some ways, but he's got a ton of love in him."

"Yes, he does," JoAnna agreed. "But I don't understand why you're planning to leave if you love him."

"I could handle my feelings for him just fine while he was still grieving for Katherine, but this last year he's been dating some and... Well, you heard him tonight, sounding like a randy old rooster. I wouldn't even mind that if I thought I had a chance with him. But he doesn't love me, JoAnna, and he never will."

"Have you told him how you feel?" JoAnna asked.

"Lord, no!"

"Then how do you know he'll never love you?"

"He treats me like a hired hand! I don't think he's even noticed I'm female."

Remembering JD's earlier remarks, JoAnna chuckled and assured the redhead, "Oh, he knows you're female, Sally, believe me. Maybe he just needs a little nudge."

"Like a whack on the head with a two-by-four?"

Laughing at Sally's dark tone, JoAnna jumped off the fence and pulled on the housekeeper's hand until her feet hit the ground. "I had something a little more subtle in mind. Come on in the house. I've got something to show you."

Five minutes later, JoAnna ushered the redhead into her bedroom and waved toward the canopied bed. "Have a seat. I'll be right back."

Sally sat down on the edge of the bed while JoAnna disappeared into the walk-in closet. She emerged a moment later with both hands behind her back. "What are you up to?" Sally asked.

Smiling, JoAnna approached, pulled a brightly wrapped dress box from behind her back and presented it to her friend. Sally's mouth dropped open in surprise, and she looked up at JoAnna. "What in the world—"

"Come on, open it," JoAnna urged. "It's your birthday present. I meant to get it in the mail on time, but I didn't get organized enough."

Needing no further encouragement, Sally tore off the wrapping and lifted the lid from the box. She gasped when she folded back a protective layer of tissue paper and found a shimmering pile of powder-blue silk. After wiping her hands off on her jeans, she reverently picked up the dress and carried it over to the mirror on the back of JoAnna's closet door. She held it in front of her, silently studying her reflection.

JoAnna walked over to stand behind her. "The minute I saw it in Marshall Field, I knew it would be perfect for you. See how the color matches your eyes?"

"It's beautiful," Sally replied breathlessly before shooting JoAnna a doubtful glance. "But don't you think it's a little...bare?"

JoAnna grinned wickedly. "Yeah, it is." Nodding toward the

adjoining bathroom, she coaxed, "Why don't you go try it on? I'll run out to your apartment and find a pair of heels for you."

Already headed for the bathroom, Sally called over her shoulder, "See if you can find my pearl earrings while you're at it. They should be in the jewelry box on my dresser."

When JoAnna returned, carrying not only the shoes and earrings, but Sally's makeup kit and brush as well, she found her friend turning this way and that in front of the mirror, trying to view the dress from every angle. JoAnna dumped the load onto the bed and hurried over to see how the dress looked for herself.

"Wow," she said, then gave her best shot at a wolf whistle. "You'll be fighting men off in droves."

"Oh, I don't know," Sally fretted, eyeing the spaghetti straps and straight neckline that dipped low enough to reveal just a hint of cleavage. She smoothed her hands down the sides of her midriff to the narrow rhinestone-studded belt at the waistline and over her hips, where the skirt fell in a straight line to just above her knees. "I've never worn anything like this before."

"Sally, it's perfect!" JoAnna protested with a laugh. "It's drop-dead sexy!"

Smiling sheepishly, Sally replied, "I can see that." Then a worried frown creased her forehead. "But what will your father think of it? He's pretty conservative."

"I can promise you one thing," JoAnna told her dryly. "It'll get his attention, and he'll like it a whole lot better than he would a two-by-four." She walked over to the bed and collected the housekeeper's shoes and earrings. "Now put these on so we can see the whole effect, and then we'll—"

Sally interrupted with wicked smile, "You know something, JoAnna?"

"What?"

"You're a lot like your father."

JoAnna halted in mid-stride, shoes and earrings clutched against her chest. "How so?"

"You both have a temper, and you seem to like matchmaking as much as he does." Sally chuckled at JoAnna's startled expression, adding, "I can't believe you're doing this after all the times you've fought with him about interfering in your life."

"Serves him right," JoAnna grumbled as she handed Sally

the earrings. "Could you believe what he said to me about Linc tonight?"

Sally leaned closer to the mirror while she inserted the pearl studs. "What was all that about the way you were looking at each other?"

JoAnna briefly told Sally about her encounters with Linc. "I don't know why Dad thinks he has to worry," she said. "There's no way Linc and I could ever get back together."

"Are you sure about that?" Sally asked, turning away from the mirror.

"Of course I'm sure!" JoAnna marched over to the bed and sat down on it with her arms crossed over her midriff. "Our lives have gone in completely different directions. And if that's not enough, our idiot fathers are still feuding."

"Forget your fathers and everything else for a minute." Sally joined JoAnna on the bed. "How did you feel about Linc? Did you enjoy talking with him? Did you still feel attracted to him?"

JoAnna tipped her head to one side while she considered Sally's questions. "Linc and I always had a special relationship," she admitted. "We were both a little, uh, different from the other kids at school."

"What do you mean by that?" Sally asked, shifting to a more comfortable position.

"Well, we both liked to study for one thing," JoAnna answered thoughtfully. "I mean, we really liked it. And we both wrote poetry. We were kind of kindred spirits, you know? My wanting to be with him went way beyond just defying JD's orders. And I did feel attracted to Linc today, but..."

She shrugged, and Sally nodded encouragement. "There just doesn't seem much point in raking up all that old history again."

"But Linc wants to."

"That's what he said, but I've already decided not to talk to him again."

"Maybe you should, JoAnna," Sally suggested. "It might settle some things in your mind about the way he left that have bothered you for a long time."

"I don't think so. I've put it all behind me and—"

"Maybe Linc needs to settle some things in his mind," Sally interrupted. "And if you've really put it all behind you, what have you got to lose by talking to him?"

JoAnna squirmed inwardly for a moment beneath Sally's challenging stare. Then she laughed ruefully. "I'll think about it if you'll wear that dress to the dance tomorrow night."

The housekeeper stood up and walked back over to the mirror. After slipping on her shoes, she straightened her shoulders and took a good long look at her reflection before smiling over her shoulder at JoAnna. "Honey, you've got a deal."

Leaning his head against the high-backed wooden rocker, one of a matched pair that had sat on the front porch of his father's house for as long as he could remember, Linc shut his eyes and let the peace of the summer evening sink into his soul. A soft, westerly breeze cooled his skin, and the only sounds to be heard came from the crickets in the grass and the rhythmic creak of the chair as it rocked back and forth. It was good to be home.

The screen door's hinges squeaked behind him, and a moment later Sean pushed a frosty bottle of beer into Linc's hand before settling into the other rocker with a weary sigh. They rocked in silence for awhile, enjoying the quiet and each other's company. Then Sean said gruffly, "I'm worried about you, son."

"No need to be."

"You still love her."

Linc stopped rocking, took a swallow of beer and set the chair back in motion without answering. Sean gave him a long, searching look before taking a gulp of his own beer. "I was afraid this would happen," he said, after wiping his mouth with the back of his hand. "When you got gored by that bull down in Houston, what was that, five, six years ago?"

"Six."

"Yeah, I guess it was six. Well, like I was sayin', when you were comin' out of the anesthetic, uh, you asked for her."

Linc planted one foot on the floor, whipped his head around and stared at his father. "I what?"

"You were still half out of your head and mutterin' all kindsa crazy things, but you asked for her. I never told you 'cause I figured you didn't know what you were sayin'. But after seein' you two together this afternoon, I realized you never got over her. What do you aim to do about it?"

"I don't know, Dad," Linc replied, shrugging his shoulders.

"I'm not sure there's anything I can do about it. What's your point? Just this morning you warned me to stay away from her."

Sean left his chair, walked over to the porch railing and looked out across his ranch. "I know I did," he admitted, with his back to Linc. "But maybe I was wrong. Jodie's a beautiful woman. Lord, she looks so much like her mother, how could she be anything but beautiful? It was always JD I couldn't stomach, not Jodie. I always thought she was an awful sweet little gal."

"I can't believe you're saying this," Linc muttered.

Grinning sheepishly, Sean turned to face his son. "Tell you the truth, I can't, either." Then his expression sobered. "The thing is, you're a lot like me, Linc."

"What do you mean?"

"You're not a loner. You need a woman in your life, but you're a one-woman man, and I think Jodie's the only woman you'll be happy with."

"Dad—"

"Now, just hear me out for a minute. Your mother was a wonderful woman, son. I admired and respected her, and we had a damn good life together. But I couldn't love her the way I did Katherine, and no matter how hard I tried to hide it from her, Mary Ellen always knew. It wasn't fair to her, and I don't want to see you make the same mistake I did. I wouldn't envy you having JD for a father-in-law. But if you and Jodie love each other, there's not a hell of a lot he could do to stop you from gettin' married. You could live here at the Shamrock and—"

Linc set his empty beer bottle down and walked over to stand beside his father. "Don't go making any plans, Dad. I don't know if I love Jodie or not, and she's made it pretty plain she doesn't want much to do with me. But just for the sake of argument, if we ever did get back together, I'd make damn sure we lived as far away from JD as possible. With all the bad blood that's gone on between you and JD and between JD and me, Jodie and I could never be happy here."

"Now, just hold your horses right there, Linc," Sean replied, widening his stance and putting his hands on his hips. "This ranch has been yours since the day you were born."

"I can buy my own ranch," Linc said, unconsciously mimicking Sean's posture.

"Why the hell would you want to? This land is your home. We can finally work it together like we always planned."

Linc's gut wrenched at the pain in his father's eyes and voice. He knew how hard this man had worked to build the Shamrock into the solid business it had become, and he knew how much it meant to Sean to give it to his only son. But he would never forget that day JD Roberts had roared up the drive, looking for blood—his blood—and gotten it with the offer of a loan.

Though Linc had bitterly resented his father for putting himself into the vulnerable position JD had exploited, he hadn't been able to stand back and watch Sean lose the ranch. Not even for Jodie. He didn't want to hurt his dad now, but he'd already paid one hell of a price for the Shamrock ranch, and he wasn't willing to pay any more for it.

Laying a hand on his father's shoulder, Linc said quietly, "I know this ranch means a lot to you, Dad. But don't count on me to come back and take over. One thing I've learned from all these years traveling around on the circuit, is that one piece of land is pretty much like another."

Chapter Four

JoAnna punched her pillow twice, flipped it over to the cool side and groaned when she glimpsed the digital clock beside her bed. The blue numbers read twelve-thirty, and here she was, still flopping around like a trout stranded on a riverbank. Willing her body to relax, she yawned, closed her eyes and was immediately tormented by yet another vision of Linc O'Grady smiling that devilish smile at her and saying, "I'll just keep poppin' up wherever you least want to see me, and I won't go away till I'm damn good and ready."

Muttering, "Well, you're sure as hell keeping your word, O'Grady," JoAnna turned onto her stomach, crossed her forearms over the pillow and rested her chin on her wrist. She darted another glance at the clock. Twelve thirty-three. It was no use trying to think of something else when even the darn numerals on the clock reminded her of the color of Linc's eyes.

Too exhausted to fight the memories any longer, she closed her eyes and let her mind drift back to a hot summer night, one just like tonight....

The full moon dappled silvery light over the pond. A breeze whispered through the cottonwood's leaves, and a pair of bats swooped after an insect overhead. The old army surplus blanket Linc kept in his pickup felt scratchy, but it protected her bare skin from the rough grass. He lay on his side next to her, his head propped up on one hand while his other hand trailed from her shoulders to her knees in a gentle, sweeping caress.

Her body still tingling in the afterglow of their lovemaking, she smiled up at him. His teeth flashed white in the darkness before he leaned down and kissed her lips. Then, putting his arms on either side of her, he slid down and rested his head between her breasts.

She stroked his back and shoulders, delighting in the smooth texture of his skin. He exhaled a contented sigh and kissed the side of her breast. A deep sense of peace and happiness flooded her soul.

She combed through his thick, glossy hair with her fingers, smiling at the thought of how much they had learned about making love since their first fumbling attempt. There was no longer any shyness or modesty between them, no awkwardness or hesitance. Other people might say that what they were doing was wrong, but nothing in her life had ever felt so absolutely right. In Linc's arms, she was free and whole and deliciously feminine.

He raised his head and looked into her eyes, the moonlight illuminating his earnest expression. His voice came out in a husky whisper. "I love you, Jodie."

"I love you, Linc," she replied, tenderly tracing his beloved features with her fingertips. "And I always will."

He moved beside her then, slid his arm beneath her shoulders and turned her onto her side facing him. "I wish we could be together more often. I hate this sneaking around," he said, stroking her long hair away from her face.

"I know. I do, too. But I'll be eighteen in six months and then—"

"Sweetheart, we've been over this before. You've got to finish high school. And then you've got college ahead of you."

"But I want to be with you, Linc."

"I want that, too. More than anything. But I won't cheat you out of your education, so we've got to be patient."

She raised herself up on one elbow. "If you think I'm going

off to college without you for four years, Linc O'Grady, you're nuts.''

"You've always dreamed of being a teacher, Jodie."

"Well, what about your dreams of being an engineer? We could both work and put ourselves through school."

"No. Your dad's willing to pay for your schooling, and you're going to let him."

"But, Linc—"

"No buts. Look around at the other couples we know who've tried it. The wife usually ends up working her tail off to get the husband through. Then he gets a job and they have to move away, or she gets pregnant and has to give up her career. I won't let you do that."

"I don't want an education if it means losing you!"

His stern expression softened as he reached up to cup the side of her face with his hand. "You won't lose me. Our parents have tried every trick in the book to keep us apart, but they haven't succeeded, have they?"

"No," she admitted softly, "but—"

"But nothing. I'm not saying it's going to be easy, but some-day we're gonna get out of this two-bit town and see the world together."

"It's not a two-bit town, Linc. It's our home. And I don't want to see the world. I just want to be with you."

"You're gonna have to cut loose sometime, babe. As long as we're here, our folks will never let us get married. You know that as well as I do. But I promise you one thing."

"What's that?"

"I'll never stop loving you. Some day we'll get married and have a place of our own."

"And babies? Lots of babies?"

Reaching up to pull her down for a kiss, he murmured, "Let's start with two. If we like 'em, we'll have more."

As their lips met, she lost her balance and sprawled across his chest. His arms clamped around her, and he rolled them over, pinning her beneath him. She ran the heel of one foot up the back of his leg, eliciting an immediate, eager response from his body.

"Don't you ever get enough?" she teased, framing his face between his hands.

"Never." Resting his weight on his elbows, he dropped hot, quick kisses on her neck, her shoulders, her breasts. "I'll never get enough of you."

Her back arched with pleasure as he took one nipple into his mouth and sucked gently. His hand caressed her waist and hip, the back of her knee, then slowly stroked its way up the inside of her thigh. His every touch brought heat and a fierce delight, and suddenly, she couldn't get enough of touching him, tasting him, breathing in the musky scent of him. She gasped when he found her slick and ready for him.

Burning with need, she whimpered when he left her to reach for another small foil packet. But soon he was back, kissing her, loving her, filling her with sensations that transported her right up to the glittering stars. She heard his tortured breathing, his ecstatic shout as he reached his climax, and then a loud, raucous chorus of male laughter coming directly toward them.

Linc froze above her for an instant as the inevitable intrusion registered in his pleasure-drugged brain. Then he flipped the blanket over Jodie and dove for his jeans. He yanked them on, but before he could zip up his fly, Bill Jensen, Wade Carter and Mike Stevens, who had all graduated a year before Linc, staggered into the clearing, singing and waving beer cans.

Bill stopped dead in his tracks when he saw them, causing Wade and Mike to stumble into him from behind. They all hooted as if they'd never seen anything so funny before. Jodie clutched the blanket with one hand and reached for her blouse with the other. The motion attracted Bill's attention.

"Well, now, what have we got here?" he asked, stepping closer and bringing the other two along with him.

Pulling on his shirt, Linc stepped between Jodie and their inebriated visitors. "You're on private property, Jensen. Get out."

"We're jus' havin' a party, Linc," Mike Stevens replied, punctuating his statement with a belch that sent the other two into a fit of giggles.

"Yeah," Wade put in. "It's so damn hot, we decided to go skinny dippin' in your pond. You can join us if you want."

Bill leered at Linc. "Or you can just go back to what you were doin'. We don't mind. We'll even help if you get tired."

Wade leaned to one side. He craned his neck around Linc and

squinted into the darkness at Jodie, then turned to his friends. "Well, I'll be damned, boys. Ol' Linc's been puttin' it to Jodie Roberts. Can you imagine what her dad would say if he knew?"

Jodie's face burned with mortification, and her stomach knotted with fear. She knew Linc would do everything in his power to protect her, but what could he do against three men if they decided...

Linc's hands closed into fists. He advanced on the men with deliberate slowness, his voice deadly calm and quiet. "Get the hell outta here, you guys. Now."

Mike's chin rose belligerently. "Who's gonna make us, O'Grady?"

"You don't want to fight with me, Mike."

"Think you can take all three of us?"

"Maybe not. But I swear, not one of you will look very pretty in the morning."

Wade clapped his hand on Mike's shoulder. "Aw, c'mon, Mike, he's right. I just wanted to have a little fun tonight, not get my nose busted again."

Bill glanced from Linc to Mike and back to Linc again. "Yeah," he finally agreed. "Let's leave these two lovebirds alone and go finish off the six-pack we got in the truck."

After a few ribald pieces of advice for Linc about "keepin' it in his pants" and "not gettin' her knocked up," they left. Tears of rage and humiliation streaming down her face, Jodie scrambled into her clothes. When she was dressed, Linc helped her to her feet and took her into his arms. He stroked her hair while she sobbed against his chest.

"I'm sorry, babe," he crooned, "so damn sorry."

"They'll tell everybody, Linc," she wailed. "What are we gonna do?"

"There's not much we can do," he answered.

She lifted her head and met his troubled gaze. "But my dad! He'll never let me see you again. I know he won't!"

He cupped his palms around her face, brushing away her tears with his thumbs. "I won't let anything come between us, Jodie. I promise."

* * *

"I promise," JoAnna whispered, wiping away the tears on her cheeks with the back of her hand.

She rolled over onto her back, and much to her disgust, more tears leaked out of her eyes. She grabbed a tissue from the nightstand, dabbed at her eyes and blew her nose. Struggling to regain her composure, she inhaled a deep, shuddering breath and let it out again.

Dammit all, she hadn't cried over Linc O'Grady in years. She was tired tonight, but she didn't have to act like a sentimental idiot. But they'd both been so young and in love, so...innocent. She had known such joy with him. And such god-awful pain.

She didn't want, didn't need, that kind of pain ever again as long as she lived. She had thought about Sally's advice, she really had. But after this, she was not—absolutely not—going to have anything more to do with him. No way.

Feeling better for having made that decision, she closed her eyes. Sleep still wouldn't come, of course, because Linc still refused to stay banished from her mind.

Muttering, "Oh, damn the man," Joanna flung back the sheet, then tiptoed through the silent house to the kitchen. She assembled the ingredients for hot chocolate, set a small pan of milk on the stove and flipped through a back issue of *The Farmer Stockman* JD must have left on the countertop while she waited for the milk to heat.

A short, sharp ring from the telephone startled her half out of her wits a moment later. JoAnna turned off the stove and hurried across the room to grab the receiver before the phone could ring again, her brow wrinkled with concern. A phone call at this time of night usually meant trouble.

Putting the receiver to her ear, she heard her father mumble a sleepy, "Hello."

JoAnna started to hang up, but the familiar voice on the other end of the line stopped her hand in midair.

"JD? It's me. We got trouble."

"O'Grady? Dammit, I told you not to call here. What if JoAnna answered the phone?"

Determined to find out the answer to that question as well as the reason her father's lifelong enemy would call him in the dead of night, JoAnna shamelessly put the receiver back to her ear and listened.

"I'd of hung up like it was a wrong number. Now quit bellerin' and listen. We got big trouble," Sean replied. "This reverse psychology idea of yours has gone too far."

"What the hell are you talkin' about? Linc looked plenty interested in Jodie this afternoon."

"Oh, he's interested in her. He wouldn't admit it, but I'm damn near positive he's still in love with her."

"So?" JD demanded. "That's what we want, ain't it?"

JoAnna shook her head as if to clear it. JD and Sean O'Grady *wanted* Linc to be in love with her?

"Course it is. But when I told him that if he wanted to marry Jodie there wasn't much you could do to stop him and they could live on the Shamrock with me, he said—"

"Now wait just a damn minute," JD protested. "Who said they were gonna live on the Shamrock after they're married? They're gonna live on the Double R."

"Don't get your bowels in an uproar, JD. I was just makin' conversation, ya know? Tryin' to feel the boy out like you told me."

"Oh, all right. But don't go gettin' any ideas, O'Grady. What did he say?"

"He said that if he and Jodie ever did get back together, he'd make damn sure they lived as far away from you as possible. And then he said he'd buy his own ranch and one piece of ground is pretty much like another!"

"Hell, he's just blowin' off steam, Sean," JD said.

"Dammit, JD, this is serious. He's got the money to buy his own spread, and he'll do it, probably in Colorado or Texas. Then our grandkids will grow up there and inherit his land instead of ours. You'd better start mendin' fences with my boy, and I mean right now."

JD exhaled a weary sigh before answering. "You know how contrary Linc and Jodie are. So far, they've played right into our hands, but if we change our strategy now, they'll get suspicious. I'll see what I can do to make up with Linc as soon as I can, but let's get 'em back together first."

"All right. But don't wait too long."

With that, Sean O'Grady hung up. JoAnna waited until she heard her father's extension click before replacing her own receiver on its hook. Stunned by what she had heard, she walked slowly back to the stove. She eyed the hot chocolate ingredients with sudden disfavor, then put them away, poured herself a glass of wine instead and carried it back to her bedroom.

Her back propped up against the pillows, JoAnna pulled her knees up to her chest and sipped from the glass while she struggled to organize her thoughts. JD and Sean O'Grady were working together? To get grandchildren? All of JD's bluster about getting her a date for the dance, his warning about staying away from Linc, had been reverse psychology?

For several minutes, she seethed in outrage, tempted to march down the hall to her father's room and hit him over the head with a blunt object. Of all the gall! After everything they'd been through over the past twelve years, how could he do this?

But suddenly, a mental picture of those two crusty old coots sitting down to play matchmaker, no doubt in a bar somewhere, tugged a smile from JoAnna. A giggle followed the smile, and finally, a semi-hysterical belly laugh erupted that had her flailing around in the bed, trying to set down her wineglass with one hand while she grabbed a pillow to muffle her laughter with the other. Wait until she told Linc about this!

The thought of telling Linc produced an abrupt, sobering effect. JoAnna inhaled a shaky breath and reached for the wineglass again, wondering how he would react. What had his father said? That he was almost convinced Linc was still in love with her? Could it be true? Could he seriously want to....

"Forget it, JoAnna," she ordered herself, draining the glass in one quick gulp.

The man was nothing but trouble. Tonight was proof enough of that; she had seen him for the first time in twelve years, and he'd already cost her a good night's sleep. And knowing JD wanted her to get back together with Linc was enough to make her even less inclined to have anything more to do with him.

JoAnna turned around and whacked her pillow in disgust, realizing she didn't have any choice now; JD and Sean had taken that decision right out of her hands. After all, Linc deserved to know what his father was up to. She would have to tell him tomorrow night at the valedictorians' photo session.

Rolling onto her side, she wondered whether the photo session had been JD's bright idea or Sean's. And what about that "accidental" meeting at the beer stand? The seating arrangements at the picnic? The reunion committee meeting after the speeches? Lord, those two must have had a grand time dreaming up ways to throw their children together.

JoAnna sighed, pulled the sheet up over her shoulders and once again willed her muscles to relax. It wouldn't be so bad talking with Linc one more time, she assured herself. After hearing about their fathers' plot, he would probably head for the nearest rodeo. But maybe, before he left, they could think of a way to teach those two would-be matchmakers a lesson.

"Okay, folks, that'll do it!" the photographer announced, mopping his perspiring forehead with a rumpled handkerchief.

The valedictorians heaved a collective sigh of relief. The gymnasium resounded with tension-relieving laughter and a steady buzz of conversation. JoAnna exchanged small talk with Dr. McMillan, the valedictorian of 1942, as she waited impatiently for the people on the bottom step of the risers to move and allow those at the top to leave.

Linc had arrived too late for her to talk with him before they were positioned for the photograph, and he'd been driving her crazy for the last twenty minutes. His warm, minty breath ruffled the fine hair at the nape of her neck. His deep voice caressed her ears every time he spoke, and even though they were lined up like Q-Tips in a box, his coat sleeve brushed against her back and shoulders more often than necessary.

How much had JD paid the photographer to position Linc directly behind her, JoAnna wondered. Or had Linc managed that himself? After his threat to act like a bad case of acne all weekend, she couldn't be sure. But it didn't matter who had arranged it; she'd never been so excruciatingly aware of another human being in her life.

She surreptitiously adjusted the left strap of her halter-necked dress and felt rough fingertips dance across her shoulders and down her spine. It was impossible to hide gooseflesh from a man standing that close, and she grimaced when she heard Linc's soft chuckle at her involuntary response. Hands clenched at her sides, she ignored the varmint's diabolical teasing as best she could, silently urging the people below her to hurry.

After taking Spook out for a relaxing ride that afternoon, she had been able to put the situation into perspective and had actually started looking forward to talking with Linc again. But now she felt all nervous and fluttery, like a teenage girl on prom night, and she didn't like it one bit. The man was simply an old friend, and he was going to stay that way.

At last a pathway opened and JoAnna carefully made her way to the floor, the wooden planks bouncing behind her as Linc matched her step for step. Before she could say anything to him, however, Mrs. Marsh, Powder River County High School's best English teacher, enfolded her in a warm hug. A moment later, Mrs. Marsh held her former student at arm's length and crowed, "Jodie, you look wonderful!"

"So do you," JoAnna replied, taking in the older woman's attractive lace dress and new, shorter hairstyle in one quick glance.

Linc approached then and casually draped his arm across Mrs. Marsh's shoulders, dropping a loud, smacking kiss on her flushed cheek. Damn, but he looked handsome in that dark blue western suit and his brand new straw Stetson, JoAnna thought as the fluttering in her stomach increased.

"Howdy, teach!" Linc grinned down at Mrs. Marsh, then threw back his head and laughed when she turned her best teacher's glare on him.

"Lincoln Patrick O'Grady, unhand me this minute," she ordered. "You'll spoil my battle-ax image."

Both Linc and JoAnna chuckled at her statement. Mrs. Marsh rarely had discipline problems in her classroom, but it was due to inspired teaching rather than any fear on the part of her students. Her eyes misted as she smiled at them.

"Oh, it's so good to see you two. I shouldn't admit this, but you were both great favorites of mine. I've thought of you often over the years."

Linc stepped back, posing for her inspection with outstretched arms. "Well, what do you think? Did we turn out okay?"

Regaining her composure, Mrs. Marsh retorted, "Jodie certainly did."

Linc's eyes darkened as he studied JoAnna from her smooth chignon to her shoulders and high, firm breasts, to her slender waist and curving hips, down her long legs to the polished toenails peeping from the open toes of her evening shoes. JoAnna couldn't stop the blush that started somewhere down around her abdomen and raced out of the neckline of her dress as his eyes made a slow, suggestive return trip to her face, but she calmly returned his appraisal, feeling her resistance to him slip another notch as her gaze locked with his.

"Yeah, she sure did," he agreed softly. "But what about me?" he asked plaintively, turning back to the teacher. "Didn't I turn out okay, too?"

"I used to think so, Linc, but..." Shaking her head at him, Mrs. Marsh let her voice trail off in mock sadness.

"But what?"

"What on earth possessed you to advertise underwear?" she asked, allowing a wide smile to come through. "I swear, I nearly had a stroke the first time I opened a magazine and there you were with your hands on your hips, wearing nothing but a sexy smile and those blue bikini underpants. They matched your eyes beautifully, by the way."

Linc's face flushed, and he squirmed visibly while his former teacher looked him over with teasing feminine lust. JoAnna laughed openly at his discomfort; after what he'd already put her through this evening, he deserved some teasing. But oh lord, she thought wistfully, that embarrassed look on his face erased the last twelve years and made him even more appealing to her.

"So now I'm just another pretty face, is that it?" he asked in a wounded tone.

"Who looked at your face?" Mrs. Marsh answered dryly. "Do you still write poetry, Linc?" she asked, changing the subject. "You had such a gift with words."

He nodded, giving her a mysterious smile, as if he had some delightful secret he enjoyed keeping to himself. "Sometimes."

JoAnna wondered what that smile was all about while Mrs. Marsh beamed with pleasure at his response. Then the teacher waved at a burly man standing by the door. "I'll be right there, Sam," she called. She turned back to her former students. "I'm so glad I saw you both. I hope we'll be able to talk again later."

JoAnna smiled as she watched the older woman hurry toward her husband.

Stepping closely beside her, Linc said, "Mrs. Marsh is quite a lady."

"She sure is," JoAnna agreed. "She was awfully kind to me during my last year here."

An eerie silence descended on the gym for a moment, bringing with it the realization that everyone else had left for the dance. JoAnna glanced at Linc and found him looking at her, the warm, admiring expression in his blue eyes reactivating that nervous, fluttery sensation in her stomach. The janitor entered the gym, jangling an enormous key ring to indicate he wanted them to leave.

Nodding toward the man, Linc offered JoAnna his arm. "Looks like it's time to go."

She hesitated a second, then put her hand in the crook of his elbow and walked out of the building with him. The high school crowned an imposing hill on the east side of town, providing a clear view of the valley. The sun had slipped behind the sage-dotted hills, bathing the stark countryside in violet shadows. The ribbon of trees edging the banks of the Powder River looked black in the distance.

They stopped in front of the main entrance by mutual agreement, absorbing the peacefulness of the scene below in silence. JoAnna inhaled deeply, drinking in the familiar aromas of sage and grass before turning to Linc.

Telling herself the sooner he left for that rodeo, the better, she said quietly, "I need to talk to you."

His eyes lit up with pleasure, and he wrapped an arm around her shoulders, giving her an exuberant squeeze. "Changed your mind about coming to the dance with me? I was hoping you would."

His eager smile reminded her again of the younger Linc she had loved with all her heart. For a moment, JoAnna allowed herself to enjoy the warmth and strength of his arm around her. It felt good, right, standing here with him like this. But she couldn't give in to those warm feelings.

Shaking her head with a nonchalance she didn't feel, JoAnna stepped away from him. "No, it's not that. We've got a problem."

He frowned. "Sounds serious," he said, dropping his arm back to his side.

She shot him a wry smile. "Well, I guess it all depends on

how you look at it. Walk me to the car, and I'll tell you about it.''

While they walked, JoAnna recounted a slightly edited version of the phone conversation she had heard, and as she had expected, Linc's lighthearted, teasing mood darkened with every step they took. By the time they reached the school parking lot and found the silver Plymouth she'd rented at the Billings airport, his hands were clenched into white-knuckled fists, his face rigid with anger.

He hit the car's roof once with the side of his fist, then cut loose with a stream of colorful descriptions of their fathers that had JoAnna alternately blushing to the roots of her hair and choking back surprised laughter. He finally wound down with, ''They're nothing but a couple of low-down, mangy, egg-sucking polecats, and I hope they both rot in hell!''

She studied the gravel at their feet while Linc fought for control. When his ragged breathing eased, she looked up at him and felt empathy wash over her at the stark emotion in his eyes. She knew exactly how he felt—manipulated and betrayed. She reached over, touched his arm and, nodding toward the car, said, ''Come on. Let's sit down for a minute.''

Linc started at the sound of her voice, as if he'd forgotten she was there. Then his face turned red, and he said, ''Lord, Jodie, I'm sorry. I shouldn't have said—''

She interrupted with a wave of her hand. ''Believe me, I felt the same way last night. You didn't say anything I haven't thought about those two, although—'' she chuckled as she opened the car door ''—you put it a little more, uh, explicitly than I would have.''

He gave her an abashed grin as he walked around to get in on the passenger side of the car. He tossed his hat into the backseat, and they both rolled down their windows to let in the soft evening breeze and the discordant sounds of the band tuning up on the town square. ''What do you want to do about our darling daddies?'' JoAnna asked, when they were settled comfortably.

Linc rubbed one hand over the back of his neck, then sighed. ''I'd like to punch their lights out,'' he said darkly.

She opened her mouth to protest, but he cut her off with a wry smile and a shake of his head. ''I know, I know. It wouldn't solve anything in the long run, but I hate feeling like a puppet dancing on the end of their string, don't you?''

"Of course I do. And I think we should teach them a lesson about minding their own business."

"How?"

She tipped her head to one side, admitting, "The only thing I've been able to come up with is to deny them what they want."

"You mean ignore each other for the rest of the weekend?" he asked.

She nodded.

Linc drummed his fingertips on the dashboard. JoAnna smiled at the gesture, remembering how he always used to do that in study hall when he was working on a particularly difficult math problem. He pursed his lips for a second, then shook his head and looked out the windshield.

"That wouldn't stop them," he said decisively. "They'd just see it as a challenge and try harder. We need something more... dramatic."

"You're probably right." She sighed in frustration before asking, "But what else can we do?"

His fingertips resumed their rhythm on the dashboard, and JoAnna unconsciously held her breath while she waited for his answer. She knew he'd come up with a plan sooner or later. Knowing Linc, it would be creative and effective. The only question was, how outrageous would it be?

As last, he turned his head toward her, his lips curved into a cunning smile, his eyes glinting with devilry. He leaned closer and asked, "You're really mad at your old man. Right?"

Fascinated, yet wary, she nodded.

"And you want to teach him a lesson he won't forget. Right?"

"Right," she repeated cautiously.

His smile became even more cunning as he moved closer to her on the bench seat. "How much do you trust me, JoAnna?"

Good question, she thought, raising an eyebrow at him while her heartbeat picked up speed. If the look in his eyes was anything to go on, he'd come up with a doozie of an idea this time. She would probably be a fool to go along with it, whatever it was, but she couldn't resist smiling back at him. "More than I trust JD or your dad."

He chuckled. "That's what I needed to hear." Then he beckoned her closer and lowered his voice to a husky whisper, as if someone might pass by the car at any moment and give their plan away. "Okay. Here's what we'll do."

The decorating committee had pulled out all the proverbial stops to turn the town square into a proper setting for the biggest party in Powder River's history. Colorful banners welcoming all graduates fluttered above the streets. Strings of Christmas lights outlined the store windows and the bandstand set up on the grass in front of the courthouse. The sawhorses erected to block traffic from the dance area sported crepe paper streamers and helium-filled balloons in the school's colors.

Enjoying the country music blasting from the band's amplifiers, Linc ambled past the drugstore some twenty minutes after his conversation with JoAnna. Clusters of people stopping to visit on the sidewalk, shouting to make themselves heard, hampered his progress toward the bar where he had agreed to meet his father. He didn't mind. He had at least a couple of hours to kill before he needed to find JoAnna again.

He grinned at the thought of what they were planning to do, and a leggy redhead in a slinky powder-blue dress grinned back at him. Linc couldn't place the woman, but he nodded politely and continued on his way until he heard a gruff male voice off to his right mutter, "My God, it's Sal."

Curiosity prompted him to glance over his shoulder. All duded up in a light gray western-cut suit, JD Roberts stood not two feet away, wearing the stunned expression of a man who has just been slugged in the gut. His gaze was riveted on the woman who had smiled at Linc, his eyes wide with shock. His mouth dropped open, shut, then opened again, his big hands crumpling an obviously expensive dress cowboy hat.

Linc stepped back and braced one shoulder against the drugstore's plate-glass window, crossing one booted foot over the other. When the band started a rip-roaring rendition of "Good Hearted Woman," a strapping young man wearing a flashy red shirt approached the redhead, asking her to dance. She smiled up at him and nodded before following him out into the street.

JD stepped forward, raising one hand as if he would stop her.

But the young cowboy twirled her away, and her delighted laughter floated over the music to the sidewalk. JD hesitated, then dropped his hand in resignation, turned and stalked off down the street.

Linc watched until he disappeared into the nearest tavern before taking another look at the redhead. Her lush curves and that mane of shining red hair would give any man a lusty thought or two. Linc guessed she was older than he was, somewhere in her late thirties maybe.

It was no surprise that JD would be attracted to the woman. But the way JD had given up and walked away when he obviously wanted her did surprise Linc. She looked a little young for a man pushing sixty, but JD Roberts wouldn't let an insignificant thing like age get in his way. The SOB Linc remembered wouldn't let *anything* stand in the way of what he wanted, no matter how many people he hurt in the process.

Shaking his head, Linc strolled on down the sidewalk. If he wasn't so hung up on JoAnna, he'd go after that redhead himself, just to give JD a hard time. He paused at that thought, then turned for another look at the dancers.

A flash of white near the redhead caught his attention, and in the next instant, his gaze focused on JoAnna, waltzing with Jordan Collins. Collins was a lanky, good-looking man who had graduated three years ahead of Linc. Linc had never liked him much in high school, and he liked him even less now. He was holding JoAnna way too closely, and the hand he held at her waist strayed over her hip as if he were tracing the bright flowers on her dress.

When Collins's hand roamed up, his thumb brushing her bare back with too damn much familiarity, Linc stepped toward the street, his hand raised in readiness to put a stop to the man's amorous attentions. The song ended before he could take another step. JoAnna pulled away from Collins with a polite smile and pivoted to say something to the redhead. Suddenly realizing he was standing in the same pose JD had held earlier, Linc snorted in self-disgust, turned and pushed his way into the bar to meet his father.

Sean waved to him from a back booth. Linc waved in acknowledgement, ordered a beer at the bar and glanced at the Budweiser clock behind the cash register. Ninety more minutes to kill. Winding his way through the crowded tables, he consciously put on a smile for his father's benefit. If he planned to teach his old man to mind his own business, there was no sense giving him advance warning.

He spent the next hour drinking beer and swapping stories with Sean and his friends. Enjoying the knowledge that he was driving his father crazy, Linc cheerfully resisted Sean's frequent suggestions that he go outside and join the party. Finally Sean stood up and crammed his hat on his head.

Though he probably wanted to go outside more than his father wanted him to, Linc baited him one last time. "What's your rush, Dad? The dance will go on all night. Let's have another beer."

Sean huffled in exasperation. "I worked hard puttin' this shindig together, and I wanna see what's goin' on out there. Now come on, Linc, you're gonna get snockered if you keep sittin' there."

Hiding a smirk, Linc polished off his beer with one swallow, reached for his hat and slid out of the booth, grumbling, "Oh, all right."

Sean halted so abruptly when he reached the sidewalk, Linc nearly crashed into him. Then he muttered, "My God, it's Sal!"

Linc noted the same stunned expression on his father's face that he'd seen earlier on JD's. When he looked to see who had captured Sean's attention, the attractive redhead in the powder-blue dress danced by with Ron Taggart, the elderly pharmacist who owned the drugstore. Leaning close to Sean, Linc asked, "Who is she, Dad?"

Sean started at the sound of a voice so close to his ear, but his gaze followed the woman until Ron steered her into the middle of the dancers and she was lost from sight.

"Who is she?" Linc repeated.

Sean shot him a sheepish glance, then looked away, craning his neck for another glimpse of the woman before answering. "Sally Metzger. She's JD's housekeeper." He paused, then added thoughtfully, "But she sure don't look like a housekeeper now."

Linc muttered an explicit curse. Sean glanced at him in surprise. "What's the matter with you? Sal's a nice little gal."

"I'm sure she is," Linc replied. "But JD's interested in her."

Sean shook his head. "I doubt it. She's been livin' out at the Double R for years, and he's never paid her any mind that I know of. What makes you think he is?"

Linc related the scene he had witnessed earlier. When he'd finished, Sean crossed his arms over his chest and smiled like a man who has just won a lottery—a big one. "Is that a fact?"

Silently cursing himself, Linc nodded. He should have known better. Knowing JD wanted the woman would only make her more attractive in Sean's eyes, and the whole situation was liable to get out of hand. And if Sean and JD started feuding again, there'd be no hope at all for him to ever get back together with JoAnna.

Granted, he wasn't ready to say he wanted that to happen yet, but he wasn't ready to say he didn't want it to happen, either. Damn those two interfering old jugheads anyway.

Putting his hand on his father's shoulder, Linc warned, "Don't do anything stupid, Dad."

Sean shrugged off Linc's hand, straightened his tie and his hat and squared his shoulders. With a devilish wink, he said, "I'm just gonna ask her to dance."

Then he turned and strode off into the crowd. Linc walked over to lean against a lamppost, shoved his hands into his pockets and crossed one boot over the other, oblivious to the people dancing in front of him until a familiar flash of white decorated with bright flowers caught his eye.

His troubled thoughts dispersed as his gaze focused on JoAnna. She was dancing with Todd Hanson, her head tipped back, exposing the graceful line of her neck, her face alight with laughter. Executing some fancy footwork, Todd whirled her around, then dipped her. The skirt of her dress billowed, drawing Linc's attention to her long, shapely legs. God, she was beautiful!

Sharp, achingly vivid memories assaulted him. His lips, kissing that graceful neck, those smiling lips. Her eyes, looking up at him with utter trust and adoration. Her husky laugh mingled with his over some silly joke he'd told her. Those long, shapely legs wrapped tightly around his waist....

Pushing away from the streetlamp, Linc decided he'd waited long enough. Following his father's example, he straightened his tie and hat, squared his shoulders and stepped off the curb. It was time to put their plan into action. It might be every bit as outrageous as JoAnna had claimed, and it might not work. But if nothing else came of it, he sure as hell aimed to enjoy executing it.

Chapter Five

Her head swimming at suddenly finding her back arched so low over Todd's arm that her hair nearly scraped the street, JoAnna clutched frantically at his shoulders and begged between gasps of laughter, "Let me up, Todd!"

He obeyed with dizzying speed, catching her in a tight embrace when she stumbled against him. Grinning like the naughty little boy he still was in many respects, Todd shook his head at her.

"Jodie Roberts, I'm surprised at you. Stumbling around in the street like a drunk out on a Saturday night toot. How much have you had to drink?"

JoAnna glared at him, but before she could answer, Linc appeared behind Todd and tapped him on the shoulder. Todd turned to see who had touched him, loosening his grip on JoAnna. As soon as he recognized his old friend, he pulled her closely again, bending down to lay his head on her shoulder.

"Forget it, O'Grady," he ordered, dancing her around in a circle. "I've got the prettiest gal in the whole county here, and I'm not sharing." He raised his head to look JoAnna in the eye.

"You don't want to dance with that broken-down old rodeo bum, do you?"

Staying mad at Todd Hanson was like trying to stay mad at a playful cocker spaniel puppy. "Yes, Todd, I do," Joanna replied, smiling. "At least—" she glanced at Linc "—I do if he promises not to dip me."

Linc traced a cross on his chest, then held his hand up in a solemn promise. "I never dip at a street dance."

Heaving a theatrical sigh, Todd straightened to his full height. He sniffed as he handed JoAnna over to Linc, "Well, I guess I know when I'm not wanted."

"Don't go away mad, Todd," Linc retorted with a chuckle, taking JoAnna's hand in his. "Just—"

"Yeah, yeah. I know the rest," Todd answered good-naturedly. "Just go away."

The band started playing a country waltz. Linc pulled JoAnna into his arms and stepped off in time with the music. Fighting a sudden attack of nerves, she put her hand on his shoulder. For a moment, she wished she had been out on a toot, or at least had more to drink than the one gin and tonic she'd sipped between dances an hour ago. At the moment, a little Dutch courage sounded like a wonderful idea.

What had possessed her to agree to Linc's plan? He was the bold, adventuresome one. She wasn't an actress; she wasn't even a good poker player. She couldn't do this in front of everyone. She looked up to tell Linc so and gasped at the intense, hungry look in his eyes. His expression softened immediately; his hand at her waist tightened, pulling her closer to him.

"Relax, honey. There's nothing to be nervous about," he said, giving her a reassuring smile.

Her heartbeat skittered at that smile and the deep, soothing sound of his voice. She leaned back to give herself more breathing space. "It shows, huh?"

"Only a little." He executed a quick turn to avoid another couple. "But we might as well enjoy ourselves. It'll be a while before they notice us."

JoAnna gradually began to relax as they talked and danced. They moved well together; Linc's strong sense of rhythm made it easy to follow his lead. But as the party continued and one song blended into the next, a new, delicious tension that had nothing to do with their fathers sparked between them.

Her field of vision narrowed until she saw only Linc's eyes, flashing with animation, his mouth, moving as he spoke and smiled. The music and laughter drifted away, leaving only the sound of his voice to fill her ears. The heady scent of his aftershave enveloped her, making her feel as tipsy as if she'd gone on a toot after all.

He cradled her right hand against his chest with his left, and she felt the fine silk threads of his suit coat against her wrist, the steady, ever more powerful thump of his heart beneath her palm. His right hand nudged her closer until their bodies brushed together with every step. Then his hand moved up to caress the bare skin above the back of her dress in tiny, rotating motions that radiated heat and excitement.

When she realized what was happening, JoAnna shook her head and looked up at the sky, reminding herself that this was all an act to teach JD and Sean a lesson. But the stern reminder couldn't stop the stars from shining brighter overhead. Or keep the crowd surrounding them from fading into a romantic, misty swirl of color and motion. Or banish the feeling that after twelve long years, she'd finally come home.

Even while she silently denied that feeling, she unconsciously pressed closer to him. Her left hand moved over his broad shoulder to the back of his neck, exploring the hard, yet supple muscles moving beneath his warm skin. He paused for a fraction of a second, then, leaving her hand against his chest, wrapped his other arm around her waist.

Unwilling to fight her emotions any longer, she laid her head on his shoulder, closed her eyes and gave herself up to the magic of being in his arms again. His lips brushed her forehead in a tender kiss. She smiled when his chest expanded and contracted with a deep, contented sigh.

During the next song, their steps slowed until they were barely shuffling in place. Her breasts grazed his chest with every breath either of them took. His hips and thighs rubbed against hers, igniting a fierce need to be even closer to him. A moment later, his arms tightened around her. She heard him whisper something in her ear, but his words failed to pierce the dreamy cloud surrounding her.

He stopped dancing and spoke more loudly this time. "They're coming, sweetheart."

She raised her head and looked up at him, her emotions laid bare under the bright streetlights. He sucked in a harsh breath and murmured, "Forget 'em, Jodie. Don't think. Just feel."

Then his face blurred out of focus as his mouth descended to claim hers, hot and demanding at the first touch. Her eyes closed automatically. Her lips parted eagerly, joyously welcoming the thrust of his tongue. He tasted wonderful—familiar and yet different, and she wanted more. She lifted her other hand to his head, plunging her fingers into the thick, dark hair below his hat, holding his lips to hers as if she needed them as much as she needed oxygen.

His arms tightened convulsively around her, pulling her up onto her tiptoes. His heart thundered against her breasts, echoing the frantic beat of her own. The hard ridge of his arousal pressed against her pelvis. She arched into him, tearing a groan of pleasure from him.

Way off in the distance somewhere, JoAnna heard whistles and catcalls. She ignored them. She'd never felt this good before—not even with Linc. As long as she could go on feeding this insatiable hunger, filling the emptiness in her soul she hadn't even been aware of until now, she didn't give a rip if the whole darn county stood there and watched them.

Then an outraged voice boomed from directly behind Linc. "Get your hands off my daughter, O'Grady!"

Though Linc's shoulders and spine stiffened, he took his sweet time about breaking off the kiss. Still lost in the sensuous mist of passion, JoAnna whimpered softly when he raised his head and glanced over his shoulder. Then Sean O'Grady joined JD. "What the hell do you think you're doin', boy?" he bellowed.

Turning back to JoAnna, Linc slowly loosened his hold on her, allowing her heels to touch the pavement. She blinked up at him in confusion, feeling as if her feet had just hit the ground with a bone-jarring thud. Snickers from the crowd finally pierced her consciousness. Her face became hot with embarrassment, and an icy knot of fear twisted in her stomach as the implication of her abandoned response to Linc's kiss began to sink in.

He inhaled a deep breath and winked at her before whispering, "Ready, babe?"

His question jerked her thoughts back to the situation at hand, namely, teaching JD and Sean a lesson. Pushing all other concerns aside for the moment, JoAnna took a deep breath, nodded, then turned with him to face their fathers. Thankful that his arm remained tight around her waist, supporting her still-shaky knees, she managed to smile calmly at both older men.

"Get your hands off my daughter," JD repeated with a fierce scowl.

Linc merely raised an eyebrow. "You really want me to do that, JD?"

"I said so, didn't I?" JD snarled in response.

All dancing ceased. The people around them inched closer, listening with avid curiosity. Somebody ordered the band to quit playing. Sean's voice carried clearly over the crowd in the sudden quiet.

"Come on now, Linc. I know what I said last night, but this ain't the way to go about it."

"Oh, I don't know, Dad. I didn't hear any complaints from Jodie." Linc paused and leered down at JoAnna. "What did you think of that kiss, honey? Was it as good for you as it was for me?"

Choking back a laugh, JoAnna pressed closer to Linc and shamelessly batted her eyelashes up at him. "Oh yeah, darlin'. It was wonderful."

The crowd tittered. JD looked around and his face flushed at all the attention they were receiving. He stepped closer, his voice lowered to a furious hiss. "For God's sake, Jodie—"

JoAnna cut him off, her face a picture of wide-eyed innocence. "But, Dad, you said you wanted me to get back together with Linc."

"What?" he sputtered, shooting an angry, desperate glance at Sean before glaring back at his daughter. "What the hell are you talking about?"

"Last night. When you were talking to Mr. O'Grady. On the phone."

JD's mouth opened and closed twice, but no sound emerged. A vein stood out in bold relief on Sean's forehead. Beginning to enjoy her role, JoAnna disengaged herself from Linc's side and walked over to stand between the two men, linking arms with each of them.

"It was so sweet of you two to be matchmakers for us. Don't you think so, Linc?" she asked, projecting her voice so that everyone could hear.

"Oh, yeah." Linc nodded fervently. "Real sweet."

She went on before either father could interrupt. "Especially since such big, macho men don't usually get into that sort of thing. And you were so clever about using the reunion to throw us together. Don't you think so, Linc?"

"Real clever," Linc agreed soberly. He widened his stance, putting his hands on his hips. "Of course, some people might think their grown children should be allowed to run their own lives, but you guys are made of sterner stuff. I don't know what would have happened to us if you two hadn't been such busybodies. I think we owe them a real debt of gratitude, JoAnna. Don't you?"

"Oh, yes," JoAnna cooed, reaching up to kiss JD's cheek, then Sean's. Both men tried to flinch away, but she wouldn't allow it. "We *do* have to thank you for getting us back together. Why, I'll bet when word gets around about how good you are at matchmaking, you'll be swamped with calls for help."

Linc turned to the audience behind him. "What do you think, folks? Are they great parents or what?"

The crowd responded with shouts of laughter. A man over by the bandstand yelled, "Hey, JD! You guys goin' into business?" Another man standing behind Sean nudged his wife in the ribs and said, "Can't you just see their sign?" He held his hands up as if framing a picture. "Roberts and O'Grady. We Make Weddings Happen. And a purty little heart at the bottom?"

His neck and ears flaming like a red light bulb, JD turned on Sean. "This is all your fault, O'Grady."

"*My* fault!" Sean took a belligerent step forward. "You old cuss, it was *your* idea in the first place!"

"That's enough," JoAnna interrupted before a full-fledged battle could erupt. "It doesn't matter whose idea it was. All Linc and I want is for both of you to mind your own business from now on."

She speared her father with a stern look. "Agreed?" After

receiving his grudging nod, she turned to his accomplice. "What about you, Mr. O'Grady?"

Sean flashed her a charming, if somewhat sheepish grin. "Whatever you say, Jodie." He extended his hand to her, and when she'd taken it, he added, "But ya know, I'd still like to see you and Linc get married and have some kids someday."

Raising her eyebrows in mock horror, JoAnna said, "Married? Me? Oh, I'm way too young for that, Mr. O'Grady." She smiled wickedly at him, then lowered her voice so that only he and JD could hear her. "But thanks to you and Dad, we'll probably have a wonderful affair. I've always wanted to try living in sin, haven't you?"

With that, she patted his cheek and walked back to join Linc, who was watching her with both admiration and unholy glee in his eyes. He put his arm around her waist and called over his shoulder as they turned to leave, "Don't wait up for us. We'll be home when we get home."

The crowd parted obligingly for them and they walked away to the sound of the band starting another song, graciously accepting congratulations from old friends and neighbors. When they were out of earshot, JD turned to Sean with a self-satisfied grin.

"We did it, O'Grady."

Sean mused with a equally self-satisfied grin, "Lord, I thought they were gonna melt the pavement there for a minute when they were kissin'."

JD chuckled in agreement. Then he said thoughtfully, "And ya know, after that stunt they pulled on us, they'll never expect us to do anything else."

"We promised to mind our own business from now on," Sean reminded his cohort, "in front of God and everybody."

"We're on a roll," JD argued.

"Hello, Sean," a soft, feminine voice broke in. "It's time for that dance I promised you."

Both men turned to find Sally Metzger standing on Sean's left. She nodded politely to JD and said, "Hello, boss," then held out her hand to Sean.

"I'm ready if you are," Sean replied. He smiled triumphantly at JD before leading her out into the dancing area. As they walked away together, JD heard Sean say, "Sally, you're sure a sight for sore eyes. If I take you out to dinner in Miles City sometime, will you wear that dress again for me?''

JD couldn't hear Sally's reply. ''Over my dead body, O'Grady,'' he muttered under his breath before he turned to head for the bar.

After escaping the crowd, JoAnna and Linc hurried across the courthouse lawn, crossed the street, then ducked out of sight around the side of the library where they collapsed against the brick wall of the building.

''I'd give a hundred dollars for a picture of your dad's face when he realized the jig was up,'' JoAnna said, wiping tears of mirth from her eyes.

''My dad's face!'' Linc hooted, holding his stomach. ''That was nothing compared to *your* dad's face when you said you'd always wanted to try living in sin! I thought his eyes were gonna fall right out onto the street!''

They rehashed every word that had been said and all the things they wished they'd said but hadn't thought of. Finally their laughter eased into quiet chuckles and broad smiles. Without either of them making a conscious decision, they drifted over to sit on the library steps.

The music from the town square floated softly to them on the cool night breeze. Linc stretched out his legs, tipped back the brim of his hat and looked up at the stars for a moment. JoAnna's delicate floral perfume filled his nostrils when he inhaled a deep breath, and a warm sense of peace filled his soul when he put his arm around her shoulders, pulling her closely against his side.

She sighed and snuggled closer, automatically wrapping her arm around his waist beneath his suit coat. He smiled down at her. ''You gettin' cold?''

JoAnna smiled back at him and shook her head before resting it against his shoulder.

''Want to go back and dance for a while or have a drink?'' he asked, hoping like hell she would refuse.

She tipped her head back and looked up at him. ''Do you want to?''

"Not really. It feels good, sitting here with you. Like old times."

Like old times. The words echoed pleasantly in her mind for a moment as she remembered some of those old times Linc was no doubt remembering as well. But then, inevitably, other memories crowded in—the night they had been caught making love; their fight the next night when Linc told her he was leaving town; the angry tears that were followed by loneliness, pain and humiliation; the eventual estrangement from her father.

The icy knot of fear she had pushed aside to confront JD and Sean in the town square returned to her stomach with a vengeance. She shut her eyes, as if she could shut out those painful memories, but they wouldn't go away. Linc O'Grady had hurt her more deeply than any other human being on earth.

So why the hell was she sitting here, practically glued to his side and loving the warmth of his arm around her shoulders? Why was it so damnably easy to know what he was thinking and feeling? Why couldn't one of those other men she'd danced with this evening spark the emotional and physical needs inside her that he did, needs that set her heart pounding and made her feel so alive. Why did it have to be Linc?

The obvious answers to those questions scared her right down to her bone marrow. She straightened away from him and folded her hands in her lap. Carefully avoiding his questioning gaze, she looked down at her hands and fiddled with the cocktail ring JD had had made for her from her mother's engagement ring. She couldn't stand it if Linc used that blasted empathy they'd always shared to read her thoughts.

When he felt JoAnna stiffen, then pull away, Linc could have kicked himself for bringing up the past. He couldn't see her expression because her head was bent, but he knew she wasn't smiling. It wasn't hard to guess what she was thinking.

His heart contracted painfully in his chest at the fear he sensed radiating from her. He pulled the heels of his boots flush against the base of the steps, clasping his hands between his bent knees, and watched the light from the streetlamp on the corner as it reflected off her glossy, black hair. He wanted to touch her again but knew he shouldn't, and frustration welled up inside him at the sudden distance he'd inadvertently put between them.

He still hated JD Roberts and probably always would. He

hated knowing he'd been manipulated by his own father, as well. If he really wanted to teach those two old buzzards a lesson, he would walk JoAnna back to her car, kiss her goodbye, and never see her again. But that old cliché about cutting off your nose to spite your face flashed through his mind, and he couldn't ignore it.

His climb to the top of the rodeo circuit had taken twelve long years of hard work, loneliness and broken bones. He'd become more cynical and jaded in the process than he liked to admit. But tonight, for the first time in a long time, he'd felt renewed and refreshed. Being with JoAnna was like getting a cold drink of water from a mountain stream after spending the day in a hot, dusty rodeo arena.

Plotting with her to embarrass their fathers had made him feel young and carefree—like a kid again. And dammit, he wanted to hang on to those gentler, happier feelings she kindled in him. Holding her again had made him feel whole, complete. And kissing her again...well, shoot, that kiss had rocked him clear down to his toenails. He'd never felt anything like it before, not even with Jodie.

That small taste of the passion they'd shared had only whetted his appetite for more. A lot more. The reunion's last scheduled event was a nondenominational worship service in the city park tomorrow morning. Was he prepared to say goodbye to her after that service and walk out of her life again? For good? No. Hell, no!

She stirred beside him, as if to rise. His left arm shot out to prevent her from leaving. She started, then gave him a questioning look. Feeling sheepish as all get-out, Linc dropped his hand to her lap, closing his fingers around her right hand. After lacing his fingers through hers, he transferred both hands to his thigh.

JoAnna turned toward him, her brows lifted in silent query. Linc cleared his throat, shifted in search of a more comfortable position on the concrete steps and looked deeply into her eyes. His heart contracted again at her anxious, wary expression, and his voice came out raspy and hoarse.

"Back there in the street, when I kissed you...well, uh, I wasn't exactly acting."

Out-and-out panic flared in her eyes for a second. Without

answering, she looked off toward the courthouse. Tightening his grip on her hand when she would have pulled it away, he cleared his throat a second time.

"You weren't acting, either, Jodie."

JoAnna blinked at his statement. It was true, of course. But the emotions she'd felt tonight were too much, too fast, too...overwhelming. And while she might admit that to herself, every instinct for self-preservation she possessed screamed at her to deny it to Linc. Then she looked up into his eyes and knew denial wouldn't do her one bit of good. He wouldn't believe her, and why should he after her unbridled response to that scorching kiss?

"No, I wasn't acting."

Heartened by her admission, Linc smiled, laid her hand on his thigh and put his arm back around her shoulders. "What are we gonna do about it?"

The sudden, cocky confidence in his voice and the easy intimacy he assumed when he caressed her bare shoulder irked her. And while heat jumped from his thigh to her palm and moved on up her arm, his blunt question sent more cold fingers of apprehension up her spine. She yanked her hand back and pulled away from him.

"What makes you think we're going to do anything about it?" she asked.

He stared at her for a moment. Then he leaned closer and gave her a smile that would have beguiled even starchy old Queen Victoria. "The magic's still there for us, Jodie. You admitted it yourself. Why wouldn't we do something about it?"

Though she felt a distinct urge to scoot away from Linc and that wicked smile of his as she had in the park the day before, JoAnna held her ground. "It's kind of like having the chicken pox, Linc," she said after a moment's thought.

Scowling at her, he drew away of his own accord. "Chicken pox? What the hell has chicken pox got to do with anything?"

"Just because you have an itch, that doesn't necessarily mean it's a good idea to scratch it."

He shook his head at her smug grin, then let out a low, rumbly chuckle. "All right," he conceded. "Maybe you have a point. But what I felt out there," he paused and inclined his head toward the town square, "was one powerful itch."

"What you felt was a powerful dose of nostalgia. Reunions are designed to resurrect good memories—"

"Nostalgia and reunions be damned. You can't honestly believe that's all it was, Jodie."

"You've just made my point. My name is JoAnna now. I haven't been the Jodie you remember for a long, long time. And you're not the Linc I knew all those years ago, either."

He lifted his hat, raked one hand through his hair in irritation, then plunked it back down on his head. "For Pete's sake, your name doesn't have anything to do with anything, either. Half the people in this town still call you Jodie. Just because I can't remember your new name every time doesn't mean there isn't one hell of a lot of chemistry between us right now."

"I didn't say there wasn't," she argued. "But chemistry doesn't make a solid relationship, and I won't settle for anything less."

"What makes you think you'd have to settle for less with me?" he asked indignantly. "I'm not looking for a quick roll in the hay for old times' sake."

She raised an eyebrow at him, and he flushed, remembering his initial reaction to her at the beer stand. Still, he held her disbelieving gaze until she looked away.

She exhaled a heartfelt sigh. "Come on, Linc. You know we could never have a serious relationship."

"Give me one good reason why we couldn't."

"I'll give you two of them," she answered, jerking her thumb toward the dancers. "Your dad and mine."

He studied her intently for a moment. "I don't think they have anything to do with this. You still haven't forgiven me. Have you?"

"I, uh, I thought I had. It's been such a long time and all..." She faltered for a second, her voice dropping to a husky murmur. "But maybe I haven't."

"Then let's talk about it," he urged. "There are some things you should know—"

She looked up at him in anguish, torn between her fear of being hurt again and her desire to hear him out. For the moment, fear won the struggle. "It's too late for that, Linc."

"No it's not," he insisted.

She inhaled a deep breath for patience. "Look, it's been a long day, and I don't feel like getting into—"

"So meet me after church tomorrow."

"I'm leaving early in the morning."

Her words hit him like a hard blow to the solar plexus. "Leaving! JoAnna, you can't!"

"I have a business to run."

Swearing under his breath, Linc stood up and paced in front of the library steps in agitation. He looked down at her and groaned silently at the mulish set to her chin. She was slipping away from him. Damn, she couldn't leave. Not when he was finally realizing how much she still meant to him. Without her, his glamorous future looked mighty damn bleak.

"Linc, I'm sorry," she said quietly after a moment. "But there's just no point...."

Halting in midstride, he dropped to one knee in front of her, put his hands on her arms and gave her a gentle shake. "JoAnna, there's every point. I know I hurt you, and I'm more sorry about that than you'll ever know."

His voice dropped to a hoarse whisper as he shook her again. "I *need* to talk to you about what happened back then, or it'll haunt me for the rest of my life."

Her expression softened, and he thought her eyes looked a little misty. He saw her throat muscles work down a gulp. Pressing his advantage, he lifted his right hand to gently cup the side of her face, caressing her cheek with his thumb.

"Please, babe, don't be afraid. And don't run from me. I promise I won't hurt you again."

JoAnna looked into his earnest, pleading eyes, and, against her better judgment, felt her resolve not to get involved with him again melt like a dish of caramels in a microwave. She had to admit Linc was right. It was time to stop running or this opportunity to clear away the debris of their past romance would no doubt haunt her for the rest of her life, as well.

Slowly, as if the very act of agreement might bring her pain, she nodded and said, "All right."

He let out a relieved sigh. "You'll meet me tomorrow at the pond after church?"

She nodded again, then said, "But I want to go home now, Linc."

He anxiously studied her face for any sign that she might change her mind. Finding none, he raised his left hand to cup the other side of her face, leaned forward and dropped a quick, tender kiss on her lips as if to seal their bargain. Then he climbed to his feet and took her hand to help her up.

They walked back to her rental car in silence. When they reached it, he took her into his arms for one last kiss. Fearing she might resist, he brushed her mouth with the barest of touches, gently moving back and forth until she relaxed against him and her lips parted voluntarily with a yearning sigh.

He teased those lips unbearably, running the tip of his tongue over her lower lip, grazing the edges of her teeth, withdrawing to glide across her upper lip. Her hands slid up his chest, over his shoulders and settled around the back of his neck. Her full breasts pressed against his chest, and her tongue darted out and touched his, sending fiery impulses to his groin.

All thoughts of keeping the kiss light and gentle evaporated like water sprinkled on a hot griddle. He wrapped one arm around her waist, pulling her flush against him and raised his other hand to the back of her head, sending the hairpins holding her chignon pinging to the street. He thrust his tongue into her mouth, savoring the taste of her while his hands hungrily combed through her long, shiny hair.

Her throaty moan of pleasure incited him almost beyond reason. He pulled her even closer, coaxing her to taste him as he had tasted her. She complied eagerly. Her hands caressed his neck feverishly, then plunged up into his hair, dislodging his hat. It slipped down over his forehead, the brim coming to rest on the bridge of her nose. She jerked back in surprise, then started giggling.

Linc yanked his hand out of her hair and snatched the hat out of the way, chuckling when she looked up at him, and observed dryly, "Well, now, that was a real mood-breaker."

He released her reluctantly, then reached down and opened the car door for her. After JoAnna had settled in behind the steering wheel, Linc shut the door and motioned for her to roll down the window. Resting his forearm on the window ledge, he stuck his head inside the car. "Good night, JoAnna. I'll see you tomorrow about one-thirty."

She nodded, but the guarded smile she gave him prompted him to add, "It'll be all right, honey. Trust me."

Then he straightened and walked away.

JoAnna watched his confident, ground-eating strides with a sinking sensation in the pit of her stomach. When he disappeared around the corner of the courthouse, she felt trembly and weak...and scared. She'd made the right decision, she told herself. But God, was she scared.

She reached out and started the ignition before resting her forehead against the steering wheel. She straightened up a moment later with an inelegant sniff, hysterical laughter welling up inside her.

"Trust me," he'd said. As if it were something she really could do. Didn't he know? Couldn't he see that she couldn't trust him again? Dear God, she'd trusted him with her heart, her soul, her virginity, and he'd left her without a backward glance. She'd sooner trust Jack the Ripper. Shoot, she couldn't even trust herself where he was concerned.

Chapter Six

Linc paced in front of the twisted old cottonwood tree that guarded their meeting place. The pond was quiet at this time of day. His father's cattle munched placidly on the thick grass that would turn brown in a few weeks from the sun's fierce heat. Occasionally they swatted their tails at the annoying insects, which never seemed to rest. Sighing with impatience, he looked at his watch again, lifted his hand and wiped his brow with a rolled-back shirtsleeve.

Memories of earlier trysts with JoAnna in this place haunted him, and he wished for the hundredth time that he'd suggested another location last night. But where else could they meet with any hope of privacy? Not in town. Not at the Shamrock or the Double R, that was for damn sure. The last time he'd been at the Double R...

Linc parked the battered pickup his father had given him in front of the long, curving sidewalk leading to the Roberts's front door. His gut twisted with dread at what he was about to do, and he paused, letting his eyes wander over the sprawling ranch house for a moment.

It was a beautiful house, he couldn't deny that. Its white brick and dark green shutters, the lush, rolling lawn smooth enough for a round of golf, and the neat, almost symmetrical shrubs around the structure epitomized everything his dad had ever wanted for the Shamrock. No wonder Jodie hated even to think about leaving it.

Well, now she wouldn't have to—at least not with him. And with the massive, forced loan from JD, maybe his dad would finally be able to realize his dreams. The thought left a bitter taste in Linc's mouth, and he wanted to holler and rage against the death of his own dreams.

Instead, he climbed out of the pickup, walked slowly up that long sidewalk and rang the doorbell. He was a man now, with a man's responsibility for accepting the consequences of his actions. He just hoped that somehow, Jodie would understand.

Heavy footsteps sounded inside. Linc's body tensed. He didn't intend to take any more abuse from JD Roberts. The door swung open then, and the big man himself stepped outside, closing the door behind him.

JD strolled over to the wrought-iron railing surrounding the veranda. Resting one hip against it, he shoved his hands deeply in his pockets and looked at Linc's truck. "Well, I'm glad to see you're all packed, O'Grady. Where ya headed?"

"None of your business."

"There's no need to be hostile, boy."

Linc's back teeth ground together as he fought the impulse to wrap his hands around the SOB's thick neck and squeeze the life right out of him. "I didn't come here to talk to you. Where's Jodie?"

JD straightened away from the railing and planted his hands on his hips. "Don't get smart with me, O'Grady."

"Look," Linc replied, struggling for a reasonable tone. "You said I could say goodbye to her. Soon as I do that, I'll be gone. Just like you wanted."

The self-satisfied smirk the older man gave him at that remark nearly undid Linc's tightly leashed control. But the look in JD's gray eyes chilled Linc to his soul, forcing him to look away and adding more rage to fester inside him.

"That's right. You'll be gone and you'll stay gone. Understand?" JD said finally.

"I'll keep my part of the deal. But I'll come back someday, and when I do—"

"Save your threats, kid." JD chuckled as he walked over to stand directly in front of Linc. "If you keep your part of the deal, you'll never be back. By the time your old man pays off that loan, if he ever does, Jodie will be married. To someone who's good enough for her."

Linc looked into those frosty gray eyes without flinching this time. "Don't count on it, Roberts."

JD's lip curled back as if he were looking at a fresh pile of dog dung he'd just stepped in. "She'll forget a no-good punk like you before Christmas."

Humiliation burned in Linc's vitals while an icy sweat broke out on his forehead. He looked away and had to clear his throat before he could speak again. "Just let me say goodbye to her. Please."

JD stared at him for another long moment, then nodded, turned on the heel of his boot and went back into the house. Linc walked over to the railing and gripped it with both hands until the bones of his knuckles threatened to poke through the skin. His eyes stung and his throat burned, but he took a deep breath and fought for control of his emotions.

Damn, but it hurt, knowing JD was probably right. The other guys in Powder River weren't blind. As soon as word got around that a pretty girl like Jodie was available again, they'd start asking her out.

The door opened behind him. He turned around and felt his heart plummet to the toes of his boots. Jodie stood framed in the doorway, poised as if she didn't know whether to run *to* him or *away* from him. Her big brown eyes were red, swollen and filled with misery. Her hair was mussed, as if she'd been lying on her bed, and her lips were pressed together in a tremulous smile.

Then she let out an inarticulate little cry and ran to him. He opened his arms to her, and she threw her arms around him and clung to him. He stroked her hair and held on tightly, memorizing the feel of her, the scent of her, the sound of her sweet voice telling him how much she loved him.

Linc shut his eyes and pressed her head against his chest. Oh, God, he couldn't leave her! But he had to.

She leaned back, looking up into his face. He knew he must look as heartbroken as she did. But he couldn't handle her sympathy. Not now. If he didn't get this over with soon, he wouldn't be able to do it at all. Taking her by the shoulders, he held her away from him. "Jodie, there's something I have to tell you."

She stared at him for another moment. Then a wary expression entered her eyes. She pulled herself up straight and stepped back. "All right. Tell me," she said with a quiet dignity that ripped at his gut.

"I'm leaving Powder River."

Jodie winced as if he'd struck her. Tears welled up in her eyes, and he shoved his hands into his pockets to keep from reaching for her. Shaking her head, she whispered, "No." She cleared her throat. "No, Linc, you can't," she said urgently. "We'll work something out—"

"I have to go." He jerked his head toward his truck. "I'm already packed."

"But why?"

"I've got to earn a living."

"You don't have to leave Powder River to do that. You can work for your dad or one of the other ranchers."

"No. I can't. I'm gonna try my luck on the rodeo circuit."

Wrapping her arms around her waist, she moved away, tracing a line on the brick floor with the toe of her shoe. Still studying her foot, she asked stiffly, "When will you be back?"

"I won't."

"I see. Then you don't want me to wait for you."

Linc shut his eyes and exhaled a ragged sigh, forcing out the painful words. "No. It's best if we end it right here."

Her shoulders slumped. Her silence nearly suffocated him, and he had to bite his tongue to keep from taking back the lie. Dammit, he *did* want her to wait for him. But he couldn't ask that of her. A moment later she lifted her head to face him, her eyes flashing with anger.

"You're a coward, Linc O'Grady. A rotten, low-down coward."

"Jodie—"

"No, we both knew we'd get in trouble if we ever got caught

together. I thought you'd be man enough to stand by me, but I was wrong, wasn't I? You're really gonna turn tail and run away."

"I'm not running."

He stepped toward her, reaching out to put his hands on her shoulders. She jerked out of his reach.

"Don't touch me!"

"For God's sake, Jodie. Stop acting like a spoiled brat and grow up. It's not as simple as you think."

"Well then, explain it to me."

He clenched his hands so hard his knuckles ached. Her sarcasm fueled his temper, but the tears she was desperately blinking back halted an angry torrent of words. He'd rather have her think him a coward than a fortune hunter. And no matter what she said, he knew she was hurting as much as he was.

Finally he said quietly, "I've gotta get out of this town, Jodie. If I don't, I'll never be anything but a ranch hand. I need more than that."

"Then let me come with you. I can work hard. I can help you."

He forced himself to shake his head. "You're only seventeen. Your dad would track us down and haul you right back here, honey, you know that. And he'd probably have me charged with statutory rape or something."

She looked into his eyes as if searching for some sign of weakening on his part. When she didn't find it, her chin wobbled and she turned her back on him. "Just go then if you're so scared of him."

"I love you, Jodie, and I know you love me. We've meant too much to each other to end it like this." She shook her head and remained silent. Finally he begged, "Don't make me leave, knowing you hate me. At least kiss me goodbye."

Her slim shoulders went rigid. She turned around slowly, her eyes bright with unshed tears, her chin lifted in wounded pride. "If you loved me, you wouldn't leave me. I'll never forgive you for this, Linc. I'll hate you until the day I die."

With that, she ran into the house, slamming the door behind her. Frozen in torment, Linc waited, praying that she would come back in a minute and say she hadn't meant it. Then, out of the corner of his eyes, he caught a motion in the second window to the right of the door. When he turned his head, he saw JD Roberts standing there with his arms crossed over his chest. The bastard was smiling.

The soft thuds of a horse's hooves striking the ground pulled Linc out of his reverie. He couldn't see the animal yet, but he knew JoAnna was close by. He walked over to his father's pickup and grabbed the blanket and cooler he'd brought along. A mixture of anxiety and anticipation knotted his stomach as he spread the blanket out under the tree. They had some mighty painful ground to cover this afternoon. But Linc hoped that when everything had been said...well, he hoped for many things. But at the very least, he wanted their friendship to survive.

He straightened up from his task in time to see JoAnna astride a big black gelding, riding over the hill on the other side of the pond. Bewitched with admiration, unable to move, scarcely able to breathe, Linc watched the horse approach at a steady walk. JoAnna sat straight and proud in the saddle, looking enticingly feminine despite the cowboy hat and boots she wore with a red short-sleeved shirt and a pair of jeans. She reined the animal to a stop, and they studied each other for a long moment before she dismounted.

As soon as her feet touched the ground, JoAnna turned to face him, her posture erect, arms hanging straight and loose at her sides. Her voice was quiet when she spoke, neither encouraging nor discouraging.

"Hello, Linc."

"JoAnna."

His heart slammed against the wall of his chest as she removed her hat and a cloud of shining black hair spilled down around her shoulders. She ran her fingers through the long, glistening strands in a natural, unself-conscious gesture. *Forget the talk,* he thought. *All I want to do is bury my face in that hair and make love to her.*

JoAnna's lips twitched in sympathetic amusement as she observed the fierce lights of desire burning in Linc's eyes. He looked so good to her wearing crisp new jeans and a blue work shirt that brought out the color of his eyes, she had to admit she wanted him every bit as much as he apparently wanted her. The strength of the physical attraction between them amazed her. All right, it thrilled her if she was going to be honest about it.

But this time, she was determined their communication would be strictly verbal. Before she went one step further in getting involved with him again, she needed some answers. And they'd better be darn good ones.

Linc gestured toward the blanket. "Uh, why don't we sit down?"

JoAnna nodded and saw to Spook's comfort, then walked over to the blanket and gracefully lowered herself to sit cross-legged, leaning back against the tree. Linc followed suit, placing himself directly opposite her. He opened the cooler and offered a choice of beer or a soft drink. When she'd chosen a Coke and he'd taken a root beer, he fastened the lid and leaned forward with his elbows balanced on his knees.

He popped his drink open, took a long swallow, then traced patterns in the condensation on the aluminum can with his fingertips. The continuing silence knotted his stomach even tighter, but JoAnna looked perfectly relaxed. Her dark eyes gazed at him expectantly, and he fumbled for a place to start.

"Do you have any idea how I felt after that last fight we had?" he said finally.

JoAnna blinked in surprise. She hadn't expected him to come to the point so abruptly, but if he could be blunt, so could she. "Since you called me a spoiled brat and told me to grow up, I've always assumed you were glad to get away from me."

He shook his head, uttering a wry chuckle. "Well, I was pretty mad at you right then," he admitted. Then his expression sobered. "But the next day, and for a long time after that, I felt pretty worthless. I never meant to hurt you. In fact, I never meant to make love to you that summer. I knew we were both too young to handle it, but you were so sweet...so damn sweet. Did you ever remember how good we were together?"

Remember? At the moment, it seemed as if all she had done for the last twelve years was try to forget those balmy summer evenings spent in rapturous excitement in his arms.

"Yes, I've remembered," she said softly. "But I did my best to forget. I didn't understand why you had to leave so...fast, but I finally decided you couldn't face my dad and all the gossip."

Linc cursed under his breath and looked away, viciously

yanking out a strand of grass and shredding it between his fingers. When he looked back at her and spoke, there was utter conviction in both his steady gaze and his voice.

"I didn't leave because of the gossip. I didn't give a damn what anybody in this burg thought."

"Then it was JD?" she asked, pleading silently, *Be honest with me, Linc. Tell me about the loan.*

Linc look into her earnest brown eyes for what felt like an eternity, then looked down at his hands. Damn! If only he could tell her the truth. He hated the thought of lying to her, even by omission. But he'd promised he wouldn't hurt her again, and wouldn't it hurt her to find out her father was a blackmailer?

At last he said, "It was a complicated decision. There isn't one easy answer to your question."

JoAnna bit her lip to hold in an aching sigh of disappointment, but she couldn't keep a touch of bitterness out of her voice when she challenged him a moment later. "So, give me an answer, anyway."

He shot her a sharp look. "All right. Even if we hadn't gotten caught like that, I would have left Powder River sooner or later. When we did get caught, I realized we were both in way over our heads. We'd talked about marriage, but neither of us was ready for that."

"No, I guess not," JoAnna admitted. "But why did you have to make it so final?"

"I was a green kid, JoAnna. I didn't know if I'd be a success or fall flat on my face. You needed some time and space to grow up, and I didn't want you to waste your life waiting for me to make something of myself. A clean break seemed like the best thing for both of us."

"Oh, I grew up all right," she muttered.

Linc paused to sip from his can. "I can see now that my timing really stunk, especially as far as you were concerned. I'm sorry for that," he said sincerely.

JoAnna sighed. While everything he'd said was true as far as it went, he was still leaving out one mighty important detail. And dammit all, if he couldn't be honest with her, there was no point in continuing this conversation. She decided to give him one more chance.

"Your decision had nothing to do with my father?"

Linc considered blurting out the truth, but the thought of seeing more pain in her eyes held him back. "I didn't say that," he hedged. "He was damn mad at both of us, and I was afraid he might lock you in your room forever if I stayed."

JoAnna snorted in disgust. "Come off it, Linc. I know about the loan."

Jerking back as if she'd hit him, Linc paled beneath his tan. "How...uh, when...did you find out?"

"About five months after you left I was looking in JD's desk for some tape to wrap a Christmas present, and I found your dad's payment records."

Linc's normal color returned as he digested that information. Then his face flushed again, and he demanded, "Why the hell didn't you tell me you knew about it?"

"Because I needed to hear about it from you, that's why," she retorted. "Why the hell didn't you tell me about it twelve years ago?"

"I didn't tell you about it then," he answered slowly, feeling his temper stirring, "because I was ashamed. I knew it would look bad no matter what I said, and JD threatened to tell you he'd bought me off like a damn fortune hunter if you ever found out about the loan."

"He did that, all right," JoAnna replied with a sad smile. "I didn't want to believe him. But when I never heard from you again, I...wondered."

"So that's why you haven't forgiven me." He tossed his hat onto the blanket and ran the fingers of one hand through his hair in agitation. "Dammit, JoAnna, that money didn't mean anything to me. But the Shamrock was my dad's whole life, and I couldn't—"

"I understand that, Linc," she interrupted. "If JD had been in your dad's position, I'd probably have done the same thing you did." She fell silent for a moment before adding, "What hurt me the most was knowing you'd forgotten me. One lousy letter or phone call from you would have made me feel so much better. I kept hoping and hoping, but I ended up feeling cheap and used instead."

Linc stood and glared down at her, his eyes practically shooting sparks of rage. "He never told you!"

"Told me what?"

"That it was all part of the deal!"

"What was all part of the deal?" she cried, scrambling to her feet.

Turning away, Linc cut loose a string of epithets that would have made a marine drill instructor blush. When he finally had himself under control, he faced JoAnna again. "I wasn't allowed to contact you in any way until the loan was paid off. If I did, JD would foreclose on the Shamrock."

Shaking her head in disbelief, JoAnna backed away until she collided with the tree. Linc grabbed her arms and steadied her before she could fall.

"No," she whispered, pushing against his chest with both hands. "He wouldn't do that to me."

"Like hell, he wouldn't," Linc muttered, letting her go. He took a step back, stating in a flat tone, "JD Roberts has always done whatever the hell he wanted, and he wanted to break us up. Permanently."

Knowing he was right about her father, JoAnna nodded grimly then looked beyond Linc toward the pond, her eyes focused on the past. "All these years, I've thought..." She swallowed hard, blinking back sudden tears. "I've thought that you never really loved me. That I was just a summer fling before you went off to find fame and fortune. That I wasn't...woman enough to...satisfy you."

The tortured look in her eyes ripped Linc's heart in two. Reaching for her with both hands, he groaned and pulled her to him, wrapping her in his arms and held her while he blinked against an unfamiliar wetness in his own eyes. He stroked her silky hair in comfort. His next words sounded as if they were wrenched right out of his soul.

"I *did* love you, dammit. No other woman has ever satisfied me the way you did, Jodie, in or out of bed. Nobody."

It felt good being in his arms. Too good. JoAnna desperately wanted to believe him. But how could she? The press adored a champion athlete, especially one as photogenic as Linc O'Grady. JoAnna couldn't count the times she'd opened a magazine or newspaper over the years and been confronted by a photograph of Linc with some gorgeous model, actress or rodeo queen, who looked as if she'd been stuck to his side with Super Glue.

Pulling away abruptly, she said, "Well you sure let enough

of them try, didn't you? How long was it before you found someone else, Linc? Two weeks?''

His arms dropped to his sides, and he gazed out over the countryside. When he turned back a moment later, his shoulders were rigid, his hands clamped on his hips.

"In the first place," he said in a dangerously quiet tone, "my love life since I left is none of your business. In the second place, you can't believe everything you read in gossip columns."

Hating herself for sounding like a jealous shrew, but unable to stop herself, JoAnna sniffed and looked away, muttering, "Oh sure."

"I'm not denying that I've had other women in my life. But there haven't been that many, and I've never felt as close to anyone else as I did to you."

When she didn't respond, he continued in that same quiet tone. But now there was a cutting edge to it. "You know what your problem is, JoAnna? You've been wallowing in self-pity all these years. You think *you* were the only one hurt?"

Her head snapped around at his harsh words, an angry protest ready to spring from her lips. But Linc put one arm on either side of her, caging her against the tree.

"You were in an uncomfortable position here, I'll grant you that. But at least you still had your home, and you had some people around who cared about you. When I left, I was cut off from everything and everybody who meant anything to me. You said some pretty awful things during that last fight we had. Things that hurt me for a long time."

JoAnna didn't want to meet the condemnation in his gaze, but she couldn't pull her eyes away. She cleared her throat, then admitted, "I guess I never thought much about what it must have been like for you. I'm sorry. But it's always felt to me—" she paused to sniff again "—like you just walked away and never looked back."

The naked vulnerability in her eyes melted the last of Linc's defenses against her like an ice-cream cone dropped on a hot sidewalk. His right hand fell to his back pocket, reappearing a second later with a leather wallet. He flipped it open, fumbled through a wad of business cards and receipts and pulled out a battered, dog-eared photograph. His hand shaking, he held it a few inches from her face.

JoAnna's heart thudded painfully against her rib cage while she stared at the school photograph from her junior year, the one she'd signed, "With all my love forever." Her vision blurred as he dropped the wallet, grasping her shoulders between his big hands.

"I tried my best to forget you," The sharp edge had left his voice. "For a long time I convinced myself that I'd succeeded. But every time I bought a wallet and switched my stuff over to the new one, I tried to throw that picture away. And I couldn't do it."

She would have shied away from the stark emotion in his eyes, but his hands moved up to cup her face, forcing her to look at him while he continued. "I can't count the times I looked at that picture and ached for you."

"Linc," she protested feebly, though why she protested at all was a mystery to her. She had never admitted it to herself before, but for twelve years, she had wanted, needed, to hear these words from him.

"Hush," he scolded gently. "Let me finish. I don't know if what I'm feeling now is love or not. But I sure as hell feel something for you, and I want to find out what it is."

"What do you mean?"

"I want us to start over."

JoAnna searched his face for even a hint of duplicity, but couldn't find one. His blue eyes, darkened now with emotion, pulled at her heart, and for an instant, it was as if she'd stepped back in time, into a romantic vision from her girlhood dreams.

Then Spook snorted at something and the present crashed back in on her. Shaking her head, she pushed against Linc's chest, fighting his grip on her heart as much as the strength of his hands on her face. "Let me go!"

Slowly, warily, he obeyed, stepping back far enough to give her some breathing room, but not so far that he couldn't catch her if she decided to bolt. *Damn you, O'Grady, you've gone too fast*, he chastised himself.

"Tell me what you're thinking," he demanded when he could no longer stand the silence.

"I can't. I'm too confused."

"Jodie," he coaxed in a soothing tone, "we had something really special once. Don't you think we should find out if it's still there?"

"Yes. No. Hell, I don't know!" she cried impatiently, then slid her back down the tree trunk to sit on the blanket again. She raised her knees, wrapped her arms around her shins and rested her chin on her kneecaps, frowning thoughtfully at Linc while he retrieved his wallet and sat down in front of her.

"You look like a bristly little porcupine, all curled up and ready for war," he said softly, a gentle, teasing light in his eyes.

Her lips twitched into an answering smile. "I feel like one. Darn you, Linc. I think I have my feelings for you all sorted out in my head one minute, and the next minute I'm all mixed up again."

"What are you mixed up about?"

"I still have some questions."

"Good. Let's get everything out into the open once and for all. Fire away."

JoAnna straightened up and after a moment's thought said, "You weren't going to tell me about the loan today, either. Why not?"

"I promised I wouldn't hurt you again. And I figured knowing what your dad had done would hurt. I guess I wanted to protect you."

She scowled at him and muttered, "You damn cowboys are all alike."

"What's that supposed to mean?"

She threw up her hands in disgust. "Protecting me is my dad's favorite excuse for manipulating me. It's all some big macho thing about taking care of the womenfolk, and I hate it. I don't need his protection. Or yours. What I do need is honesty. Complete, total honesty."

Linc bristled momentarily at being lumped with JD, then bit the inside of his lip and nodded thoughtfully. "All right. I won't do it again. What other questions have you got?"

"You've been pretty successful for a long time," JoAnna said slowly, groping for the right words. "If you really felt that strongly about me, why didn't you help your dad pay off the loan? It wouldn't have been hard to find me."

"Don't think I didn't try." He shook his head, as if at a bitter memory. "It took four years to get to the point where I had some money, but my dad's just as proud and stubborn as yours. He kept saying it was his debt and he'd pay it off and that it was too late for me to get you back. And..."

"And what?"

He shot her a wry, self-conscious grin. "It bothered the hell out of me to know you still had a hold on me after all that time. I resented you for it." He hesitated for a second, then added, "And I was scared to death that if I ever did find you, you'd spit in my face and tell me to get lost."

"I wouldn't have done that."

"Oh yeah? Well, you sure made me work hard enough to get you to talk to me this weekend."

"I wouldn't have spit in your face," she assured him with a wry chuckle. "I probably would have slammed a door in it."

They grinned at each other for a moment, until the tension spiraled up between them again. JoAnna glanced down at her hands. Linc watched one of his father's cows amble down to the pond for a drink. "What do you say, JoAnna?" he said. "Are you willing to give a broken-down old rodeo bum another try?"

She snorted at his self-description while she stretched out her legs. Then, tipping her head to one side, she asked, "What did you have in mind?"

"I think we should spend some more time together. Get to know each other again."

"You mean have an affair?"

"Did I say that?" His mouth quirked up at one side at her skeptical look. "All right. The thought has crossed my mind. But I want more than sex from you."

"What do you want, Linc?"

After pulling the cooler closer, he rested one forearm across the top and drummed his fingers on the plastic lid while he considered her question. Then he spoke. "Right now I want a friend. Someone who cares about the real me—not the rodeo star or the guy in the ads."

"But why me?" JoAnna asked when he fell into a thoughtful silence. "Surely after all this time you've met some folks you feel close to."

"I have. But some weeks I do two or three rodeos in different states.'' He gestured with his right hand, as if groping for the words he wanted. ''It's like, you're around good people, but not the same ones. And you're always focused on this particular rodeo, and the horse or bull you've drawn to ride. You get acquainted with people, but you don't really get to know them. Does that make any sense?''

She nodded, and he continued. ''You and I have a history that goes back to the grade-school playground. You know all my old friends, my hometown. You knew my mother, and I knew yours. And you've always been easy for me to talk to. Shoot, I've told you things I've never told anyone else. The kind of friendship we had is damn hard to find, JoAnna.''

''I know it is,'' she said quietly. ''But do you really think we could be, uh, just friends?''

''I don't know,'' he admitted. He drummed his fingers on the cooler again for a moment. ''Look, you said you wanted complete honesty, and I want to be straight with you. The truth is that neither of us is ready for any kind of a commitment, but I think on some level, we still love each other.''

JoAnna shook her head in automatic denial and opened her mouth to protest, but he stayed her with a hand on her arm.

''Maybe if we spend enough time together we'll find out we really do love each other and get married and do that whole bit. Maybe we'll find out it was all just infatuation or nostalgia, and we don't have enough in common anymore to make a relationship work. But I think we owe it to ourselves and to each other to find out. That's what I meant when I said I wanted to start over with you.''

He made it sound so simple, so appealing. She knew, however, that it was neither. ''But what if I find out I love you, and you find out you don't love me? Or vice versa?''

''That's a risk we'll both have to take,'' he answered. ''But is that risk any worse than spending the rest of our lives wondering if we could have had something dynamite together?''

She shook her head. ''I don't know, Linc. Even if we did love each other, I still see too many problems for us.''

''Like what? Give me an example.''

''There's your life-style for one thing. You're used to lots of excitement, and you travel all over the place. But my business is in Madison, and I live very quietly. I can't, or maybe I should say I won't, follow you around on the rodeo circuit or wait at home for you, knowing the groupies are crawling all over you.''

"I won't be in rodeo much longer. Only a year or two at most. What else?''

She thought for a moment. "When I was eavesdropping the other night, your dad told JD what you said about us living far away from him if we ever got back together."

"So? You live far away from him now."

"My mother worried about him growing old alone. Before she died, I promised her that I'd come home if Dad ever needed help running the ranch. I have to keep that promise. And..."

"And what?"

"Well, you hate JD so much. I know you've got good reason to, Linc. But he's my father. Much as I'd like to change him sometimes, I love him. Could you ever make peace with him?"

Linc reached across the space between them and gently tipped her chin up, forcing her to meet his eyes. "I don't know, but I think you're borrowing trouble, honey. The first thing we need to settle is how we feel about each other. If we don't love each other, there's no point in worrying about any of this stuff. If we do, we'll find a way to work it all out."

She gulped at the tenderness and the determination in his gaze. "I'm scared, Linc. I can't help it."

"I know, and I don't blame you. I don't want to get hurt again, either. But we've come full circle now, so what do you say, JoAnna? Will you spend some time with me?"

In spite of her misgivings, there was really only one answer she could give him. "All right. But how are we supposed to get together? Long-distance phone calls? Quick weekends sandwiched in around your rodeos?"

"Doesn't sound too great when you put it that way," he admitted. "But I'm booked at least through the end of August."

"And I really can't get away that much right now. I've just added another employment counselor to the staff, and my receptionist and bookkeeper are both getting ready to go on maternity leave."

"I'll take care of the geography problem," Linc said after a moment's consideration.

"How are you going to do that?"

"I''ll take some time off and come see you in Madison."

JoAnna raised an eyebrow at that. "Won't that hurt you in the standings?"

He shrugged and climbed to his feet, offering her a hand up. "I need a break anyway. I'd rather spend it with you than anyone else."

"Linc, don't do anything that might jeopardize your career. I'm not making any promises."

"Don't worry your pretty little head about it, honey." Linc answered with a devilish twinkle in his eye. "That's my problem. Not yours."

She smirked at his obvious attempt to bait her. Then her expression sobered. "Until we're more sure of how we feel about each other, I really don't want to, uh, sleep with you."

He put his hands on her shoulders, answering in a serious tone. "I know. And I'll try not to pressure you." His eyes took on that wicked twinkle again. "But do you think I could have one kiss now? To seal our bargain?"

JoAnna stepped closer to him, raising her hands to the sides of his strong neck as she smiled up at him. "Oh, I think I could be talked into that."

He put his arms around her waist, and, lowering his head, he muttered, "I've had about all the talk I can stand for a while, babe."

Then his mouth closed over hers, tenderly wooing a response that was swift in coming. Her lips parted to admit his tongue, and he accepted her silent invitation with a muffled groan. Their breathing grew ragged; their hearts pounded in unison.

His hands roamed over her back before reaching up to tangle in her hair. She caressed his neck and shoulders, then made a tactile exploration of his strong jaw and teased his wiry sideburns with her fingertips. Finally, when he knew he either had to quit or risk losing control, Linc sighed and turned his head to bury his lips in the center of her palm.

JoAnna's lashes slowly opened, revealing a sweet, bemused expression that nearly undid all his good intentions. After a moment, her eyes focused, and she smiled up at him self-consciously. Knowing it would be a long time before he could hold her again, he let her go reluctantly. She stepped away from him and started looking around for her cowboy hat.

"Well," she said as she picked it up and tucked her hair under it, "I guess I'd better get home."

He nodded, and together they walked over to the patient black gelding, who nickered a greeting as they approached. JoAnna tightened the cinch, then gracefully mounted Spook.

Linc patted the animal's glossy neck. "It'll probably be the second week of September before I can get away, but I'll see you in Madison as soon as I can."

"All right," she told him with a smile. "I'm listed in the phone book under J. Roberts. On Nevada Road."

Then she reined the horse around and nudged him into a walk, turning once in the saddle to send Linc a cheery wave before giving Spook his head. Linc watched them canter away with conflicting emotions rolling in his chest. When they disappeared from sight, he shook his head, carried the blanket and cooler to the pickup and dumped them into the back.

He was relieved that she'd believed him about the money and the agreement with JD, relieved that all the old secrets from the past had finally been aired. Although he ought to be ashamed of himself for feeling so damn smug that she'd been jealous over the women in his life, he wasn't. And, of course, he was glad that she'd agreed to see him again; he'd wanted that all along when he'd suggested this meeting.

But he couldn't help wondering if he wasn't making the biggest mistake of his life. His old pal Marty Taylor continually teased him about being a romantic, sentimental slob. Linc had stubbornly denied the charge, but maybe Marty was right.

The JoAnna Roberts he'd been with this afternoon was not his old, beloved Jodie. But deep down in his gut, Linc knew it wouldn't take much for him to fall in love with her. If he hadn't already done it.

He'd been mighty damn quick to reassure JoAnna that they could work out all their problems if the need arose. But could they? Could he ever make peace with JD Roberts? Even for JoAnna's sake?

"Well, it's too late to worry about that now, O'Grady," he muttered as he climbed into the truck and reached out to start the ignition.

The engine roared to life. Linc turned the pickup around toward the Shamrock. When he hit the gas, however, the engine sputtered, then died. He turned the key again. The vehicle didn't respond.

He climbed out, walked around to the front and lifted the hood, but everything checked out as far as he could tell. He got back in and tried the key again. This time, the engine caught and ran long enough for him to check the gauges before it coughed and died.

The needle in the gas gauge didn't move off the E for empty, not even by a millimeter. Linc stared at it in consternation. Dammit, he'd filled the tank this morning, just before he'd told his dad—

He finished the thought aloud. "That you were going to see JoAnna this afternoon."

Linc rubbed one hand over his eyes and let out a deep, frustrated sigh. Then he started to laugh. If he was a romantic, sentimental slob, then he came by it honestly. The way he had it figured, JoAnna must have informed JD of her plans for the afternoon. The old matchmakers had gotten together on the phone, compared notes and decided it would be a good idea for JoAnna to have to give him a ride home.

Riding double with her would have been romantic, Linc supposed, if the pickup had run out of gas before she left instead of afterward. As it was, he had a five-mile walk ahead of him.

He climbed back out of the truck, dug a cold beer out of the cooler and headed off down the dirt road that would eventually lead him back to his father's house. With every step he took, the conviction that he'd been right when he'd told his father that he and JoAnna could never be happy living here deepened.

Even if their fathers were all for them getting married this time, neither one of them would ever be able to resist butting into their lives. Every time he and JoAnna had an argument, they'd be right there in the middle of it. Knowing those two, they would try to tell them how many children to have and how to raise them.

No, Linc told himself as he trudged along under the hot sun, *if you want any hope of a life with JoAnna, it'll have to be someplace far away from JD and Dad. Someplace far from Montana.*

Chapter Seven

JoAnna held Spook to a canter until they reached a long, relatively flat field four miles west of her father's house. Then, leaning low over the horse's neck, she urged him on. "Okay, big fella, go for it!"

Spook eagerly stretched out, streaking across the prairie like a comet. JoAnna laughed, leaving her troubled emotions behind in the exhilaration of the gelding's smooth, powerful gallop, enjoying the sun on her face, the wind in her hair. But when they reached the jagged rock she used as a mile marker and she gradually reined the big animal back to a walk, thoughts of Linc quickly caught up with her.

She knew she'd made the right decision in agreeing to see him again. Whatever was between them needed to be settled once and for all. Given their fathers' sudden interest in their relationship, it made a great deal of sense for any future meetings to take place away from Powder River.

A jackrabbit bolted out of a clump of sagebrush in front of Spook, and living up to his name, he skittered sideways until JoAnna brought him back under control, scolding, "Stop that, you big baby. I've got enough unruly males in my life right now.''

Spook bobbed his head as if he understood and set off for the barn. JoAnna smiled, patted his neck, then went right back to worrying. Yes, it made sense to see Linc away from Powder River, but should she have agreed to his coming to Madison?

She planned to live there at least another five years if JD remained in good health. After her turbulent last year at home, she had found contentment among Wisconsin's generous, friendly people with their devotion to beer and brats, the Milwaukee Brewers and the Green Bay Packers. She had built a good life for herself there, and she couldn't shake an uneasy premonition that Linc's arrival would change it. Irrevocably.

"Now who's being a big baby?" JoAnna muttered to herself when she realized she was doing exactly what Linc had accused her of doing earlier—borrowing trouble.

As long as they didn't make promises or commitments they couldn't keep, or jump into a passionate affair, there was no reason to believe Linc's visit would rip her life apart again. For all she knew, he might not even show up. When he got back to the rodeo circuit and had time to put this weekend into perspective, he could well decide that he didn't want a relationship with her after all.

That thought brought a piercing stab of disappointment. JoAnna reined Spook to a halt at the top of a big hill. The gelding pranced impatiently and swung his head around to look at her, his expression clearly saying, *Look, lady, I'm ready for my oats and a rubdown.*

JoAnna reached out and scratched him behind the ears, crooning, "Just give me a minute, Spooker."

He settled down at her soothing tone, and she took a few moments to gaze out over the Double R. The rugged land with its alternating barren, rocky bluffs, and lush, irrigated pastures tugged at her heartstrings. Her friends from Wisconsin, accustomed to rolling green hills and huge oak and maple trees, would probably find this little corner of southeastern Montana about as inviting as the moon. But even though she didn't choose to live here at the moment, to JoAnna it was home. It would always be home.

She loved these wide-open spaces with no sign of civilization but the narrow gravel road, the power lines and the miles of barbed wire fence. This land was her heritage. The sleek Black Baldys grazing in the fields represented years of her father's sweat.

JD drove her crazy with his bossy orders, his underhanded manipulation, his just plain ornery cussedness. But her promise to her mother aside, JoAnna knew she could never throw back in his face his dreams of passing onto his only child what he'd spent a lifetime building.

"Oh, Spooker," she murmured, "what the hell am I gonna do if I fall in love with him again?"

The horse raised his head at the sound of his name and blew out an impatient snort, his hide shivering with eagerness to be off. JoAnna held him steady for one last look around, then nudged him into a walk with her knees. When they reached the last gate into the ranch yard, she dismounted and led the gelding the rest of the way to the corral.

JD stepped out of the barn as she loosened the cinch, his bushy eyebrows raised in surprise. "Back already?"

JoAnna grinned. "Were you hoping we'd taken off for Reno?"

"Ya know, you're not too big to spank just yet," her father threatened, walking over to take the heavy saddle from her.

She challenged him with a smile. "Oh, yeah?"

"Yeah."

Folding her arms across her chest, she waited until his stern expression softened into a wry, answering smile. Then she followed him into the tackroom and collected a currycomb and a bucket of oats while he took care of the saddle. When they went outside again, she set to work grooming Spook. JD leaned one hip against the corral fence and crossed one foot in front of the other.

"I'm sorry I interfered again," he said finally.

JoAnna raised her eyes from Spook's broad back and looked at her father. "Why'd you do it, Dad?"

"When Sean paid off the loan, well, we got to talkin' about you and Linc." He shoved his hands into his pockets. "And it occurred to both of us that all our damn feud ever did was drive you two away. We thought if we could get you back together, maybe you'd...come home."

"And produce grandchildren for your ranches."

"Well, yeah. But it was more than that, I swear it. I just wanted you to be happy."

"A woman doesn't have to get married and have children to be happy these days, JD."

"Maybe that's true for some women, honey." He crossed to stand on the other side of the horse from her. Then, looking her right in the eye, he said, "But not for you."

"Dad—"

"No, now hear me out. You've built up quite a business back there in Wisconsin, and I'm damn proud of you. But it would be a waste for you to spend your whole life alone. You've got so much to offer a husband, and just look at the way Timmy Scott came arunnin' to see you on Friday. You love kids, and you always have. Tell me one thing. Do you really enjoy coming home to an empty house every night?"

JoAnna moved up to work on Spook's tangled mane. Avoiding her father's intense gaze, she admitted, "Not always. But that doesn't mean Linc is the answer."

"Maybe he's not. I sure don't want you to rush into anything. But some day I want you to have the happiness your mother and I did. As far as I know, Linc's the only man you've ever loved like that."

"I thought you hated him."

"No, it was his old man I hated. I always thought Linc was a pretty good kid until...well, you know."

"Then why wouldn't you let him contact me again?"

JD flushed. "Oh. He told you about that, did he?"

JoAnna nodded. "He sure did. And you know something, Dad? Never hearing from him again hurt me more than anything else that happened. So why did you do it, and why the hell didn't you tell me when I found out about the loan?"

"I did it for your own good, Jodie. I was afraid you'd never get over him if he was writin' to you and callin' all the time."

Thinking that over, JoAnna removed Spook's bridle and turned him loose in the pasture. She stood at the gate for a moment, resting her elbows on the top rail. The big animal trotted over to his favorite spot, lay down and rolled from side to side in the soft dirt.

"Linc and I would have run into each other at the reunion

anyway, Dad. Why did you think you had to throw us together?''

His lips twitched into a teasing grin. "I figured you'd feel
pretty skittish about seein' him. And let's face it, Jodie, you're
not exactly a spring chicken anymore. Not for havin' babies.''

"I have a *few* good years left in me," she retorted.

He shrugged. "Maybe so. But let me tell you somethin' about
Linc O'Grady. It took a lot of guts for that boy to start off with
nothin' and become a national champion the way he did. And
he kept his word about not comin' back or contacting you until
the loan was paid."

He paused and chewed on his lower lip for a moment. "I've
always felt bad that he didn't make it for his mother's funeral.
I told Sean it was fine with me, but that stiff-necked old cuss
wouldn't let him. Anyway, I admire him. I'd be proud to call
him my son-in-law."

"If you mean that, you might want to think about apologizing
to Linc," JoAnna said, her eyes still trained on the gelding.

JD drew back, his jaw tilted at a defensive angle. "I've got
nothing to apologize for. Any decent father would have done
what I did to protect his daughter."

"He doesn't like you much."

"If he loves you enough to deserve you, he'll swallow his
pride and learn to tolerate me."

JoAnna rolled her eyes at JD's stubborn expression then
pushed away from the fence and turned back toward the barn.
"Well, I guess we'll have to wait and see about that. He's coming to visit me in Madison."

JD's eyes lit up, and he rubbed his hands together in delight.
"He is? That's great."

Laying a hand on his arm, JoAnna cautioned him, "Don't go
counting grandchildren yet. I don't have any idea how this will
turn out."

"Of course you don't, but—"

"But nothing. You stay out of it."

"Well, I will, but—"

"I mean it, Dad."

Their eyes locked in a battle of wills. Then JD said grudgingly, "Aw, all right."

JoAnna eyed him sternly for a moment before releasing his

arm and heading back to the barn. Her father walked beside her, waiting outside while she put away the bridle, currycomb and grain bucket. "You know," she said when she returned, "instead of worrying about my love life, you ought to be thinking about your own."

Digging the toe of his boot into the dirt, he muttered, "There's nothing wrong with my love life."

"Mom's been gone a long time," JoAnna said quietly. "She wouldn't mind if you found somebody else, and I wouldn't, either."

"I've been datin' some." He shrugged. "But I just haven't found anybody who'll...oh, I don't know."

"Anybody who'll what, Dad?"

"Most of the gals I've taken out are just so damned eager to please. It's like they're wearin' this big sign that says, Marry Me, JD and I'll Do Anything You Want." He shifted his weight to the opposite foot and sighed. "I guess what I've been lookin' for is somebody who's not afraid to stand up for herself and fight with me once in a while like Katherine did."

"Sally's not afraid to fight with you," JoAnna observed in a mild tone. "But I understand why you've never asked her out."

JD shot JoAnna a sharp glance. "What's that supposed to mean?"

"Oh, nothing, really. It's just that I can see why you might feel a little intimidated about asking her for a date."

"Intimidated!"

"Let's face it, Dad," she needled him with an innocent expression on her face. "You're no spring chicken, either."

"I ain't dead yet," JD snapped.

"Of course you're not. I only meant that, well..." JoAnna shook her head in admiration of the housekeeper. "She's so pretty and sweet and intelligent, you'd probably have a lot of competition. Just about every man in the county asked her to dance last night."

"And you think I couldn't cut the competition?"

Biting the inside of her cheek to keep from chuckling, JoAnna studied her affronted father for a moment. "Oh, maybe you could," she said. "Since she lives right here, you'd have the inside track with her. But you might feel more comfortable with someone a little closer to your own age."

He scowled at her for a moment before asking suspiciously, "You wouldn't be tryin' to give me a dose of my own medicine, would you?"

She raised both hands in a "who me?" gesture and lied. "After all the times I've yelled at you for butting into my business, would I do that? I was just trying to point out that if you think you're too old for Sally—"

Before she could get out the rest of her sentence, JD turned on his heel and stomped off toward the house, muttering under his breath, "We'll just see who's too old."

JoAnna waited until the screen door on the back porch banged shut. Then she collapsed against the barn in a fit of laughter. She told herself she really ought to be ashamed of herself for manipulating her father that way. But she wasn't. JD had deliberately pushed her hot buttons too many times for her to feel any guilt over hitting a few of his.

A moment later she heard the crunch of tires on gravel. Wiping her eyes with the backs of her hands, she straightened up and saw a red Toyota wagon pull into the driveway. To JoAnna's surprise, Gaye Scott jumped out of the car before the dust had even settled and headed for the front door.

Cupping her hands around her mouth, JoAnna, called, "Over here, Gaye!"

The blonde turned, raised a hand in greeting and hurried to meet JoAnna in the ranch yard. After a quick hug, she said fervently, "Thank God you're still here."

JoAnna put her hands on Gaye's shoulders and held her at arm's length. Her brow puckered with concern as she noted her friend's red nose and puffy eyes. Gaye made a brave attempt at a smile, but tears welled up in her green eyes, and a second later her features crumpled into a mask of anguish.

"What's the matter?" JoAnna asked, putting an arm around her friend.

Gaye clamped her mouth shut and shook her head, obviously struggling for control. JoAnna led her to the patio, and after seating her at the redwood picnic table, went into the house for a pitcher of lemonade. When she returned a few minutes later, she found Gaye sitting as still as a statue, staring off at the hills surrounding the ranch.

After setting the tray containing the glasses and pitcher in the middle of the table, JoAnna sat down across from her friend. She filled the glasses with the icy liquid, handed one to Gaye, and striving for a light tone, said, "If you're ready to talk, I'm ready to listen."

"Remember when I told you about my worst nightmare the other day?" Gaye replied. "Well, I think it's about to come true."

JoAnna let out a surprised gasp. "Brady's back?"

"Not yet. But he called me this afternoon."

"What did he say?"

Gaye linked her fingers around the glass and swiveled it back and forth for a moment. She sighed. "He wants to see Timmy."

"Just Timmy?"

"That's what he said, but he...well, he hinted that he'd like to see me, too. Lord, I'm so confused."

Join the club, pal, JoAnna thought with a grim smile. Aloud, she asked, "What did you tell him?"

"That it'd be a cold day in hell before I let him get within ten miles of my son."

"Can you do that? He's Brady's son, too."

"I know," Gaye answered, shaking her head. "And I'm not even sure I want to keep them apart."

"Why not?"

Gaye reached up and twirled one of the bouncy curls behind her right ear around her finger. "Timmy doesn't remember Brady, but he's been asking lots of questions about him. And when he starts kindergarten in the fall, I'm sure he'll have plenty more to ask when he figures out most of the other kids have dads at home. He gets plenty of attention from my dad and my brothers, but it's not the same as having his own father around."

"Wouldn't it hurt him more though," JoAnna said thoughtfully, "if his dad breezed into his life for a while and then breezed out again?"

"It might, and that's what scares me. But Brady's not really a bad guy, JoAnna." Gaye's eyes took on a dreamy cast. "He was a wonderful father to Timmy before he left."

"Before he abandoned you," JoAnna corrected her, fearing that her friend might allow romantic memories to cloud her judgment.

"Well, he's never forgotten to send Timmy a birthday or

Christmas present, and his child support payments are always right on time. A lot of divorced fathers don't do that," Gaye argued. Her eyes took on that wistful, faraway look again. "And on the phone, he sounded so...lonely."

"He acted like a selfish jerk, and he hurt you both. It's his own darn fault if he's lonely. You can't afford to get all soft-hearted over him now."

Gaye looked at JoAnna abruptly, as if the harsh words had finally brought her back down to earth. "He wasn't the only one who acted like a selfish jerk, JoAnna."

"That's not what you told me before."

"I was angry then," Gaye replied, looking away self-consciously.

"And you're not now?"

"Well, yes, I am. I still think he should have stuck it out with us. But I've had time to look at my own behavior, too, and I wasn't blameless."

JoAnna reached out and patted Gaye's hand. "I didn't say you were, pal. But you don't deserve to drown yourelf in guilt, either." She gave her friend a rueful smile. "Frankly, I think I'm about the last person you should ask for advice."

"Why is that?" Gaye asked.

After JoAnna briefly recounted her earlier conversation with Linc and confessed to her own confusion, Gaye threw back her head and laughed. "Aren't we a pair—almost thirty years old and still tied up in knots over our first lovers? We sound like a couple of ditzy bimbos in a made-for-TV movie."

"Yeah," JoAnna agreed. "We could call it *Return of the Long-Lost Lovers*."

They fell silent then for a moment, each lost in her own thoughts. Finally JoAnna asked, "What are you going to do about Brady?"

"I don't know," Gaye grumbled. "He sounded so determined to see Timmy, I don't think he'll give up. I suppose I should call him back and try to talk to him like a rational adult. What are you going to do about Linc?"

JoAnna propped her elbow on the table and rested her chin on the heel of her hand. Mimicking her friend's glum tone, she answered, "I don't know. I guess I'll just have to take it one day at a time and see what happens."

"That sounds like a pretty reasonable approach." A twinkle of humor entered Gaye's eyes a second later. She leaned closer to JoAnna and, lowering her voice, said, "Now that I'm faced with seeing Brady again, I'm beginning to understand why you were so flipped out when Linc showed up at the reunion."

"I wasn't flipped out." When Gaye gave her an oh-sure-you-weren't look, JoAnna shrugged. "Well, not *that* flipped out."

Gaye held up her palms in surrender. "All right. But even though it's been rough seeing him again, aren't you glad you did?"

JoAnna nodded slowly. "Yes, I am. It's nice to know he didn't just walk off and forget me."

"And even though you're feeling scared about what might happen in the future, aren't you a little bit excited about seeing him again?" Gaye persisted, an impish grin spreading across her features.

"I guess you could say that," JoAnna replied, unable to resist giving Gaye an answering grin. "What's your point?"

"You're a worrywart, JoAnna. You always have been, and you probably always will be. I'm not denying you've got plenty of reasons to worry when it comes to dealing with Linc, but I don't want you to forget the good feelings you have for him because you're afraid things won't work out."

"In other words, enjoy it while it lasts?" JoAnna asked dryly.

"Why not? I think he's a pretty terrific guy, and if you'll be honest with yourself, you do, too, or you wouldn't have gotten this involved with him."

"Are you planning to follow your own advice with Brady?"

Gaye wrinkled her nose at JoAnna and chuckled. "Okay, so it's easier said than done. We both have a lot at stake here, but worrying won't really help anything. And you don't have a kid to consider, so why don't you pretend you've just met him? Forget about the past and JD and the ranch and get to know him again."

JoAnna raised a skeptical eyebrow at her but didn't respond. After a moment Gaye glanced at her watch, let out an exasperated sigh and stood up. "Come on and walk me to the car. I've got to pick Timmy up at my folks' house."

When they reached the Toyota, Gaye climbed into the driver's seat and rolled down her window. JoAnna reached in and squeezed her friend's hand. "You keep me posted on what happens with Brady."

"I will," Gaye promised. "You do the same. And think about what I said, kiddo. I mean, you've got a wonderful opportunity for a second chance with the only man you've ever really loved. Why not take advantage of it?"

JoAnna stood in the driveway, watching the little car until it disappeared around a curve, asking herself, *Why not indeed?*

Chapter Eight

"Oh, for Pete's sake!"

JoAnna dropped to her knees and patted the plush blue carpeting in front of her dresser in search of the earring clasp that had slipped through her fingers. Chad Winslow, her date for the evening, would arrive soon, and she wasn't even close to being ready. She spotted the clasp a moment later and scrambled to her feet with an aggravated sigh.

She'd spent a long, hectic day at the office. Even though it was Friday night, she would much rather have stayed home and put her feet up than go out. But it was too late to cancel, and she'd probably end up thinking about Linc all evening if she didn't have something to occupy her mind.

It had been almost seven weeks since she'd last seen or heard from him. It would be at least another three weeks before she saw him again—if he came to Madison when he'd said he would. With every day that passed, the reunion weekend became more dream than reality to her. Did Linc feel the same way?

JoAnna inserted her earring, then picked up a brush, hoping to get her hair under control before Chad showed up. When the doorbell rang a second later, she plunked the brush back down in resignation and hurried to the front door in her stocking feet. "Come on in," she said, opening the storm door. "I'm almost—"

"Almost what?" the man on the other side of the screen door asked, chuckling at her astonished expression as he opened it and stepped inside.

"Linc!" Automatically moving back to give him room, JoAnna stared at him, blinked, then stared again. "What are you doing here?"

Instead of answering, he shut the storm door with a resounding thunk. Before she could react, his arms surrounded her, hauling her into a rough embrace while his mouth lowered to cover hers in a hungry, searching kiss.

JoAnna's head whirled, and her knees turned mushy. Her heart pounded as if she'd just sprinted a mile. Oh, God, how she had longed for this moment, even while she hadn't quite allowed herself to believe it would really come. But the broad, muscular shoulders beneath her palms were real enough, as were the eager hands combing through her hair and the warm lips planting sweet, nibbling kisses across her cheekbones, her eyelids, the tip of her nose.

"Oh, babe," he murmured in a husky tone, "Lord, but you feel good."

Her eyes flew open. Her palms pushed against his chest, and she shook her head as if to clear away the sensual mist surrounding her.

"Aren't you glad to see me?" he asked, grinning down at her.

Glad didn't even begin to describe the way she felt, JoAnna thought with a smile. "Of course, I am. It's just that I didn't expect you until September."

"I couldn't wait another day. In fact, you're lookin' at a retired cowboy."

"Retired?" JoAnna stepped back and gaped at him as if he'd just sprouted another head.

His grin faded. He shifted his weight to the opposite foot and winced before shifting it back. "Could we sit down?"

"Oh! Sure." Feeling foolish for keeping him standing at the door so long, she led the way to the living room. Linc followed much more slowly, and when she turned and noticed he was limping, JoAnna frowned in concern. "What happened to your leg?"

He lowered himself gingerly onto the sofa, giving her a grateful smile when she brought an ottoman for his foot. "Just a few bruises," he assured her. "I didn't get out of a bull's way fast enough, and the sucker kicked me."

JoAnna sat down beside him, turning sideways in order to see his face more clearly. He looked tired, and she could see lines of pain around his eyes and his mouth. His chin and lower cheeks were dark with a day's growth of whiskers. But she'd never seen a man look more handsome. "It's not bad enough to make you retire, is it?" she asked, nodding toward his leg.

Linc chuckled. "Nah." Then his expression sobered. "But it started me thinkin', and I decided I've had enough."

"Are you sure that's why..." She faltered when he raised an eyebrow at her. "I mean, uh, I told you not to make any sacrifices on my account."

"I didn't. I've got a few other irons in the fire, and only had a few more years in rodeo at best. Why not get out while I'm still on top and in one piece?"

His explanation sounded reasonable to her. Smiling at him, she asked, "What are you going to do now?"

He leaned over and took her hand in his. "Have dinner with me and I'll tell you all about it."

At the word dinner, JoAnna gasped and jumped to her feet. "Oh Lord, I forgot!"

"Forgot what?"

"I have a date tonight," she explained, glancing at her watch. "He'll be here any minute."

Linc struggled to his feet, bellowing, "A what?"

"A date." JoAnna grinned at his affronted scowl. She hadn't known Linc could be so possessive. Still, she had to admit she kind of liked the idea as long as he didn't get out of hand. "You know, where a man and a woman go out for dinner or to a movie?"

He planted his hands on his hips and asked, "Why are you doing this, JoAnna?"

"Did you expect me to put my life on hold until you turned up?" she shot back, mimicking his stance.

"I see," he said more quietly. "You didn't really trust me to come."

She shrugged. "I wanted to. But I haven't heard from you since the reunion. For all I knew, you might have changed your mind."

"Well, I didn't." He hobbled close enough to put his hands on her shoulders. "And now that I'm here, are you still going to date other men?"

"I take it you don't like the idea," she replied, shooting a teasing grin up at him.

"Damn right I don't." He exhaled a sigh before giving her a wry smile and pulling her closer. "I've come a long way to be with you, and I don't want to waste our time together playing games. Are you serious about this guy?"

JoAnna shook her head. "He's just a friend. And I don't want to play games, either, Linc. So after tonight—" she paused, reaching up to stroke his bristly chin "—we'll go steady."

Linc snorted with laughter, as she had hoped he would, then swooped down to kiss her breathless. She responded eagerly, reveling in the strength of his arms, the musky male essence of him, the hardness of his body pressed against hers. When she began to think and hope the kiss would never end, he turned his mouth aside, brushing his lips against her neck.

"Don't go, Jodie," he murmured. "I need you tonight."

She hugged him tightly for a long moment before pulling away. "I have to, Linc. I can't just stand him up."

He leaned his forehead against hers, growling, "All right. But don't kiss him, whoever he is."

She chuckled, kissed him on the chin and stepped back. "Where are you staying?"

"I don't know yet. I rented a car at the airport and came straight here." He put his hands back on his hips and sent her a challenging smile. "My stuff's right outside."

Well aware of what he was hinting at, JoAnna shook her head at him. In Powder River, the neighborly thing to do would be for her to invite him to stay with her. She had plenty of room, after all. But she wasn't ready to do that. Not by a long shot.

"You might try the Holiday Inn," she suggested, walking to the front door and opening it. "I hear they have a nice pool."

Linc remained where he was and studied her. His gaze roamed

slowly from her tousled hair to her well-kissed lips, over her smooth shoulders, bare but for the spaghetti straps of her lavender sundress, and on down to her toes, before reversing direction and climbing back up to her face. JoAnna's skin tingled with heat wherever his eyes focused, but she stood her ground, waiting silently until he limped over to her.

Leaning down, he kissed her cheek. ''I'll see you later, honey,'' he said, and walked out the door.

JoAnna watched while he got in his car and drove away, then raced for her bedroom. She brushed her hair, applied fresh lipstick and a light cologne. She hummed to herself as she strapped on high-heeled sandals and found her purse, pausing for one last glance in the mirror above her dresser.

The woman reflected there didn't look as if she'd had a rough day at work. Her eyes were shining. Her cheeks were flushed more than the blush she'd applied earlier could account for. Her lips were curved into a silly grin. She looked happy and excited and...in love.

''Don't do it, JoAnna,'' she scolded herself in a whisper.

But the woman in the mirror didn't appear to be listening. Her lips stretched into a radiant smile, and the sparkle in her eyes intensified. Frightened by what she saw, JoAnna turned away from the mirror in protest and inhaled a deep, calming breath. When the doorbell rang a second later, she sighed and hurried to greet Chad.

Chad Winslow was an ex-hockey player turned businessman. JoAnna had met him at a chamber of commerce dinner a few months ago. He reminded her of a big, cheerful teddy bear, and she enjoyed talking with him. The evening would be no different from the others she had spent with Chad, she promised herself, Linc or no Linc.

It wasn't an easy promise to keep, however. Her thoughts continually strayed to Linc even while she shared an intimate dinner with Chad at a quiet restaurant on Washington Avenue near East Towne Mall. If Chad noticed her distraction while they sipped after-dinner drinks and listened to a couple singing humorous duets at the piano bar, he didn't mention it. But when he suggested that they leave early, JoAnna was more than ready to end the evening.

She had to choke back a surprised laugh as Chad pulled his

car into her driveway twenty minutes later—the half of her driveway that wasn't blocked by a small camper. Linc's rental car was parked in front of the house. And there he sat on her front steps with a bottle of beer in his hand, chatting with her next door neighbor, Artie Schellenberger. Oh Lord, he looked like an impatient father waiting for his wayward daughter to come home.

JoAnna waited for Chad to open her car door, then walked up the sidewalk with him. She ought to be madder than hell at Linc for pulling such a stunt, but somehow, she knew she would have been disappointed if he'd meekly taken a room at the Holiday Inn. She met his oh-so-innocent smile with a bland smile of her own and introduced Chad to the other two men.

Linc's eyebrows shot up as he noted Chad's burly physique. During the small talk that ensued, he conveyed his possessive attitude toward JoAnna without much effort at subtlety. Before long, Chad dropped a chaste kiss on JoAnna's cheek, promised to call her soon and left.

When Artie wandered back to his own yard a few minutes later, JoAnna sat down beside Linc. The evening was warm and humid, scented with the smell of freshly cut grass and flowers blooming in the beds next to the steps. A pair of squirrels performed a high-wire act on the power lines crossing the street. She clasped her hands around her knees, inhaling a deep breath of the summer air.

Linc reached over, lifted her right hand from her knees and held it, lacing his fingers through hers. He rubbed his thumb across her palm, idly stroking the backs of her fingers with his free hand in an affectionate, companionable gesture. Neither spoke, but the simple touch communicated a sense of peace between them, a gladness to be together again.

At last, JoAnna broke the silence. "You've been busy while I was gone."

"I was damn lucky to get to the rental place before it closed. How mad are you?"

"Does it matter?" she said dryly. Before he could answer, she asked, "Just how long are you planning to stay?"

"At least for the fall semester. After that, I guess it depends on you."

"What's the fall semester got to do with your plans?"

"I'm gonna register for school next week."

She turned to him in surprise. "At the unversity?"

"Yup. Think I'll be the oldest freshman on campus?"

"I doubt it. But why, Linc? You don't really need college now."

"I always wanted to go, but it wasn't possible. And I can't just sit around while you're working, so this seemed as good a time as any to give it a try." He grinned. "Who knows? Maybe they'll polish off some of my rough edges."

"What are you going to major in?" JoAnna asked, intrigued.

He shrugged. "I don't know. I'm just gonna take what any freshman takes." He pulled a slip of paper out of his shirt pocket and read from it. "English, history and music appreciation. The counselor tried to get me to take some math and science, but I decided three classes were enough for starters. I want to have plenty of time for you."

Shaking her head in amazement, she glimpsed the corner of Linc's trailer in the driveway. "You can't stay in that thing, you know," she said, nodding toward it. "Especially once the weather gets cold."

Linc rubbed his chin while he glanced from JoAnna to the trailer and back again. "Well, I'll admit, the shower's not great and the kitchen's pretty small. But I figured you might be willing to let me use yours if I clean up after myself."

"But, Linc, you must be used to—"

"I'm used to motel rooms and campers. But that's not the point."

"Oh? And what is the point?"

"I came here to spend time with you. Normal, everyday living time, so we can really get to know each other again. We're not gonna get that if I'm living way off somewhere in an apartment. Where did you think I'd stay when I got here?"

"In a motel, I guess. I thought you'd just come for a couple of weeks."

Linc stretched his legs out, turning his head to frown at her. "We need more than two weeks. I want to be close to you, JoAnna. And since you don't want me living in your house, the camper seems like a good compromise."

She considered that for a moment, then said, "You've done a lot of thinking and planning about this."

"Yes," he agreed. "It's important to me. *You're* important to me." He paused. "Look, I know you're jittery about us making love again, and I don't blame you for that. I'll admit I want you like hell, but you've got to start trusting me. I won't jump your bones or pressure you, honey."

JoAnna gave him a dubious glance. Maybe he wouldn't jump her bones, but she wasn't so sure she could resist jumping his. Linc smiled and softened his voice to a coaxing tone.

"I'll find someplace else to live if you really want me to, but I'd like to give this a try. I'll be a good neighbor, I promise."

JoAnna looked into his serious eyes and knew she was licked. "All right. We'll try it. But the first soggy towel I find on the floor, you're off to the Holiday Inn."

Linc's teeth flashed white in the darkness. He let go of her hand and wrapped his arm around her shoulders, giving her an affectionate squeeze. "Atta girl. Now just quit your frettin' about every little thing. We're gonna have a great time together."

"I'll try."

They were quiet for a while then. Linc's arm slid down to her waist. JoAnna relaxed against his side and lay her head on his shoulder. It felt good, being with him like this. And he was right, she admitted. Living in such close proximity, they were bound to learn more about each other. That was what they'd both wanted back by the pond in Powder River.

From now on, she would keep her wits about her, but she wouldn't waste this time with Linc by agonizing over the past or the future. It was time to let go and live in the present.

Then Linc observed in a dry tone, "You didn't get much of a good-night kiss from the Incredible Hulk."

"I sure didn't." Grinning inwardly at Linc's description of Chad, JoAnna heaved an exaggerated sigh. "Gee, I wonder why not. Do you think there's something even my best friends aren't telling me?"

Linc pulled away slightly and studied her face as a man inspecting a work of art. He shook his head slowly. "I don't think so. You look damn kissable to me. Smell good, too."

She wiped her brow with the back of her hand. "Boy, that's a relief. Well, maybe Chad thought there was too big an audience."

"Could be."

They fell silent again, each making a show of watching the stars emerge. JoAnna felt a pleasant tension escalating within her and sensed Linc was experiencing similar feelings. *Lord,* she thought with a silent, bemused laugh, *all we have to do is talk about kissing and our engines rev up*. Then Linc swore softly and swatted the back of his neck. A second later he slapped at his forearms.

"What's the matter?" JoAnna asked.

"I think these damn mosquitoes are tryin' to carry me off to Canada," he complained, swatting the side of his neck this time.

"We'd better go in, then."

"Your place or mine?" Linc asked, leering at her until she laughed.

"Neither. You're not going to pressure me. Remember?"

He rose to his feet, then reached down to help her up, pulling her closely against him in the process. "You could at least offer me a cup of coffee."

"It's getting late, and I have to work until noon tomorrow." She softened her refusal with a grin. "But I could take you on a driving tour of Madison in the afternoon."

"Sounds good. You can have dinner with me tomorrow night, and we'll have a good long talk."

"I'd like that."

She held his warm gaze while he lowered his head, then closed her eyes when he kissed her with a hot, breathless passion that left her knees quivering and her pulse racing. He released her much too abruptly a few moments later and limped across the lawn to his camper.

"What was that for, O'Grady?" she called indignantly.

He turned and held out his hands in an innocent pose. "That was just for the good-night kiss I cheated you out of."

Then he was gone, leaving her standing there, smiling idiotically after him and looking forward to tomorrow like a kid on Christmas Eve.

Linc shut the camper's door and leaned against it while he fumbled for the light. After finding the switch, he opened the tiny refrigerator, pulled out a bottle of beer and plunked himself down on the padded bench behind the table. He took a long drink then slouched back against the seat, silently congratulating himself on a job well done.

He was frustrated as hell, and his first meeting with JoAnna hadn't exactly gone the way he'd envisioned it. But he felt reasonably satisfied. At least they'd made a start.

"You should have called her, O'Grady," he muttered, easing off one boot. "Or at least sent her some flowers."

It wasn't that he hadn't thought of doing both of those things. He had. But after the first few days back on the circuit, the reunion had taken on the feeling of an illusion, something he'd dreamed up because he'd wanted it for so long.

Much as he hated to admit it, he'd been scared to death to dial her number and find out none of it had happened or worse yet, that it had all happened and she'd changed her mind about seeing him again. The longer he waited, the harder it had become to contact her. It seemed silly for a man who made his living by climbing onto crazed Brahmas, most of them weighing over fifteen hundred pounds, to act like such a coward. But he had.

He took another long drink, then pulled off his other boot and carried his beer over to the small bunk. After shucking his clothes, he stretched out on top of his sleeping bag, absently massaging the purple bumps on his right hip and thigh where the bull's hooves had caught him two days ago. Closing his eyes, Linc diverted his attention from his aches and pains by picturing the way JoAnna had looked when he'd surprised her.

Her dark eyes had widened before lighting up with pleasure. Her sweet lips had curved into a welcoming smile, and her arms had reached for him. And that dress...

He loved that dress. It was simple, but feminine. It flattered her curves without flaunting them, and its pale lavender color and low, square neckline showed off her dark tan.

At this very moment, he knew he'd die a happy man if he could only march right back into JoAnna's house and help her remove that little number. He would take his sweet time about it, kissing and caressing her while he slipped those skinny straps off her shoulders. Then he would slide down that long zipper, one notch at a time, and hold his breath while the material pooled around her feet.

Linc groaned and grabbed for his beer bottle. Lord, it was going to be hard to keep his promise about not pressuring her. Glancing down at his groin, he muttered, "That ain't the only thing around here that's goona be hard, either."

But at least he was finally in Madison. He could see her, talk to her, touch her. The last seven weeks had been hell. He hadn't ridden worth a damn. He'd hated the traveling, the crowds, even the rodeo clowns who had saved his miserable hide more than once. All he'd wanted was to get back to JoAnna.

He had made such careful plans, repeatedly cautioning himself not to get his hopes up, not to expect too much. When he contacted the University of Wisconsin about starting school, he had decided to take a wait-and-see attitude and be logical about his feelings for JoAnna. Hah!

The minute she opened that door tonight, looking all rushed and flustered, his heart had turned right over in his chest and he'd been lost. He'd tried to deny it. But when she told him she had a date, what had he done? Gone out and rented a damn trailer, for God's sake. Now that was the act of a desperate man.

Even though she'd told him her date was just a friend, the hours he'd spent waiting for her to come back had been ugly. He'd never felt such gut-deep jealousy before, hadn't even known he was capable of it. Winslow had seemed to be a nice enough guy, but Linc had wanted to rearrange his handsome face so bad his palms had itched.

It was time to stop kidding himself. He was in love with JoAnna Roberts. He always had been. And God help him, he always would be.

Linc swung his legs over the side of the bunk, stepped into the kitchen and splashed some water on his face. Then he opened the window over the table and stood beside it, looking at JoAnna's house. He hadn't seen much of the interior, but he supposed it was a typical suburban rancher. Probably had two or three bedrooms, maybe a family room downstairs. Right now, that house sheltered his hopes for the future.

Yes, he loved JoAnna Roberts. He wanted to marry her, have children with her, grow old with her. But if he wasn't damn careful, he knew he would lose her again.

She had trusted him implicitly once, but her trust had been shattered. If he'd only told her about the loan and the conditions

JD had put on it twelve years ago.... Well, he hadn't and he couldn't change that now. So he'd have to earn her trust again.

But he couldn't tell her how he really felt. Not yet, anyway. He couldn't rush her at all. It would take a cool head, determination and patience. He could handle the cool head and determination parts, no sweat. But the patience? Well, he'd just have to develop some. Somehow. Even if it killed him.

[faded text from previous page showing through]

Chapter Nine

Smiling with satisfaction, JoAnna closed the last file her new employment counselor, Alice Henderson, had left for inspection. The cheerful, middle-aged woman was competent and thorough, and she had the ability to put even the most nervous client at ease. JoAnna had already made Alice her assistant, and she was fast becoming a dear friend, as well.

JoAnna glanced at the clock, noting with a start that it was after seven. She carried the stack of files to Alice's office, then went back to her own office for her purse. But before she could get out the door, the phone rang.

Sighing, JoAnna perched on the corner of the desk and picked up the receiver. "Roberts Personnel."

"Why aren't you home with Linc, *idjit?*"

"Hello to you, too, Gaye," JoAnna answered with a smile.

Gaye laughed. "Actually," she said more seriously, "I'm just as glad you're at the office. Got a few minutes?"

"Sure. What's up?"

"Oh, nothing much. I've lost five pounds, Brady's back and Timmy's got the chicken pox."

"Whoa. Brady's in Powder River?"

"Yeah. Timmy's so excited, I can hardly stand him. All he talks about is his dad."

"Do I detect a note of jealousy in your voice?" JoAnna asked.

"Well, of course you do," Gaye retorted. "I mean, wouldn't you think the ungrateful little wretch could remember who's been here taking care of him day after day for the last three years?"

"Timmy's only five, Gaye. You know he adores you. Brady's just a novelty right now."

"God, I hate it when you're logical."

"Okay. The kid's a brat, and shooting's too good for him. Does that make you feel better?"

JoAnna smiled at her friend's responding giggle. Then Gaye sighed. "Just be glad you're having your reunion with Linc in Wisconsin. Brady's been back for four days, and you'd think it was the Second Coming."

"I can imagine."

"No, you can't. My folks are beside themselves with joy, my son's gone berserk, and everybody I run into wants to know when we're going to reconcile."

"Are you?"

"Who knows? But he looks good, JoAnna. Darn good."

"Has Brady said he wants to try again?"

"No. I've only seen him twice when he's come to visit Timmy. But when he looks at me, I get all hot and itchy inside, and I can't think of a single intelligent thing to say. I don't know what I'd do if he made a pass."

"Melt in a puddle at his feet?" JoAnna asked, moving around to sit in her chair.

"Probably. Is that the voice of experience I hear?"

"No. Linc's been a perfect gentleman." *Too darn perfect,* JoAnna thought with a grimace, remembering several nights of aching frustration in the last week alone.

"You mean he's been there for three weeks and he's still sleeping in that camper? Sheesh! I thought you'd be having a passionate affair by now."

"Sorry to disappoint you. We're having a lot of fun, though. You should see him, Gaye. He's like a little kid. He's so excited about his classes, and he wants to go everywhere and do everything.''

"I'll bet he's playing hard to get. You know, bring you to your knees by playing it cool.''

"I don't think Linc's playing anything. He's just giving us both time to get used to each other. Frankly, I appreciate it.'' *Most of the time,* JoAnna added silently.

"Uh-huh. And you don't get all itchy and hot inside when he looks at you with those sexy blue eyes?''

"I didn't say that. Lord knows I've had a few moments when I'd love to haul him off to bed. But we're rebuilding our friendship first. We both need to do that.''

"So, you think the affair part could start soon?''

"I doubt it. We're still being…well, cautious with each other.''

"For Pete's sake, JoAnna, what are you waiting for? You love the guy, and you might as well admit it.''

"It's not that simple. And if you're so hot about affairs these days, have one with Brady.'' JoAnna rubbed her eyes with one hand and sighed. "I'm sorry, Gaye. It's just that—''

"No, *I'm* sorry,'' Gaye said quietly. "And I do understand it's not that simple for you. But hang in there, kiddo. I still think Linc's a great guy, and who knows? Maybe it'll work out for you this time.''

"Yeah. Maybe. Maybe it'll work out for you and Brady, too.''

"Hey, before we hang up, I've got some other news for you.''

"What's that?''

"You know Sally Metzger was dating Linc's dad for a while last summer?''

"Are they getting serious?'' JoAnna asked.

"No, I don't think she's been out with him for at least a month. But guess who she *has* been seeing?''

"Who?''

"*Your* dad. They went to the farmer's union dinner the week before last and to the movies last week. And Jennie over at the bank was telling me that she saw them together in Miles City on Saturday night. She said they were dancing up a storm and acting like quite the lovebirds.''

"That's nice.''

"Is that all you've got to say? I mean, we're talking about your dad and a much younger woman."

"He's a big boy, Gaye," JoAnna assured her. "And Sally's a nice person. How's Linc's dad taking it?"

"Fine, as far as I know. In fact, Sean and Nancy Edwards were in Miles City with JD and Sally."

"I'm glad to hear that. Listen, Gaye, I've got to go. Call again if you need to talk. Any time."

"You, too. And JoAnna? Don't leave Linc out in that camper too long. At least one of us deserves to have some fun."

"Goodbye, Gaye."

JoAnna hung up the phone, leaned back and draped her right leg over the chair arm, smiling at her friend's parting shot. So JD was courting Sally. And they were double-dating with Sean O'Grady. JD and Sean must be getting along fairly well to do that.

If they could patch up their relationship after all those years of hostility, perhaps she and Linc could do the same thing. He certainly appeared to be making every effort to make their living arrangements work.

He cleaned up after himself, did his own laundry, took out the garbage and mowed the lawn without waiting to be asked. He was a tad cranky when he first got up in the morning, but once he'd had a shower and a cup of coffee, he made a better breakfast companion than Bryant Gumbel or Willard Scott. If he didn't take her out to dinner, he usually had something cooking by the time she got home from work.

They had settled into a comfortable routine, and there was no doubt in JoAnna's mind that they could live together quite compatibly for the rest of the semester and beyond. But as she had told Gaye, they hadn't talked about their feelings much or argued about politics or anything else, for that matter. They were just so excruciatingly polite with each other.

JoAnna smiled ruefully at that thought, realizing that many women would have snatched Linc up after the first week and thanked God such a man existed. She certainly wasn't complaining about his behavior, but something told her they were living a fairy tale. It was pleasant, but...passionless.

Oh, the passion was there between them, simmering just below the surface. She sensed it in the casual, affectionate touches they couldn't help, in their warm camaraderie and teasing, in the brief good-night kisses they occasionally shared. But real people with real relationships just weren't always so blasted nice to each other all the time.

They had to learn to take the bad with the good. Though she wasn't quite ready to haul Linc off to bed yet, she *was* ready for something more honest, something deeper, something less cautious with him.

She glanced around the office, absently admiring the tasteful prints on the walls, the sleek Scandinavian furniture, the plush gray carpeting. It was a functional room, but a homey, restful one as well.

It had taken five years and countless hours of hard work to build her business to the point where she could afford such furnishings. She used to relish the quiet hours after five o'clock, when the phones stopped ringing and the staff left for the day. But since Linc's arrival, she couldn't wait to go home.

She had only stayed late tonight to prevent the paperwork she normally handled in the evenings from completely overwhelming her desk. Had her feelings about work changed because she knew Linc would be waiting for her? Or would having a dog or another roommate make her feel the same way? Somehow, she doubted the latter.

"Well, Gaye's right about one thing," JoAnna muttered, glancing at the clock on the wall and reaching for her purse. "What are you doing at the office when you could be home with Linc?"

Linc checked on the chicken casserole he'd put in the oven over an hour and a half ago, cursing when the potholder slipped and he burned his finger on the oven rack before closing the door. He turned down the oven temperature for the third time and glanced at the clock. Where in the hell was JoAnna?

If she didn't get home soon, their dinner would be dryer than the grass back home in August. He stomped into the living room and looked out the window for some sign of her car, trying to keep a lid on his rising impatience and irritation. But dammit, where the hell *was* she?

He paced around the living room, feeling as if he had ants

crawling under his skin. Picking up his history text from the coffee table, he flopped down on the sofa and opened the book, but at the moment, he didn't give a hoot about the ancient Greeks. Finally he slammed the book shut and stomped back to the window.

The last three weeks were among the best he could remember. They had also been the longest weeks in recorded history as far as he was concerned. Oh, JoAnna and he hadn't fought or anything like that. In fact, they'd gotten along surprisingly well.

But all this cheerfulness and politeness was slowly driving him nuts. He didn't want to play "house" with JoAnna anymore. He was sick and tired of kissing her on the cheek—or on the lips when he felt in control of his baser instincts—and going back out to that damn camper every night.

Running a hand through his hair in frustration, Linc turned away from the window and returned to the sofa. He wanted to see her crabby and out of sorts, just once. He wanted to fight with her and know they would eventually make up—preferably in bed. He wanted to know how she felt about him, dammit.

But he *didn't* want to rush her or scare her off, and so he would go on being a model guest—if he didn't wring JoAnna's neck when she finally waltzed in the door. Just then he heard the familiar thump of her car door in the driveway.

"Patience, O'Grady. Hold on to your damn patience," he ordered himself, opening his history book again and pretending to study.

JoAnna breezed into the room a moment later with a cheery, "Hi, sorry I'm late." She dropped her purse on the coffee table and sniffed appreciatively. "Something smells great."

Linc plastered a welcoming smile on his face and glanced up from his text. She looked cool and relaxed, and so damn beautiful in a hot pink, short-sleeved sweater and matching skirt, that his belly and groin tightened painfully. "Well, I'm sure glad you're not dead in a ditch somewhere," he blurted, unable to censor his mouth in time.

Oh, that was a great opening, O'Grady, he chided himself. *Just dandy.*

JoAnna raised her eyebrows in surprise at his harsh tone. "I had some work to catch up on," she replied evenly.

Before he said anything else he knew he'd regret, Linc tossed his book on to the table and headed for the kitchen. "Dinner's ready," he called. "Let's eat."

"I'll be right there."

JoAnna shook her head at his stiff, retreating back, silently telling herself, *Be careful what you wish for.* Then she went into her bedroom, changed into jeans and a T-shirt and washed her hands. When she entered the kitchen, Linc was serving a concoction of chicken, vegetables and rice.

They took their seats at the small, round dinette table, and for the first time in three weeks, JoAnna felt as if she were eating with a blind date. A silent, moody one. A moment later, Linc left the table and walked over to the refrigerator. He returned with the catsup bottle and proceeded to smother his dinner.

JoAnna nearly gagged at the sight of his plate. Enough was enough. She put her fork down. "Why did you do that?"

"Dam stuff's so dry it tastes like straw." He shot her a scowl, then took another bite.

"I said I was sorry I was late," she pointed out, pushing her plate away as her own temper heated at least ten degrees.

Linc gave her another dark look, telling himself he was acting like an ass, but feeling unable to hold in his anger any longer. "You should have called."

JoAnna rolled her eyes and said, "Oh, brother. I lost track of time, and then I got a phone call from Gaye. All right?"

"You knew I'd be fixing dinner. Seems to me, it would have been simple common courtesy to let me know you'd be late."

"I didn't ask you to cook—"

"Well, thanks a helluva lot." He pushed back his chair, carried his plate over to the sink and dumped the contents into the garbage disposal, muttering, "Some appreciation I get for slaving over a hot stove."

JoAnna laughed incredulously. "I've been neglecting my work to spend time with you. What's the big deal if I stay a little late one night catching up? For Pete's sake, Linc, you sound like a nagging wife!"

His nostrils flared, and his face flushed. He marched over, planted his hands flat on the table and loomed over her, yelling, "Didn't it ever occur to you that I might be worried?"

"That's ridiculous!" she yelled right back. "I've been working late at the office for years."

"In case you've forgotten," he ground out, "Madison isn't exactly a small town. You're a woman, JoAnna. Sometimes women get raped and murdered when they're out alone after dark."

"It's not dark yet. And our parking lot's well-lit when it is."

"Oh yeah? Well, you could have had car trouble or been in an accident."

JoAnna jumped to her feet, put her fists on her hips and met him nose to nose over the table. "You sound like JD."

"That was a low blow. Where'd you learn to fight dirty?"

"It's not my fault if you're acting just like him."

Linc's voice softened to a dangerously low tone. "Cut it out, JoAnna. Now."

She poked him in the chest with her forefinger. "Look, I haven't answered to anyone since the day I left home. And I'm not gonna start again with you, you big...poop!"

Linc straightened to his full height, glaring at JoAnna while she did the same. Then his sense of the ridiculous took over, and one corner of his mouth twitched up. "Did you say...*poop? Big poop?*"

Oh, hell, I can't believe I said that, she thought with chagrin. Knowing her face was probably as red as her Bucky the Badger T-shirt, she gave him a shamefaced grin. "I'm sorry, Linc. That was, uh, childish."

His shoulders shaking, Linc sagged onto a chair, threw back his head and howled. JoAnna felt the tension ease out of her body at the sound of his laughter. It was absolutely infectious, and before long, she grabbed for a chair as well because she was giggling too hard to stand up.

"Ah, JoAnna," he gasped a few moments later, wiping his eyes with his fingertips. "That was rich."

"I suppose I'm never going to live that one down, am I?"

"Probably not," he agreed, "but I guess I had it coming." Then he asked wryly, "A nagging wife, huh?"

JoAnna tipped her head to one side, giving him am impish smile, "Well, just a little."

They both chuckled. "You know something?" JoAnna said a moment later, "I'm not sorry you got mad. It was more than my being late though, wasn't it?"

Linc nodded. "Yeah. I've been trying to be the perfect guest so you wouldn't throw me out."

"And I've been trying to be the perfect hostess so you wouldn't leave."

"Really? Kinda like havin' me around, do ya?" he drawled with a smug grin.

"Yeah," she drawled in return. "But I'll still send you packing if you leave soggy towels in the bathroom."

"Fair enough." He glanced at the casserole dish and grimaced before turning back to JoAnna. "I'll make you a deal. You go order a pizza and put on some music, and I'll get rid of that mess."

"Hey, it isn't *that* bad." She laughed at his deadpan stare, then headed for the phone, saying, "All right, all right."

After placing the order, she went into the living room and sat down beside the stereo. She flipped through her albums, grinning when she heard Linc whistling over the clatter he was making with the dishes. A lifelong fan of country music, she had collected recordings of every major artist from Hank Williams, Jr., and Randy Travis to George Jones and Loretta Lynn. But her all-time favorite was Marty Taylor. She reached for his "Greatest Hits" album and set it on the turntable before going back to the kitchen for napkins and paper plates.

Linc looked up from wiping off the counter and smiled when the sound of his old friend's husky baritone drifted into the kitchen with JoAnna. He rinsed out the dishrag and draped it over the faucet, watching JoAnna bend over to dig paper plates from a cabinet. Her jeans pulled tightly across her delectable bottom, and his mouth suddenly went dry.

He crossed to the refrigerator and pulled out a can of Old Style beer, holding it up to JoAnna. "Want one?"

"Sure."

They moved into the living room to wait for the pizza to arrive. Angling herself into one corner of the sofa, JoAnna propped an elbow on the back, resting her head on her palm. Linc sat down beside her, smiling when she closed her eyes with an expression of pure enjoyment on her relaxed features.

He patted her bent knee affectionately, and she said, "I love this song. Whenever I get homesick for Montana, it always makes me feel better."

"Which do you like more, the words or the music?"

She opened her eyes, giving him a questioning look. "I don't know. What difference does it make?"

"I wrote the words."

There, Linc thought while he waited for her reaction. It was finally out. The one last secret he'd kept from JoAnna.

"You did not," she chided him with a grin. "Marty Taylor's lyricist is a guy named Patrick Dobson. It says so right on the album jackets."

"My mother's maiden name was Dobson. My middle name is Patrick."

"Get outta here, O'Grady. The man's a recluse. He doesn't even show up for the award shows."

"You always liked my poetry. That's where the lyrics come from."

"Linc, you don't have to try to impress me just because we had an argument. I already think you're special enough."

He chuckled. "Good. You can go into detail about that later. But I'm telling you the truth, honey."

"You're kidding."

"Nope."

"You're not kidding!"

Laughing at her incredulous expression, he cupped her face between his hands. "I'm honest-to-God not kidding. I *am* Patrick Dobson, and I wrote every one of those mushy, sentimental songs Marty sings. I'll give you his number so you can call him if you want."

"But why the big secret? Why not use your own name?"

"And wreck my tough-guy image?"

She shook her head as if to clear it, dislodging his hands. Then she studied him critically for a moment. "That doesn't seem to bother George Strait, and he's been in rodeo."

"Well..." He shrugged. "It's a matter of protecting my privacy."

"A guy who models underwear worries about his privacy?"

"Gimme a break. I write from the heart, you know? Some of my poems are pretty personal."

"Where did you meet Marty Taylor?"

"At a rodeo in Houston about seven years ago. We were invited to the same party and got to talking. We've been working together ever since. He's the only one besides our lawyer and the IRS who knows I'm Dobson. And now you, of course.''

''Why did you tell me?''

''Because I trust you. And, uh...I guess I thought if I opened up a little more with you, you might do the same with me. I'm tired of us holding each other at arm's length and tiptoeing around each other like we have been. Aren't you?''

The doorbell rang before she could answer. Impatient with the interruption, JoAnna hurried to the door, paid for the pizza and brought it back to the coffee table. Linc served the slices onto the paper plates, looking at her expectantly while she sat cross-legged on the floor on the other side of the coffee table from him.

''I know what you mean,'' she said slowly, accepting the plate he held out to her. ''But I'm not sure where to start. What do you want to know?''

''Everything.'' He chuckled at her perplexed expression. ''For starters, I'd like to know what you want to do with the rest of your life?''

''Oh, is that all?''

''C'mon, you know what I mean. You've said a couple of times that you'll probably help JD run the Double R someday. But is that what you really want to do? Or would you rather stay here and run your business?''

Giving herself a moment to consider the question, JoAnna took a bite of her pizza. When she'd finished swallowing, she said, ''I enjoy what I'm doing, especially when I can match someone up with a great job. I've made some good friends here, and I like being my own boss, but I've always missed the ranch. I guess I've been waiting for my dad to mellow out a little before I went home.''

Linc eyed her skeptically. ''Do you honestly think that's possible for JD?''

''I can always hope, can't I?''

''Get serious, Roberts. From what I can see, you've been pretty successful here. What can the Double R give you that you can't give yourself?''

''I am being serious. And there's a lot the ranch can give me that I can't get myself.''

''Such as?''

She shot him an exasperated glance. "A bigger challenge for one thing. It's more of a gamble, more exciting pitting yourself against the weather and cattle prices than sitting behind a desk at an employment agency. And I miss the variety of things you have to do and being outside and working with the animals. It's a whole different life-style."

"So it's the work rather than the Double R itself that appeals to you?"

"I don't know about that. I've never separated the two before."

"But it's possible?"

"I guess so." Reaching for another slice of pizza, she said, "Now it's your turn. What do you want to do with the rest of your life? Model? Write songs? Become a rodeo commentator?"

Linc shook his head. "I've had it with modeling. And writing songs isn't a full-time job for me. It's more of a hobby. I've had a couple of offers about being a commentator, and it might be fun for a while, but I can't see myself doing that forever."

"So what do you want to do?"

He grinned. "I'd like to get back into ranching, but with horses, not cattle. And maybe start a rodeo school as a sideline."

JoAnna leaned forward, resting her forearms on the coffee table. "What kind of horses? Thoroughbreds?"

"Nah, they're too high-strung. I was thinking more along the lines of quarter horses."

"Won't you get bored staying in one place all the time?" she asked.

"I won't know until I try, will I? Besides, I've got enough money to hire good help. I figure if I want to take a trip now and then, there's no reason I couldn't do it."

"I see."

Do you really, babe?" he wanted to ask. Instead, he finished eating in silence, allowing her some time to think over what he'd said. While JoAnna cleared away the debris from the meal, he put another record on the stereo and sat back down on the sofa.

She returned to the living room a moment later, carrying a fresh beer for each of them. He patted the cushion beside him and she took it with a smile. Resting his arm behind her on the sofa back, he asked, "Well, what do you think?"

''Of your plans?'' When he nodded, she said, ''They sound wonderful.''

''Can you see yourself being a part of them? We'd make a good team.'' He held his breath as he waited for her answer.

She turned to face him more directly. ''Maybe.''

Linc set his beer on the table, gave her a lopsided grin and raised his hand to caress her cheek. ''Only maybe?''

JoAnna lowered her eyes. ''After what you told me tonight, I'm even more worried about your life-style, and—''

''Why? I'm gonna be a rancher. You said you wanted that, too.''

Her gaze shot up to meet his. ''It sounded more to me like you want to play at being a rancher. You'll own the land and the stock, but you'll still be free to pick up and leave whenever you want.''

''Even ranchers need vacations sometimes. That's all I meant.''

''I'll grant you that. But what if somebody finds out you're Patrick Dobson? You've created such a mystery surrounding him, the press will go nuts and you'll *really* be famous. And then you'll have people calling you from all over the place, wanting you to—''

''For God's sake, JoAnna, will you quit borrowing trouble?''

''I can't help it. And—''

''There's more?''

''Yes! You know it as well as I do. Where did you plan on having this ranch of yours?''

''We can have it right here in Wisconsin if you'd like, so you can keep your employment agency. You can raise horses just about anywhere.''

''Anywhere but Powder River?'' His silence was answer enough. ''See?'' she said sadly. ''We still have all these problems, Linc. Nothing's really changed since the reunion.''

''You're wrong,'' he said quietly, leaning toward her. ''As far as I'm concerned, everything's changed.''

''What do you mean?'' She swallowed at the intense look in his darkened, mesmerizing eyes.

''I love you, JoAnna. And you love me. You're just too chicken to admit it.''

JoAnna stiffened but couldn't look away. His words, his eyes, the tenderness in his voice made her ache with wanting and scared her witless at the same time. "That's not fair," she whispered, drawing closer to him in spite of herself.

The naked desire in her eyes and in her hoarse whisper undid what little restraint Linc had left. He slid both arms around her, muttering hoarsely, "So? Who said life was fair?"

Then his lips captured hers in a kiss ripe with hunger. He plunged his tongue deeply inside her mouth, tasting spicy traces of pepperoni and beer. She moaned in response, the throaty sound of pleasure igniting his need for more of her.

He wanted to touch her everywhere, taste her everywhere, all at once, but he struggled for control. His hands explored her back, gliding over the soft cotton of her T-shirt as they outlined her spine and shoulder blades, encountering baby-soft skin when they found her nape. Lord, she felt good, smelled good, tasted good.

Her hands were trapped between the two of them. She pressed against his chest until he loosened his hold enough for her to free them. Her touch was as feverish as his—on his chest, his shoulders, his biceps—telling him how much she wanted him more plainly than spoken words could have done.

Blood pulsed hot and fast through his body, and he knew that somehow, he had to slow down. He leaned sideways until he was lying on the sofa, then pulled her down on top of him and rolled over until they lay facing each other. They gazed into each other's eyes, their ragged breathing drowning out the stereo. His heart lurched in his chest when she gave him a smile as seductive as Delilah's must have been and traced his lower lip with her index finger. So much for slowing down.

He caught the tip of her finger between his teeth, licking it while he pulled the hem of her T-shirt out of the waistband of her jeans and slid his hand inside to caress the small of her back. Her skin felt like warm silk beneath his fingertips. Her eyes closed, and a blissful smile spread across her lips as he became bolder, stroking over her waist and midriff.

Kissing that sweet smile, he gently cupped her breast, relishing her sigh of delight against his lips. She reached up and ran her hand over his hair, the motion pressing her hardened nipple more firmly against his palm. He'd waited forever to touch her like this again. He groaned with his own delight, finally pulling his mouth from hers when she suddenly stiffened in his arms.

Dropping sweet, nibbling kisses on her cheeks, her eyelids, her earlobes, he asked, "What is it, honey?"

"The phone's ringing."

"So let it ring," he coaxed her, moving under her chin with his lips.

She arched her neck to give him greater access, shivering when he found the juncture of her neck and shoulder with his tongue. "All right."

But now that he could hear the damn thing, he couldn't concentrate on JoAnna the way he wanted to. Whoever was trying to reach her was persistent as hell. Sighing with regret, he pulled his hand out of her shirt and raised his head.

"Maybe you'd better answer it."

She disentangled herself and grabbed the extension on the end table, grinning at him as he sat up beside her. Her "hello" came out low and husky.

"Oh, hi, Dad. I was, uh, a little busy. No, that's all right."

Wouldn't you know, Linc thought darkly, *that JD would be the one to interrupt.*

JoAnna's face lit up with happiness. "Really? Well, you sure didn't waste any time. Oh, no, I'm happy for you, Dad. For Sally, too. Well, of course I want to talk to her."

Linc started to stand up, intending to give JoAnna some privacy for her conversation, but she motioned him back down with one hand.

"Hi, Sally. Congratulations. I told you that dress would get his attention, didn't I? I wouldn't miss it for the world. I'd love to. Thanks for for asking me. Okay, put him back on."

Linc surreptitiously adjusted his fly. But while his body gradually relaxed, he started feeling damned uneasy as he watched JoAnna. Her dark eyes glowed softly with affection, her laugh was warm, her free hand made animated gestures. The closeness she shared with JD was evident and he felt threatened by it.

At the same time, he found himself feeling a twinge of envy and guilt. He'd been close to his own father like that once....
JoAnna's eyebrows shot up in surprise, and he turned his attention back to her.

"He is?" She looked at Linc, her eyes dancing with mirth.

"Yes, he's still here. I'll ask him and let you know. Okay. Talk to you later, Dad."

JoAnna hung up the phone, then let out a loud whoop and jumped to her feet. Turning to Linc, she bubbled over with excitement. "They're getting married!"

Well, goody for them, Linc thought darkly, wishing she'd get even a quarter this excited about the thought of marrying him. But when he'd hinted at it, what had he gotten? A lousy maybe.

Oblivious to his mood shift, JoAnna chattered on. "Sally asked me to be a bridesmaid and get this—your dad's going to be the best man!"

Not wanting her to know just how ugly his thoughts were at that moment, he stuck a polite smile on his face and said, "That's, uh, real nice. When's the wedding?"

"November first." JoAnna paused and shot him a quizzical look, as if she finally sensed his inner turmoil. Then smiling, she sat back down at a right angle to him, pulling one knee up onto the cushion. "JD made it a special point to invite you to come to the wedding with me. You'll come, won't you?"

He gave her an "are you out of your mind?" look and slowly shook his head. "I don't think that's a good idea."

"Come on, Linc," she chided him softly. "If JD and Sean can bury the hatchet, can't you at least try?"

Attending JD Roberts's wedding would be about as much fun as getting stomped and gored by a bull as far as Linc was concerned. But if he wanted to marry JoAnna, sooner or later he would have to establish some kind of a civil relationship with the old SOB for her sake. And if he could show JoAnna that he'd try to get along with her dad, maybe he could also convince her to live someplace besides Montana.

Nodding thoughtfully, he said, "All right. I'll go."

Balancing on her knee, JoAnna leaned forward, threw her arms around his neck and hugged him. "It won't be so bad." A second later, she rested her forehead against his and grinning wickedly at him, asked, "Now, where were we?"

Linc put his hands on her waist and kissed her quickly before gently pushing her back onto her own sofa cushion. She looked at him with a mixture of hurt and confusion in her eyes. He gave her a crooked smile. "I guess I'm just not in the mood anymore."

She leaned back against the armrest. "We would have made love if Dad hadn't called," she said quietly.

"Yeah, we probably would have. But I'm not sure we're really ready to do that now."

"Why not?"

The last thing he wanted to do at the moment was get into an argument with JoAnna. "It's not that I don't want you, honey," he said, reaching out to take her hand. "But you said it yourself. We still have some problems. We made love impulsively when we were kids, and we both got hurt. I don't want any regrets this time for either of us."

JoAnna smiled sadly. "I understand. But I wish you could... Well, maybe if I explain something to you you'll understand my dad a little better."

"I'll try."

"JD didn't come out of that mess twelve years ago without being hurt, Linc. After you left Powder River, he about drove me crazy trying to arrange dates for me." She sighed at the memory. "And then, when I found out about the loan, I just wanted to get as far away from him as I could. I started applying to schools on the east coast."

"So Wisconsin was a compromise?"

"Yes. Luckily for me, it turned out to be exactly what I wanted and needed. But Dad was crushed that I wouldn't stay in Montana."

"How did your mother feel about having you so far away?"

"She wasn't much happier than JD was, but she understood why I needed to get away and establish some independence. I almost moved back home when she got sick, but she wouldn't let me."

"Why not?"

"I'd just started my business for one thing. And she didn't want Dad to get dependent on me."

Linc frowned at her. "I can't see him being dependent on anyone."

JoAnna chucked. "That's because you don't know him at all. Not really. You've only seen his hard side."

He raised a skeptical eyebrow. "You mean he has a soft one?"

"Of course he does. Especially for kids. He'd have spoiled me rotten if my mother hadn't put her foot down."

"Why didn't they have more kids then?" Linc asked, intrigued by her story in spite of himself.

"They tried. But Mom had three or four miscarriages, and the doctor finally convinced her to quit trying. That's why Dad's always been so protective of me."

"You make him sound like Santa Claus."

JoAnna shook her head impatiently. "No, I'm not denying he can be a real turkey when he wants to be, Linc. I know he was really rough on you, and I'm not trying to excuse what he did. But he's meanest when he feels that his family or his land is threatened. And from his viewpoint, you were a threat to everything he wanted for me."

"I'm supposed to forgive him because of that?"

"Just think about it. If you can't forgive him, at least try to understand him."

He smiled at her. "You should have been a lawyer." Still holding her hand, he stood up and pulled her to her feet beside him. "It's getting late. Walk me to the door?"

She nodded her agreement and went willingly into his arms when he turned to her before letting himself out. Their goodnight kiss was tender and heartfelt, leaving them both trembling and aching for more. "If we're going to abstain, we'd better think up lots of activities to keep us busy," Linc said hoarsely when he finally found the strength to pull away.

Then he slipped out the door and was gone. JoAnna gazed thoughtfully after him for a long moment before starting to smile. She did love Linc O'Grady. She always had, and she always would. She believed that he loved her, too.

But would love be enough to hold them together this time? If Linc could get past his hatred of her father, she figured they had a fighting chance. And if she could stop being such a worrywart, their chances of making it would be even better.

Only time would tell. But JoAnna knew one thing for sure—whatever pain or anxiety might lay ahead, she wouldn't give Linc up easily this time.

Chapter Ten

Over the next month, Linc did plan lots of activities to keep them busy. JoAnna stifled her fears about him as best she could. And she had fun in the process—glorious, carefree fun such as she hadn't had since, well, she didn't think she'd ever had fun like this.

Linc dragged her to the malls and made her help him choose some non-western clothes so he'd "blend in a little better on campus." She doubted she would ever get used to seeing him in Reeboks instead of boots, but she loved having him come jogging with her before work every morning.

They went to a Wisconsin Badger football game and screamed themselves hoarse. She helped him study for the first exam he'd taken since high school and felt as proud of his grade as he was. They went to a drive-in movie to celebrate and necked in the backseat of her car like a couple of teenagers.

One Friday he surprised her with plane tickets to Nashville, and they spent a weekend with Marty Taylor, his wife Janice and their two sons. The Taylors were both witty and down-to-earth. Their obvious devotion to each other and their children warmed JoAnna's heart, and their affection for Linc was extended to her so naturally, she felt right at home.

Each day became an adventure in laughter and loving. They went to concerts, plays and movies, visited museums and the tourist traps in Wisconsin Dells. Linc hid love poems in her car, in her desk at the office and in delightfully unexpected places in her house. Some of them were so sweet and whimsical they brought tears to her eyes; some were torrid enough to torch her socks off.

There were times when she ached all over with wanting him, but he insisted on courting her "just a little while longer." She was alternately amazed, amused and irritated with his continued restraint and teased him unmercifully about all the cold showers he was forcing them both to endure. But she loved being courted by him almost as much as she loved Linc himself.

On the third Saturday in October, Linc hurried her out to the car after breakfast and headed west. After some intense badgering from JoAnna, he finally admitted he wanted to see the House on the Rock near Dodgeville. They arrived at the bizarre, fifteen-room house perched on top of a sixty-foot chimney rock by midmorning.

Holding hands, they wandered through rooms carved out of stone with plush carpeting on the walls and even on the ceilings. They spoke in hushed tones, enjoying the mystical atmosphere provided by twisting, turning staircases; closed-in, dimly lit rooms; and breathtaking vistas to the valley floor over four hundred feet below.

Exquisite, oriental objets d'art, gorgeous leaded glass lamps and a three-story bookcase delighted the eye, while sweet, tinkling music from the waterfalls and the rich notes from a grand piano in the music room caressed their ears.

After lunch in the Bavarian Beer Garden, they toured the cavernous museum attached to the house, marveling over the incredible collections of dolls and dollhouses, music boxes, mechanized orchestras, and on and on until JoAnna felt as if every one of her senses had been pleasantly assaulted.

At last, they came to the world's largest carousel. They stopped and stared in open-mouthed wonder at the exotic animals and thousands of sparkling lights. To the delight of the other visitors, Linc swept JoAnna into his arms and waltzed her around the platform until she was breathless and dizzy. She looked up into his eyes, and everything around them—the applauding tourists, the glittering, raucous carousel and the unending exhibits—faded into a misty background.

His steady gaze held such love for her, such tenderness, her heart surely stopped beating. He whispered her name, and then he kissed her with a hungry, searing urgency. When he released her and murmured urgently, "Let's get out of here," JoAnna could only nod her heartfelt agreement.

They drove back to Madison with barely a word spoken between them. She tried to coax him through her front door, but he shook his head with a smile and said, "You've got an hour to get dressed up for dinner. We're going someplace special."

The magic continued at a restaurant in a restored Civil War era mansion. They were seated at an intimate corner table in a small dining room on the first floor. A shimmering harvest moon cast its light through slender French doors on Linc's left. Every look, every word, every casual touch they exchanged, heightened the exquisite tension growing between them.

JoAnna sipped champagne and wondered how a man could be so perfect. Linc's dark hair gleamed with health, and the moonbeams reflected off the silver strands in his sideburns. His blue suit coat hugged his broad shoulders while his snowy silk shirt emphasized his deep tan. The strength of character in the creases and angles of his face, the laugh lines around his eyes and his self-confident carriage stirred every feminine instinct she possessed.

All she had to do was look at him and she felt swamped with the desire to run her fingers through his hair and cover that rugged face with kisses.

Caught up in the same enchanted spell, Linc studied JoAnna as she studied him. Her hair glistened with blue-black highlights in the candlelight. Her dress was an utterly feminine, peach-colored confection with a strapless bodice that clung to her curves, then flared into a fluffy, billowing skirt. Her smooth shoulders invited his touch, and her light, provocative perfume made his head swim.

He barely noticed his dinner; all he wanted was to be alone with her and tug on that bodice until the dress slithered down her body into a shimmering heap on the floor.

After coffee and turtle pie for dessert, JoAnna sat back with a sigh of repletion. "It's been a wonderful day," she said.

"It's not over yet, honey." He covered her hand with his own, sending shivers of delight through both of them.

"I know." She lifted his hand to her lips, brushing a kiss across his knuckles. "Let's go home."

"Don't you want an after-dinner drink? There's a tunnel to the carriage house we could explore and—"

Giving him a bewitching smile, JoAnna slowly shook her head. "I don't want to explore a tunnel."

Linc sat back in his chair and fiddled with his coffee cup for a moment. Then, looking her square in the eye, he asked, "What do you want?"

"You. I want you, Linc."

"Are you sure?"

"Absolutely."

"Then let's go."

He signaled the waiter for their check. The rest of their exit from the restaurant passed in a blur for JoAnna, as if someone had hit the fast-forward button on a VCR. When they arrived at her house, Linc hustled her up the walk, opened the front door and yanked her inside, then slammed and locked the door behind him.

Leaning against the coat closet, he blew out a gusty sigh and drew her into his arms with a devilish smile. "Alone at last."

She slid her hands beneath his suit coat, rubbing the warmth and hardness of his chest with her palms. "You're lucky you didn't pass a cop, O'Grady."

"Cop, schmop. Kiss me, woman!"

She obeyed with pleasure while he removed her shawl, draping it over a chair. One hand dove beneath her hair and caressed her nape. The other traced the zipper at the back of her dress. As the kiss deepened, his hips moved in slow, erotic circles against hers.

JoAnna fulfilled her earlier fantasy and combed her fingers through his thick glossy hair. He tasted of coffee and chocolate and caramel. The spicy scent of his after-shave filled her head. Her breasts flattened against his chest, and she felt the thunderous beat of his heart racing with hers.

When his mouth left hers, nibbling the length of her throat, she arched her neck for him. Her hips began moving in counterpoint to his, as if seeking the part of him that could fill the aching emptiness inside her. Without warning, he scooped her up and carried her to the bedroom, setting her down beside the queen-size bed and turning on the bedside lamp.

His eyes never leaving her, he tossed his jacket and tie onto the floor and tugged off his dress boots. Then he took her into his arms again and kissed her until her knees buckled. He supported her easily with the strength of his arms, and a moment later, she felt her zipper give, heard the soft whir as it slid to the bottom of the track.

"Can you stand now, honey?" he asked, stroking her back and shoulders.

"I think so."

He tugged on her dress, his eyes darkening as he watched his earlier fantasy become reality. She held her breath while his eyes blazed over her lacy, strapless bra and half-slip, and on down her long legs to her strappy evening sandals.

"You're absolutely gorgeous, babe," he whispered.

Before she could respond, his hands traced the lace edges of her bra, then cupped the aching fullness of her breasts. He dipped his head and kissed the deep cleavage, unfastening the garment with deft fingers an instant later. He knelt at her feet and slowly drew the half-slip to her ankles, offering a steadying hand while she stepped out of it.

"Oh, Lord," he breathed when he looked up again and saw the frilly garter belt, the sheer stockings, and the wispy bikini panties peeking out at the juncture of her thighs. "You wore that to drive me crazy."

He stroked her hips and down her thighs and calves, kissing the warm bare flesh at the tops of her stockings while he slipped off her sandals. Feeling her knees weakening again, she grasped his shoulders as his nimble fingers unhooked the garters and rolled down her stockings. He dispensed with the garter belt and panties, then pulled back the covers on the bed for her.

She collapsed gratefully onto the smooth sheets, stretching out on her side and propping herself up on one elbow to watch him finish undressing. Her heartbeat accelerated with each article of clothing he dropped, and she wolf-whistled at the skimpy powder-blue underwear she recognized from his magazine ad.

When he copied the cocky pose he'd held for the ad's photographer, she giggled. "Mrs. Marsh was right. They match your eyes beautifully."

Chuckling, he swooped down and kissed her before hooking his thumbs into the waistband and peeling off the briefs. The sight of his proud nudity stole her breath. She held her arms out to him and he sat down on the bed, bracing one hand on either side of her to support his weight.

"Are you protected, honey?"

"Yes." Smiling, she rolled onto her back and ran her fingers over his chest. "One way or another, I intended to jump your bones tonight."

His skin felt hot to her fingertips, his muscles taut and trembling with restraint. She wouldn't have been surprised if he'd gone ahead and made love to her at that instant. Instead, he smiled down at her and reached out to smooth the tousled hair back from her forehead. Her heart opened up at his tenderness, and she whispered, "I love you, Linc."

His hand became still in her hair. He closed his eyes and gulped. Looking at her a moment later, he said hoarsely, "I know you do. We wouldn't be here if you didn't. But I was beginning to think you'd never say that to me again."

Sudden tears pricked the backs of her eyes. Blinking them away, she reached up to frame his face with her hands. "I'm sorry it took me so long. It's just been hard—"

"Hey, none of that," he chided her gently. He stretched out beside her and gathered her into his arms. "We're together again now. That's all that matters."

She linked her fingers behind his neck and rubbed her cheek against his chest, savoring the closeness between them. Then his free hand started to roam slowly over her body, reigniting arousal wherever he touched. His lips worshipped the length of her neck, the curve of her jaw, then settled hungrily on her mouth. His tongue teased the sensitive flesh inside her lower lip, danced across her teeth and finally searched out her tongue.

She moaned with pleasure and let her hands explore the different textures of his body—the slightly damp, silky hair curling above his collarbone, the smooth hard flesh of his back and shoulders, the wiry tufts of hair on his chest. She inhaled deeply of the clean, soap-scent of his skin, tasted and tormented his nipples.

"Darlin'," he gasped, pulling himself above her and pinning her hands beside her head. "If you don't stop that, I won't last two seconds."

"I thought we were doing pretty well."

He flashed her a wicked grin. "Honey, you ain't seen nothin' yet."

Sliding back, he lowered his mouth to investigate her neck and shoulders. Then, with tantalizing slowness, he moved toward her breasts. His hands fondled their swelling firmness while his lips came ever closer in tighter and tighter circles that brought an echoing tightness to her womb.

Her back arched. Her heart hammered against her breastbone. Her veins felt as if liquid heat flowed through them as his mouth finally closed over her extended nipple. She writhed under the erotic suckling of her breasts; her arms wrapped around his head, holding the source of her pleasure to her.

Just when she thought she couldn't bear the burning ache for fulfillment raging inside her, he shifted, insinuating his hand between her thighs, tenderly parting them. She gasped as his gentle fingers danced over her skin, coming enticingly close to the center of her need, then sliding away again, only to return and intensify the delightful torment seconds later.

She released his head with a soft ecstatic cry when his fingertips entered her, caressing her for long, breathless moments.

"Sweetheart, I don't think I can wait much longer," he murmured, his voice rough and aroused as the rest of his body.

"Love me, Linc," she begged, grasping his waist to urge him closer. "Now."

"I will, JoAnna," he vowed, carefully positioning himself while his eyes burned into hers.

Her soft, joyous cry as he entered her came only a heartbeat before his own louder one. He held himself absolutely still for a moment, as if savoring the sensations. His biceps bulged and his forehead glistened with perspiration as he struggled for control.

JoAnna reached up to wipe his brow, then traced the corded muscles standing out along his neck and down his long arms.

He groaned as she stroked the contours of his chest and rib cage, his flat belly, and on around to the rigid curve of his buttocks.

"God, I love it when you touch me," he moaned.

He leaned down to capture her lips in a demanding kiss. Her fingers dug into the flesh of his hips as he started to move inside her. Wrapping her legs around his waist, she matched his cadence, her head thrown back in abandoned delight.

She felt her body, her very soul, lifting to ride a shining cloud as tension built within her, part pain, part bliss in its intensity. She grasped his straining shoulders, clinging as if she might fly off the face of the earth if she didn't hold on with all her might.

"Ride with it, honey," he coaxed, his voice a husky thread of sound mingling with her whimpers of pleasure.

His thrusts became stronger, deeper, until she convulsed in his arms, then slowly relaxed, her eyes glowing with such wonder, he followed her over the brink of ecstasy to his own fulfillment.

JoAnna's arms closed around his back as he collapsed, holding him close while their thundering hearts gradually slowed and their tortured breathing returned to normal. His weight was welcome, wrapping her in the security she had never found anywhere else but in his arms. She licked a drop of sweat from his neck, making him shiver and roll to one side, gathering her into his embrace.

Their hands stroked, petted and caressed each other as they cuddled in the warm afterglow, as if they each had to be constantly reassured that the other was really there and wouldn't fade into yet another lonely dream. At last, Linc broke the silence, his voice filled with contentment.

"It's still there for us."

"Yes, Linc."

"It's even better than it was before."

"Yes, Linc."

"I feel like I oughta stand up and beat my chest and yell or something, but I'm too tired."

"Are you sure? I'd love to see that."

"Are you laughin' at me?"

"Yes, Linc."

He leaned over and swatted her rump, a fierce scowl on his face that sent JoAnna into gales of laughter. He laughed with her, a joyous, carefree sound that filled her with happiness. She wrapped her arms around his neck and pulled him down for a searing kiss that sent fresh tingles of electricity to the tips of her fingers and toes. She pouted when he pulled back, telling her firmly, "JoAnna, we should talk."

"About what?" she asked innocently, sliding her hand across his hip at a slow, tantalizing pace.

"About...JoAnna, behave yourself!"

"Later," she coaxed, rising up to push his shoulders flat on the bed.

Smiling with a sense of her feminine power, she straddled his hips, brushed her breasts against his chest and nibbled at his neck and earlobe until he surrendered with a muttered, "You're right. Later."

JoAnna woke up the next morning to find Linc's head pillowed on her breasts, his arm wrapped around her waist like a small boy clutching a teddy bear. Though one of her arms was pinned beneath him and felt decidedly numb and his whiskery chin felt scratchy as woolen underwear against her tender skin, she'd never known such peace before. She stroked a lock of hair from his forehead with her free hand.

Linc opened one bleary blue eye, smiled a sweet, sleepy smile, and closed the eye again. He burrowed his face between her breasts and squeezed her tightly.

"Mornin', gorgeous," he mumbled, dropping a loving kiss on the side of her breast.

"Good morning yourself, sleepyhead," she retorted, twining her fingers through his hair. "I've got good news and bad news for you."

"What's the good news?"

"I love you." She smiled, giving his whiskers a playful scratch with her fingernails.

"I already knew that," he answered smugly without opening his eyes. "What's the bad news."

"If you don't get off my arm soon, it's going to fall off."

"What?" He looked around in confusion, then rolled aside, lifted her arm and started rubbing it briskly. "Why the heck didn't you say something sooner?"

The only word JoAnna could manage at first was a strangled "aaagh!" as the blood rushed back into her arm with a battalion of electric needles.

Linc massaged her until she could speak coherently enough to say, "It's fine now."

"I'm sorry, honey," he replied, turning his attention to her naked torso. The cool morning air had a predictable effect on her nipples. "Aw," he said sadly. "Poor things look all puckered and cold."

He bent his head to remedy the situation. Then, to JoAnna's chagrin, he pulled away, flipped back the tangled sheet and blanket, and swung his legs over the side of the bed.

"Where do you think you're going, O'Grady?" she demanded with a surprised laugh, scooting after him. Putting her arms around him from behind, she hugged him and planted kisses across his shoulder blades.

He flashed her a devilish grin. "Haul it out of there, Roberts. I've got something to show you."

She propped her chin over his shoulder, rubbing her breasts against his back. "I already saw it last night. Several times. And just look at the poor thing. It's all swollen and hard."

"That's not what I wanted to show you."

"Later." She licked the rim of his ear while she reached down, boldly caressing him.

Groaning, he turned to her, kissing her breathless as he pressed her back down on the bed. "All right, you insatiable wench. Later."

Much later, JoAnna sat primly on her own side of the car, enjoying the vivid golds and reds of the oak and maple trees flying past her window. When Linc turned onto County Road M toward Middleton, she asked, "Haven't we done enough sight-seeing yet?"

"Not quite."

"Sure you won't tell me where we're going?"

"Nope."

Smiling at his suppressed excitement, JoAnna decided to let him keep his secret and settled back against the seat. She didn't really care where they were going, after all, as long she could go with him. They passed through Middleton, then turned west on Highway 14.

About ten miles down the road, Linc switched on the blinkers and slowed down for a right turn. JoAnna caught a glimpse of a yellow For Sale sign. Then the car crested the top of a hill and a picturesque, white, two-story farmhouse came into view.

A freshly painted picket fence surrounded the yard. One of the mature oaks inside it sported a tire swing. Fifty yards behind the house, a red barn with an attached blue silo rose in stately splendor, and flashes of sunlight reflecting behind it suggested the presence of a stream.

Linc parked next to the house and switched off the ignition. "This is what I wanted to show you. Come on. Let's get out and take a look around."

JoAnna gazed at the house for another moment, feeling as if her bubble of happiness had just developed a slow leak. Linc had been studying more at night lately. She had assumed that he'd been working harder because midterms were coming. And with all the activities he'd been planning for them, she simply hadn't questioned how he spent his time. Obviously he'd used some of it visiting real-estate agents.

She turned to him, a protest forming on her lips, but he leaned over and hushed her with a quick kiss. "Just give it a chance, darlin'. Please."

How could she refuse when he looked at her like a darn puppy begging for attention? she wondered indignantly, slowly nodding her head.

The air was crisp and clear when she stepped out of the car, the sunshine golden. The house was set far enough back from the highway to give it an aura of peace and welcome. JoAnna took a moment to absorb the atmosphere and couldn't resist smiling as she followed Linc through the gate and around to the back door.

"The whole place has been modernized," Linc told her enthusiastically, leading her into a huge, sunny kitchen. "But it still has a lot of old-fashioned charm."

As if he feared she might start finding fault, though that would have been difficult to do even if she'd wanted to, he whisked her through the first floor in a hurry. In minutes, she'd seen the formal dining room, the spacious living room with a fireplace and bay windows on two walls, the cozy den, a half-bath and the combination laundry/sewing room. "What's your rush, O'Grady?" JoAnna had to ask. "Is somebody gonna throw us out of here in five minutes or what?"

Linc chuckled and gave her a self-conscious grin. Putting his arm around her waist, he urged her up a broad stairway. "I'm just anxious for you to see it, that's all. There's four bedrooms and two more bathrooms up here."

"Why this house?"

He didn't answer until they reached the landing, where he gestured toward a cushioned window seat beneath a slender, arched window. "Sit down and I'll tell you," he said.

JoAnna followed his suggestion, feeling tension radiating off him as he sat down beside her. Her pulse rate picked up speed when he turned to her with a solemn expression in his blue eyes.

Clasping JoAnna's left hand, Linc cleared his throat. "These last few weeks and last night especially, have been like a dream come true for me," he said. "I don't want it to end when the semester's over."

He tipped his head to one side and looked at her expectantly. A moment of sheer joy bubbled up inside her until he shifted impatiently on the cushion and she remembered where they were sitting. Her chest suddenly felt tighter than a pair of designer jeans, and she had to look away.

Linc gently palmed the side of her face, forcing her to meet his gaze. "What are you thinking?"

"I don't want it to end, either," she admitted softly.

Sliding both arms around her, he tucked her head into the curve of his shoulder and said, "Then marry me, JoAnna. I want you to be my wife and have my babies and be there to hold me in the night."

JoAnna wrapped her arms around his waist and pressed closer to him for a moment, savoring those words she'd ached to hear for such a long time. She felt his lips brush the top of her head, heard the deep, steady cadence of his heart beneath her ear, smelled the scent of the soap they'd shared in the shower this morning on his skin. A hundred yeses hovered on the tip of her tongue, but before she could get one out, Linc continued speaking.

"Imagine climbing these stairs with me every night. We'll

stop at each room and check to make sure the kids are covered up, and then we'll walk down the hall to the master suite and shut out the rest of the world. We'll set up a huge Christmas tree in the living room every year and string all the trees outside with lights. We'll take the kids sledding and ice skating in the winter, and there's even a pond out back so they can swim in the summer.''

It sounded so wonderful, JoAnna could have wept. In fact, when Linc held her away from him a moment later, hot tears clogged her throat and stung her eyes. Forcing them back, she said huskily, "Oh, Linc."

His smile uncertain, he asked, "Is that a yes or a no?"

"I want to say yes, but..." She held out her hands palms up and glanced around the landing.

"If you don't like the house, we can find another. Or we can build a new one."

"It's not the house. You knew I'd love it when you brought me out here, and I do. But I have to go home."

"JoAnna, I've seen your business, met your friends.... You've built a good life for yourself here in Wisconsin. Powder River's not your home anymore."

"Yes, it is. I promised my mother I'd go back, and I have to keep that promise, Linc. I told you that right from the beginning."

"But JD's getting married next week. He's not gonna grow old alone now. Surely your mother would understand—"

"Maybe she would. But Sally's more interested in cooking and taking care of the house than she is in running the ranch. What'll happen to it if something happens to Dad? And what about your dad? He's going to need you one of these days, too. Don't you feel any responsibility toward him at all?"

Linc's nostrils flared as he sucked in an angry breath. "Of course I do. Hell, I let him send me into exile to save his land, didn't I?"

"But that's just it, Linc. I've been in exile, too, and I'm ready for it to end. I want, I need to go home for me. And you do, too, or you wouldn't still feel so bitter."

"Don't tell me what I need, JoAnna. And don't try to tell me you don't love Wisconsin. It's got wonderful people, all the water anyone could want and all these gorgeous trees. And the land is sure as hell better than it is in Powder River.''

She shook her head at him. ''I do love Wisconsin, but you've only seen it at the most pleasant time of the year. The humidity in the summer will drive you buggy, and the winters can be unbelievable.''

''It snows in Montana, too.''

''Not like it does here, believe me. And at home, if it's not pouring down rain or snowing, the sun is out. Here in about three weeks we'll get this gray crud in the sky, and it'll stay there until April. Sometimes I think I'll scream and jump into Lake Mendota if I don't get to see some real sunshine.''

Rubbing the back of his neck, Linc muttered, ''I can't believe we're arguing about the weather. For God's sake, if you don't want to stay in Wisconsin, we could live in Colorado or Arizona.''

JoAnna sighed in exasperation. ''We're not arguing about the weather. We're talking about loyalty and family responsibility. Our families settled that land, and our fathers have worked their whole lives to build it into something special for us.''

''That was their choice. We don't owe them our whole lives.''

''Well, what about our kids? That land will be their heritage as much as it is ours. Would you deny them the chance to know the only grandparents they've got?''

''Considering the two they'll have, they'd probably be better off. And speaking of kids, think about how far it is from the Double R to a hospital. You really want to drive a hundred miles of two-lane when you're in labor?''

''Oh, piffle! Women have been having babies out there for years. What's the matter, Linc? Scared you'll have to deliver one in a pickup?''

Swearing under his breath, he got up to pace the landing. JoAnna blinked back a fresh batch of threatening tears as a wave of despair washed over her. Lord, how were they ever going to be able to come to an agreement? She couldn't lose Linc now. Not again.

Despite her best efforts, however, one tear spilled over, then another. She dashed them away with the back of her hand but couldn't help sniffing. Linc pivoted at the sound. The sight of JoAnna rummaging furiously in her purse with one hand and wiping away tears with the other literally brought him to his knees in front of her.

"Aw, honey, don't," he begged, fishing a handkerchief out of his back pocket. "We'll find some way to work it out. I promise."

She used his handkerchief to blot her eyes and blow her nose, then raised her gaze to met his. "But how? You c-can't stand the thought of l-living in the one p-place I h-have to live."

Linc gathered her into his arms and stood, pulling her up with him. He buried his face in her hair. "I don't know, babe," he murmured. "But there's got to be a way."

He held her for another moment, rocking her back and forth. When she pulled away and looked up at him with a shaky smile, he said, "Listen, we don't have to decide this right now. We'll be going to Powder River next week for the wedding. Maybe by the time we get back, we'll see the whole situation in a new light. Let's give it a rest until then. What do you say?"

"All right." She smiled at him more naturally then. "We won't talk about it again until after the wedding. But do me one favor?"

"Anything."

"Get rid of that stupid camper and move into the house with me."

"You mean," he drawled with a wicked grin, "you really do want to try living in sin?"

"Yeah. You wanta make something of it, O'Grady?"

"Nope. Want to see the rest of this house now? Just in case you change your mind?"

Seeing the hopeful look in his eyes, JoAnna couldn't refuse. But as she accompanied him up the next flight of steps, she silently prayed that Linc would be the one to change his mind. Because if he didn't... Well, she couldn't bear to think about that.

Chapter Eleven

There were so many people packed into Powder River's Congregational church, the ushers had to open the curtains at the back of the sanctuary and set up folding chairs. Linc shifted impatiently on the hard pew and wished the wedding would just hurry up and start. He'd been on his best behavior since he and JoAnna had arrived in Powder River the day before. But even though JD had been cordial, almost friendly, Linc still felt about as comfortable as a hog on a high wire.

He glanced at his watch and sighed. The ceremony would take half an hour tops. Allowing a couple of hours for the reception and a couple more for transporting gifts back to the ranch and cleanup, Linc figured he and JoAnna could be on their way back to Billings in plenty of time to catch their plane for Madison.

That should have been a comforting thought. It would have been if he and JoAnna were the couple about to be married this afternoon. Living in the house with her this past week had been the most profound experience of his life and he couldn't wait to get back.

He loved the way she smiled at him when she first woke up,

the intimate talks they shared in the dark just before they went to sleep. He loved watching her get dressed for work in the morning, knowing she'd be coming home to him in the evening. He loved her for the simple, honest affection she lavished on him without stopping to think about it. He didn't dare think about their lovemaking or he wouldn't be able to stand up without embarrassing himself when the bride walked down the aisle.

It was ironic that JoAnna worried about his life-style, Linc thought. They'd stayed home every night last week, but he hadn't felt bored or restless at all. No, for the first time since he'd left Powder River for good, he'd felt as if he really belonged somewhere. And it was all because of JoAnna.

Gaye Scott slid into the pew beside Linc, followed by her ex-husband, Brady. Linc shook hands with both of them, noting that Brady looked darn near as uncomfortable as he felt. Gaye smoothed the skirt of her light blue suit over her knees, then leaned over and whispered to Linc, "They're almost ready. Lord, I hope Timmy doesn't drop the pillow."

Linc grinned at her mother's nerves. "He'll do just fine. How's JoAnna?"

"She's fine now that she's stopped running around like crazy, checking on details," Gaye replied, her big green eyes sparkling with amusement. "She looks absolutely gorgeous. How are things going with you two? Any chance of another wedding soon?"

"If I tell you, are you gonna blab it all over town?"

"Only if it's good news."

Linc chuckled at her reply. He'd always liked Gaye, and it sure wouldn't hurt to have her on his side if JoAnna proved difficult. Leaning closer, he told her, "I've asked her to marry me, but she hasn't said yes."

Gaye's eyebrows shot up, and she forgot to whisper. "Why not?" She received several reproving stares from the people around them. Lowering her voice again, she added, "I know she loves you."

She listened sympathetically while Linc briefly explained the situation. When he'd finished, she said, "Don't worry, Linc. She'll come around."

Before he could respond, the minister entered the sanctuary, followed by JD, Sean and Ron Simpson. Elsie McKenzie began the processional on the organ, and JD and his attendants turned to face the back of the church. Linc felt an unexpected twinge of sympathy when JD tugged at his bow tie and cast a nervous glance out over the rows of expectant faces.

Then a broad smile spread across JD's mouth, and his eyes lighted up with pleasure and unmistakable pride. Linc turned to see what had brought about the transformation and saw JoAnna start down the aisle. Again, he felt a twinge of sympathy for the older man. What man wouldn't be proud to have her for his daughter?

She wore a floor-length velvet gown the color of a Montana sky in summer. It had long sheer sleeves, a scooped neck and a high waistline, but it wasn't the dress that locked Linc's breath in his chest and made his heart hammer against his sternum. It was JoAnna.

Approaching the altar at a smooth, steady pace, she carried herself like a queen. She looked poised and confident, and her serene smile outshone the dozen candles embedded in glass chimneys in the flower arrangements behind the chancel rail. Her eyes met Linc's as she turned to face the congregation. She gave him an impish wink and his heart turned over.

He was so lost in admiration of JoAnna, Gaye had to nudge him to stand up when the bride entered the sanctuary. He looked over his shoulder, his glance sliding over Sally's sister Betty, the maid of honor, Timmy Scott, proudly bearing his precious pillow, then Sally. Betty looked stunning in a dress matching JoAnna's; Sally was the epitome of a radiant bride in her pale blue gown. But the lovely redheads held Linc's attention for less than a second before it snapped right back to JoAnna.

Lord, she was beautiful, inside and out. The ache of wanting her tore at his vitals. As the ceremony proceeded, he tried to envision himself living peacefully in Powder River with her, raising their children, getting along with JD and his own father at family dinners and branding parties. Linc figured he could handle Sean all right. But what about JD?

He had to admit he'd seen a different side of JD Roberts during the last day and a half. He wouldn't exactly call it a softer side; there just wasn't anything soft about the guy. JD was an old-fashioned patriarch, used to ruling his family and employees for their own good. Their own good as he saw it, anyway.

Linc's father and most of the other ranchers of their generation operated the same way. A ranch was a business like any other, after all, and somebody had to be in charge. Linc suspected he had some of those patriarchal tendencies himself. Of course, JoAnna would never let him get away with dominating her the way JD had dominated her mother.

But last night at the rehearsal dinner, Linc had discovered that JoAnna's father did have a sense of humor. In fact, when the man wasn't sneering or bellowing or glaring at you, he possessed a fair amount of charm. And when he looked at his bride or his daughter, even JD Roberts couldn't completely hide his deeper emotions.

It was those deeper emotions that concerned Linc. JD didn't just love JoAnna; he was possessive and protective of her, as well. If they didn't agree on what was best for her, JD would land on him with both feet. That would put JoAnna right smack in the middle, and they'd all wind up miserable.

At that moment, Gaye sniffed, then let out a soft sigh and reached for Brady's hand. Linc glanced toward the front of the church in time to see Sally slip the wedding band onto JD's finger. The minister pronounced them husband and wife and invited JD to kiss his bride. JD beamed down at Sally with such love and tenderness in his eyes and kissed her with such passion, the whole congregation echoed Gaye's sigh.

Linc grinned as a new thought struck him. Was it possible JD would be so wrapped up in his new wife, he wouldn't have the time or inclination to interfere in his daughter's life? From what he'd seen of Sally, Linc doubted she would let JD get away with much. Maybe... Doggone it, maybe it *could* work. After all, it wasn't Powder River itself he objected to.

His heart swelled with hope, and when JoAnna flashed him a brilliant smile as Ron Simpson escorted her down the aisle, Linc knew he'd do just about anything to make her happy. Feeling as if a huge load had just slid off his back, he followed the Scotts to the fellowship hall.

Making his way through the receiving line, Linc shook hands with his father and Ron Simpson. He paused when he got to JD, looking deeply into the older man's eyes. He couldn't honestly say he liked the man, but for the moment anyway, the old, burning hatred wasn't there. Extending his hand, he said sincerely, "Congratulations, JD."

JD studied him soberly for a moment, then smiled, took his hand in a near bone-crushing grip and pumped it enthusiastically. "Thanks, Linc. I'm glad you came."

Linc moved on, kissing the bride's cheek, shaking hands with her sister and kissing JoAnna's smiling lips. Leaning close to her ear, he whispered, "Just wait until I get you alone."

As if sensing his lighter mood, her eyes quickly scanned his face before she answered with a chuckle, "Later, O'Grady. Later."

The small, intimate joke warmed him like a fire on a frigid winter night. He enjoyed the rest of the reception, eating cake with JoAnna, talking with folks who might well become his neighbors before long. Through it all, his anticipation for the evening ahead built, and he found himself fantasizing about the look on JoAnna's face when he told her he'd changed his mind about going back to Powder River.

Finally the bride and groom retired to change into traveling clothes. Linc accepted a small bag of rice from Timmy Scott, who was passing around a huge tray, then turned when a hand clapped him soundly on the back. His father stood there grinning at him like a man who has just struck oil and can't wait to tell someone.

"What's up, Dad?" Linc asked, suddenly feeling a shade less comfortable.

Sean inclined his head toward a doorway. "Come with me for a minute, son."

Mystified, his uneasiness growing with every step, Linc followed his father down a shadowy hall to a Sunday school room. Sean opened the door and stepped aside for Linc to enter first. JD Roberts glanced up from fastening a shirt cuff and smiled, and Linc felt his stomach clench with apprehension.

"Come on in, Sean, and shut the door," JD ordered, reaching for his suit coat. "Have a seat, Linc. We don't have much time."

"I'll stand, thanks," Linc replied. "Much time for what?"

"To settle your future, son," Sean answered jovially, moving farther into the room. "Yours and Jodie's."

Linc broadened his stance, folding his arms over his chest and drawled, "And you two think *you're* gonna do that?"

JD shot Sean a warning glance before looking back at Linc. "I wouldn't put it that way, Linc. Naturally we're interested in your plans. And I just wanted to be a hundred-percent sure you knew that if you wanted to marry Jodie now, well, I wouldn't have any objections."

Undiluted rage suddenly boiled up inside Linc, and the old burning hatred rushed back with a vengeance. Despite what he'd said, it was obvious that JD *did* plan to settle their future the way *he* wanted it settled. From the confident look on his face, the arrogant bastard fully expected Linc to go along with whatever his scheme was without so much as a token protest. "You think I'd give a rat's ass if you did object?"

"Now, Linc, there's no call to be that way," Sean said in a placating tone that only made Linc madder. "We got a proposition for ya if you'll just listen."

"I've heard enough."

JD grabbed Linc's forearm before he could turn to leave. "Don't be a damn fool. Hear us out, now."

Linc shook him off with a glare hot enough to melt asbestos, halting his progress toward the door only when JD added a husky, "Please."

His hand already on the doorknob, Linc shut his eyes and sucked in a deep breath. He let it out a moment later, then turned to face the older men. Leaning one shoulder against the door casing, he muttered, "I'm listening."

JD cleared his throat and shoved his hands into his trouser pockets. "Before we get into that, there's something I want to tell you," he said. At Linc's curt nod, he continued, "What I did to you way back then wasn't anything personal, Linc."

"It felt damn personal to me."

One side of JD's mouth quirked up in a wry smile. "Well, yeah, I can see how it would. But what I meant was, I'd have done the same thing to anybody who messed with my little girl."

"Is that supposed to be an apology?"

Ignoring Linc's sarcasm, JD replied bluntly, "No. And I'm not gonna give you one, either. I had every right to protect my daughter, and I did it the best I knew how. But that's all in the past. Jodie's happier than I've seen her in a long time, and I want her to stay that way."

"Just as long as she stays right under your thumb," Linc muttered.

"It ain't like that, Linc," Sean protested. "We just want you kids to come home where you belong."

Linc turned on his father, snapping, "We're not kids anymore, Dad."

Sean rolled his eyes in exasperation. "Well, hell, don'tcha think we know that?" He blew out a gusty sigh, then said more quietly, "Look, I'll give you the land down by the pond as a wedding present. You can build your own house there and have all the privacy you want. We'll make you full partners in both ranches. You'll have a say in everything, and one of these days, you and Jodie'll have over five thousand acres. Now I think that's a pretty damn generous offer."

Linc shook his head. "Boy, you two just don't know when to quit."

"Why should we?" JD demanded irritably. "We've got an opportunity to build the best damn ranch in Montana. You're the only one hanging on to the past. Jodie's ready to come home. If you love her, you'll drop this damn fool grudge and come with her."

Shaking his head again, Linc straightened away from the door casing and propped his hands on his hips. Looking from one older man to the other, he said, "Well, you almost got what you wanted."

"What do you mean?" JD asked.

"I almost had myself talked into coming back during the wedding," Linc answered, letting out a mirthless chuckle. "I told myself I could handle you, Dad, and that JD would be so busy with Sally, he wouldn't have time to bother Jodie and me. But you two couldn't resist, could you? You just *had* to interfere."

Sean's voice took on a desperate edge. "Dammit, Linc, listen to—"

Linc cut him off with a glare. "I'm done listening to either one of you. And I'm sure as hell done letting you manipulate me. Now, I'm going to marry Jodie. If you two keep your noses out of our business, we might let you see your grandchildren once in a while. But it'll be a mighty cold day in hell before I ever agree to move back here."

He jerked open the door, then paused for one last shot at JD. "Have a nice honeymoon, Roberts."

With that, he stormed down the hall to the back door of the church. He slammed on the safety bar and stepped outside, cursing violently under his breath.

JoAnna dumped her overnight case on the floor beside her bed, then stretched her arms out to the side and flopped back on the mattress. Linc dropped the suitcase in the middle of the room, sat down beside her and lifted his left foot to pry off his boot. She groaned when he jostled the bed getting at his right one.

"How can you even move? I think I died somewhere over Minneapolis."

"It's been a long day, all right," Linc answered, unbuckling his belt.

Rolling onto her side, JoAnna opened one eye and watched him strip. Lord, but he was magnificent. Exhausted as she was, the sight of his big strong body still aroused her. Unless his mood changed for the better, however, she doubted they would make love tonight.

The weekend hadn't been easy for him; she'd expected that. But she'd been proud of the way he had handled being with her father, and she would have sworn that at least during the reception, Linc had finally unclenched his hair and enjoyed himself. He'd been laughing and telling stories and sending her teasing lascivious glances. And then his good spirits had vanished, and he'd been quiet and withdrawn ever since.

He leaned over her, bracing his weight with one hand on the bed while he went to work on the buttons of her blouse with the other. "I can do it," she murmured, though she really didn't mind having him undress her.

"My pleasure," he told her with a wry grin, tossing each article of clothing he removed onto the growing pile on the floor.

When he'd finished, he grasped both of her hands and pulled her to a sitting position. "Come on, honey, you'll feel better after a shower."

"It's too late for that, Linc," she protested, leaning toward her pillow. "Just let me sleep."

Chuckling, he grabbed JoAnna under the arms and hauled her to her feet. "You can sleep in tomorrow. Besides, I don't sleep with stinky women."

She grumbled every step of the way to the bathroom, but she had to admit the hot water felt wonderful. Leaning back against Linc's chest, she turned her face up to the spray. She sighed with pleasure while his soapy hands moved over her, gently scrubbing away the grittiness and fatigue from the trip, leaving tingles of excitement in their wake.

By the time he turned her around to face him, she was wide awake. She kissed his neck and collarbone and ran her hands over his lean flanks as he washed her back and hips. His muscles twitched when she grazed a ticklish spot, and glancing down, she noted that Linc's mood had definitely improved. She smiled and reached for the soap.

"Don't start anything you don't aim to finish," he warned in a husky tone as she spread the fragrant lather over his chest and abdomen.

Going up on her tiptoes, she kissed his stubbly chin, then scrubbed his neck. "You started it," she informed him. "Besides, I don't sleep with stinky men." She turned him around to work on his back and shoulders.

"I thought you were tired."

She reached around him, deliberately rubbing her breasts against his soapy skin while she caressed his rigid manhood. "That was before this incredibly handsome man took off all my clothes and dragged me in here."

He moaned with pleasure. When she released him, he turned and pulled her against him, kissing her with a hungry passion that made her mind reel. She clutched at his shoulders as he bent her back over his arm. Then slowly his kiss became gentler and she raised her hands to his thick, wet hair and gave him back her own fierce ardor.

Still kissing her, he shut off the water and stepped out of the glassed-in cubicle, bringing her along with him as if he couldn't bear to let go of her even for an instant. He groped along the wall with one hand, and when he found what he wanted, wrapped her in a fluffy towel. At last, he broke the kiss and his hands raced over her, drying her off. He barely flicked the cloth over his own wet skin before whisking her back to the bedroom.

She climbed into the bed and he was already reaching for her as he slid in beside her. She went into his arms, and he crushed her to him, burying his face against her neck and murmuring, "Oh, God, babe. I need you so much tonight."

The desperation in his voice sent a frisson of alarm up her spine. He sounded as if...as if this might be the last time they would ever make love. Stroking the back of his neck, she asked, "Did something happen at the wedding we need to talk about?"

He raised himself up on one elbow and gave her a smile tinged with...what? Sadness? Regret? Fear? She couldn't tell, but something was there. Before she could question him further, he said softly, seriously, "I don't need to talk about the wedding. I just need to show you how much I love you."

"Linc—"

His lips stifled any further protest, demanding a response from hers she couldn't have withheld if she'd wanted to. But she didn't want to withhold anything from him. If Linc needed some kind of reassurance, she would give it to him gladly. With that as her last coherent thought, she wrapped her arms around him and surrendered to his passion.

While he had always been a considerate lover, he had also been a demanding one. Tonight, he was insatiable. He kissed her again and again and again, stripping her of all defenses and inhibitions. His hands moved over her with a fierce gentleness, as if branding her with his possession. He told her what he intended to do to her in a low, rough voice that filled her mind with erotic visions and her body with burning anticipation.

Straddling her thighs, he feathered his fingertips over her hair, her eyebrows, eyelids, cheekbones, nose and mouth, praising each feature, following with his lips in hot, moist kisses. He repeated the procedure with her neck, her shoulders, her arms and hands, sucking each of her fingers into his mouth and bathing them with his tongue as if she were some incredible delicacy and he had to have another taste. She reached for him, needing to touch him and taste him, but he firmly put her hands at her sides and moved on to her breasts.

He stroked and shaped them with his hands, worshipped and loved them with his words. His lips and tongue caressed them to an aching fullness, and when he drew her engorged nipples into his mouth and suckled, she felt as if he were pulling her very essence from her body.

Refusing to be hurried, he worked his way down to her toes, pausing it seemed, at every curve and indentation, making her feel utterly beautiful and cherished and igniting every nerve ending along the way with yearning. She whimpered when he parted her legs. Moaned when he ran his hands up her inner thighs. Cried out when at last, he touched her most vulnerable, needy flesh.

"You're so beautiful here," he said, his voice thick and heavy with his own desire. Lowering his head he muttered, "Gotta have a taste."

She gasped at the first contact, then groaned in delight as his lips and tongue grew more bold and insistent. Her hips lifted to meet his burning mouth as the tantalizing sensation built in wave upon wave. His big hands cupped her bottom, and he drove her into a frenzy of ecstasy that made her cry out again as she peaked, then shuddered in fulfillment.

Before she could lose that glowing, floaty feeling, he guided her legs over his shoulders and entered her with a full thrust. She clutched at his bulging biceps as the delicious tension spiraled out of control within her again.

"Come with me, babe," he panted, rocking smoothly, fiercely. "We'll fly."

And fly they did, souls joined as well as bodies. Their cries of rapture filled the room. Finally Linc collapsed into JoAnna's arms with a rough sigh of completion. Her hands reached around him, stroking the fine sheen of perspiration on his back while their hearts thundered as one.

She wasn't even aware of the tears of release trickling down her cheeks until Linc rolled onto his side and brushed them away with his thumb, crooning, "Sleep now, sweetheart. Just sleep."

He held her as she drifted off, and for a long time after, his eyes burned with his own unshed tears. Hope warred with his fear of losing JoAnna when it came time to talk about marriage again. Surely after what they'd just shared, she would realize they were meant to be together. After giving herself to him so completely, she wouldn't choose JD and the Double R over him. Would she?

Chapter Twelve

When they finally got up the next day, Linc and JoAnna unpacked, then fixed a hearty breakfast of blueberry pancakes, bacon and juice. They lingered over coffee and the Sunday newspaper, trading sections and talking desultorily. After the dishes were done, Linc buried his nose in his history text. JoAnna credited his reticence to lack of sleep and spent the afternoon catching up on her laundry and puttering around the house.

But as the day wore on, she noticed Linc was staring out the window more than he was reading. The notes and papers that usually cluttered the entire surface of the coffee table remained in a neat stack. And he was sitting up straight with his feet flat on the floor, rather than sprawling comfortably in the corner of the sofa with one leg up on the cushions and the other stretched out between couch and table, as was his usual way.

Memories of his withdrawn attitude on the trip home and the desperate way he'd made love to her the night before began to torment her. JoAnna told herself she was overreacting because she was still tired herself, and went out to the kitchen to start dinner. But when Linc complimented the lasagna she'd made and retreated right back into his preoccupation, she couldn't ignore her growing anxiety any longer.

He helped her clear the table and stack the dishes in the dishwasher, then turned as if to go back to the living room. She deliberately stepped in front of him. He stopped short and gave her a questioning look, but didn't speak.

JoAnna laid one hand on his chest and gazed into his eyes before asking, "What's bothering you?"

Linc glanced down at her hand for a long moment. A smile curved one side of his mouth, but his eyes were guarded when he looked back at her again. "It shows, huh?"

She nodded, feeling a tightening in her chest. "Care to tell me about it?"

He raised one hand and brushed it across her cheek in a gentle caress. "I guess we'd better." Inclining his head toward the refrigerator, he asked, "Is there any more of that wine we had for dinner?"

"Yes, but—"

"Go on over and sit down," he ordered, indicating the kitchen table. "I'll get it."

JoAnna complied reluctantly, her anxiety growing as she watched his unhurried movements. When he took the chair opposite hers, she said, "You're scaring me, Linc. What's so bad we need a drink to talk about it?"

"Tell you the truth, I'm a little scared myself," he admitted, fiddling with his glass. He sighed, then continued, "It's about the trip we just took. I did a lot of thinking while we were in Powder River...."

"About what?" she prompted when his voice trailed off and his eyes remained fixed on the wineglass.

His head jerked up, and he looked straight at her. She saw a chilling bleakness in his eyes and unconsciously held her breath while she waited for his answer.

"About us. About living there again."

"And what did you decide?" she asked, feeling as if the bottom of her stomach might just drop out.

He reached across the table and covered her hand with his. His deep voice took on a husky edge. "I tried to see it your way, babe. I really did. But I just can't go back there."

Disappointment, sharper than a scalpel, sliced through Jo-

Anna. She'd had such high hopes, such damnably high hopes. Tears were suddenly close to the surface, and she couldn't bear to meet his gaze any longer. "I see. Then last night was a... goodbye."

"No, dammit! I don't want that, and I hope you don't, either." He grasped her chin and tilted it up, forcing her to look at him. "I love you more than anything else on this earth, JoAnna, and I intend to marry you. But I can't live in Powder River. Not even for you."

She pulled back out of his reach. "How can you be so sure of that? We were only there for two days. Considering how you felt about going in the first place, I thought everything went pretty well. I mean, you didn't fight with my dad or yours."

Something in his expression changed. She couldn't put her finger on what it was, but it prompted her to ask, "Did you?"

Anger at Sean and JD surged through her as Linc described his encounter with them in the Sunday school room. What in the world had those crazy old coots been thinking of, cornering him like that? But when Linc explained their proposition, she began to feel irritated with him, as well.

"For heaven's sake, Linc," she said, struggling without much success to control her impatience. "I know they must have been about as subtle as a garbage truck, but can't you see? They were just trying to tell you that they want to work with you. I'm sure we can negotiate anything you're not comfortable with."

He shook his head at her, dark blue fire flashing in his eyes. "No, they were trying to manipulate me. Buy me off like they did before. They're not going to give up control of anything. I'd end up being their errand boy."

"That's ridiculous."

"Is it? Hell, your dad couldn't even keep from poking his nose in our business on his wedding day! And my dad's not any better. I'm telling you, they won't give us a minute's peace if we go back there. I'll be damned if I'll let you or our kids live in a war zone."

"Lord, you still really hate them both," JoAnna muttered incredulously.

"Well, what do you expect, JoAnna? They ran me out of town when it suited them. And now because it suits them again, they want me to come back. They don't give a damn how I feel, and they never did. I don't trust either one of them, and I sure as hell don't want to be their partner. For the life of me, I can't figure out why you would, either."

She bit down on her lower lip to hold back an angry torrent of words and counted to fifteen. Maybe she was asking too much of Linc. Maybe he would never be able to get over what their fathers had done to him. But there *had* to be some way to compromise. They were reasonably intelligent adults. Weren't they?

"What if..." she began thoughtfully, then paused to develop the idea more carefully.

"What if what?"

"Well, what if we didn't live right on top of them? We could buy some land around Miles City. They have better transportation facilities up there, and that would be better for your rodeo school. But we'd still be close enough to lend a hand if they ever needed us."

Linc considered her suggestion for less than five seconds before shaking his head. "They'd still drop in on us any time they felt like it."

"We'd be almost eighty miles away, Linc!"

He snorted. "That's nothing to them. People out there go to Miles City for a hamburger."

"Why are you being so stubborn?" she demanded.

"Why are you?" he shot back. "Don't you think it's about time you grew up and stopped trying to be JD's little girl?"

She quelled the urge to throw her wineglass at his head. Just barely. "I am *not* trying to be JD's little girl. I'm just trying to keep my promise to my mother and be practical."

"What's practical about putting up with their bull every day of our lives? Look at us! We're already fighting about them and we're not even married yet."

"Sooner or later we're going to inherit that land."

"We don't need it, JoAnna. We can build our own place. Make a fresh start. When the time comes, we'll sell the Double R and the Shamrock."

Incensed, JoAnna planted both hands flat on the table and leaped to her feet, sending her chair screeching across the tile floor. "Over my dead body! The Double R is my home and it always will be."

A crushing silence followed her blunt statement. Masking the gut-ripping hurt it caused him behind a glare, Linc fumed silently, *Just once, I'd like to be more important to someone than a damn ranch!*

JoAnna looked away for a moment, then walked over to the refrigerator for the wine bottle. She took several deep, calming breaths and returned to the table. Avoiding her eyes, Linc remained silent as she refilled their glasses. But when she pulled her chair back up to the table and sat down, his stony expression softened and he leaned forward, bracing both elbows on either side of his glass.

"There's another way around this, JoAnna," he said quietly. "You marry me and we'll stay right here in Wisconsin or go wherever you decide as long as it's two days' drive from Powder River. You can go home for a visit any time you want and stay as long as you want, take the kids with you or leave them with me."

She started to shake her head, but he held her off by raising one hand. "I won't complain or pester you to come back, I promise. I'll come with you if you need me, and stay for as long as you need me. I'll do anything I can to help you fulfill your responsibilities to JD. Isn't that enough?"

JoAnna sipped her wine, but had a hard time swallowing around the lump in her throat. Linc's offer was a generous one, and she wanted to accept it so badly, she feared her heart would shatter if she didn't. But she couldn't. Holding her hands up in a plea for understanding, she said, "No. I'm afraid it isn't enough."

"Why not?"

"Because of my mother."

"JoAnna, that promise wasn't reasonable—"

"No, it's not the promise. It's the way she died."

Linc shook his head in confusion. "You've lost me."

"Well, I told you before that I thought about going home when she got sick, but she wouldn't let me. She was sick for over two years, Linc. And during that whole time, I felt so helpless. So damn far away. Every time the phone rang, my heart would sink. And then, at the end, she just went really fast and I didn't...couldn't get home in time. I don't ever want to go through that again."

Linc came around the table and took her into his arms.

"There's nothing for you to feel guilty about, honey. Knowing JD, your mother had excellent care," he said.

"I don't feel guilty, exactly. Not about her care anyway. But I missed a lot of opportunities to be with her. There were so many things I needed to tell her, needed to ask her about. But every time I went home, there just never seemed to be enough time or she wasn't up to talking or there was somebody else around...it wouldn't have been like that if I'd lived closer."

"I feel the same way about my mother," Linc admitted quietly. "But you can't torment yourself over something you can't change, JoAnna."

"I don't. But I've already lost too many years with my dad, Linc, and so have you. And that's something we *can* change."

Linc closed his eyes and rested his forehead against hers, struggling with his conscience, wracking his brain for a way to meet both her needs and his own. Then he sat down in JoAnna's chair and pulled her onto his lap. She put her arms around his neck, and he cherished the moment of closeness.

Finally he asked, "Why didn't you move back there a long time ago?"

"Dad and I didn't get along all that well until the last couple of years or so. I finally took some assertiveness training classes and learned how to keep him off my back, but it was hard. The agency kept me pretty busy, too. Going home was just one of those things I was going to do someday. I didn't really think about it all that much until I saw you again."

"Is it still hard for you to stand up to him?"

She nodded and gave him a wry smile. "You know, it's funny. I don't have much trouble being assertive with anyone else, but Dad's in a class by himself."

Linc turned her to face him more fully. "That's why we can't go back there to live, babe," he said seriously. "You'd be caught in the middle of every argument I had with him, and believe me, there'd be a lot of 'em. I love you too much to put your through that kind of stress."

Scowling, JoAnna climbed off Linc's lap and took the chair adjacent to his. "So you're refusing to live there for my own good. Is that it?"

"Now, JoAnna—"

"No! I told you, I don't need your protection. Certainly not from my own father. It may be hard for me to stand up to him, but I can do it. Give me a little credit.''

"Well, how about giving me a little trust? How about showing me you care about what I need?''

"That's not fair, Linc! Of course I trust you and care about you.''

"Enough to compromise?''

"I offered you a compromise, and you turned it down flat.''

"Because I know damn well it won't work and so do you.''

"It would if you'd stop feeling sorry for yourself and let go of the past, Linc.''

"I'm not doing this because of the past. I'm doing it for our future.''

"Are you? I don't think so. I think you've found the one perfect way to get back at both your dad and mine. How can I believe you really love me—the me I am now—if you won't stop hating them?''

"I don't want to get back at them. I just want to marry you and raise a family in peace. Is that really too much to ask?''

"Of course it's not. I love you, and I want to marry you, but I have to live with my conscience. Going home is what's right for me, and I have to do it.''

"Is this some kind of test?'' he demanded with a harsh laugh. "If I love you, I'll come back to Powder River even if I know we'll be miserable? Take it or leave it?''

"You could at least give it a try!''

"And you could try it my way. I'll do anything for you, babe. But not that.''

JoAnna threw up her hands in exasperation. "You're telling me I can have you or my father in my life but not both. How do you expect me to make a choice like that?''

"You can't have everything you want, JoAnna. If you really loved me, there wouldn't be any question in your mind about who was more important to you.''

With that, he turned on his heel and stormed out of the kitchen. Tears puddled in JoAnna's eyes, then poured down her cheeks. Furiously wiping them away with the backs of her fists, she cursed him under her breath, calling him every vile name she'd ever heard her father's ranch hands use. When she ran out of epithets, she heard a dresser drawer bang shut, then the thunk of a suitcase lid hitting the frame.

Charging for the front door, she planted herself in front of it and folded her arms across her chest. A moment later, Linc walked out of the bedroom, suitcase in hand. He set it in front of her, then opened the coat closet and dug out the parka he'd bought in preparation for a Wisconsin winter.

JoAnna watched in silence while he shrugged into the coat, her insides twisted into icy knots of fear. She promised herself that no matter what, she wouldn't beg him to stay, but when he turned back to face her with a distant, almost aloof expression in his blue eyes, she blurted, "Don't do this, Linc."

"Changed your mind?"

The cold, indifferent note in his voice stiffened her spine and quelled the trembling of her chin. Raising that chin to a defiant angle, she said, "No. But walking out at the first sign of trouble isn't the answer."

His lips tightened at that. "This isn't the first sign of trouble," he said. "It's been there between us all along."

"We can still work it out."

He looked down at his feet and let out a deep sigh. Finally he looked up at her again, his eyes filled with regret. "I don't think so, babe. If I stay, we'll just keep hurtin' each other. It's time to cut our losses."

"Just like that? Cut our losses and get on with our lives?" she demanded, clamping her hands on her hips.

"You know better than that, JoAnna," he said, reaching into his shirt pocket. He pulled out a white business card and handed it to her. "Marty'll know how to reach me if you do change your mind, or if you should need me."

She tossed the card over her shoulder and told him in a deadly quiet tone, "If you walk out that door, Linc, I won't need you. Not ever."

He reached out and grabbed her by the shoulders, giving her a hard shake. "In case you've forgotten, we didn't use any protection last night. If you're carrying my baby, I'd damned well better hear from you."

"What difference would a baby make?"

"Dammit, JoAnna, haven't we hurt each other enough? Don't make this any harder than it already is!"

The raw pain in his voice took the fight out of her. Her shoulders sagged and she had to blink back tears as she reached behind to open the door for him. "All right. Just...go. Please."

Linc retrieved Marty Taylor's card from the floor, pressed it into her hand and picked up his suitcase. Pausing beside her, he tipped up her chin with his free hand and kissed her. Then he said hoarsely, "I'll always love you. Don't ever forget that."

"Then don't go."

"I have to. You can tell JD he's won again."

"No, Linc," she choked, "we've all lost."

Chapter Thirteen

Too numb even to cry, JoAnna went into the living room, dropped Marty Taylor's card onto the coffee table beside the books Linc had left behind and sat down in the overstuffed chair that faced the front entry. She stared at the closed door for a long time, telling herself Linc would surely come to his senses any minute and return. But as the minutes stretched into an hour and a half, then two hours, and the silence of the house closed around her like a suffocating blanket, the tears started to fall.

Knowing they were part of the healing process, JoAnna let them come. Losing Linc the first time had plunged her into despair for months. She wouldn't let that happen again. No matter how much they might want to, people didn't die from broken hearts. This god-awful pain and emptiness would pass. Life would go on and so would she. Eventually.

In the meantime, she would be kind to herself. She would weep when she wanted to, rage when she wanted to, do whatever she felt like doing whenever she felt like doing it. She would stay busy. She would contact the friends she'd neglected during the past weeks. She would...she would...she would drown in these damn tears if she didn't get off her butt and go find a tissue.

JoAnna blotted her eyes and blew her nose, then systematically went through her house, eradicating every sign of Linc's presence. His books ended up in a grocery sack under the stairs in the basement. The special mustard he'd bought, the horseradish he loved and all the other goodies he'd stuck in her refrigerator and cupboards filled the trash can.

She shoved hangers across the bar in her bedroom closet, filling in the space where Linc's clothes had hung beside hers, wishing she could close the gaping hole in her life as easily. She scoured the bathroom fixtures and dumped the towels in the washer. When she went back into the bedroom, though, the queen-size bed taunted her with memories.

Gritting her teeth with determination, JoAnna stripped the bed right down to the mattress. She shook the pillows out of their cases and carried the pile into the laundry room, holding her breath so as not to inhale any lingering traces of Linc's masculine scent. Gathering fresh linens from the hall closet, she went back to the bedroom.

She moved around the bed, tucking and smoothing with brisk efficiency. The activity brought blessed relief from the urge to cry until her foot hit something just past the edge of the bed frame. Getting down on her hands and knees, she reached under the bed and pulled out a navy blue, size eleven Reebok.

The air rushed out of her lungs, and she sat back on her heels, staring at the shoe like a prairie dog facing a rattler. After a moment, she picked it up and clutched it against her breasts, muttering, "Damn you, Linc," as a new wave of tears gushed from her eyes.

The next morning, JoAnna went to work despite a raging headache and puffy red eyes no amount of makeup could hide completely. Since Linc hadn't spent much time at her office, she hoped it would be easier to hold memories of him at bay there. By the end of the day, however, she was ready to admit defeat.

She never should have allowed him to come to Madison and imprint himself on every facet of her life. She never should have made love with him again. She should have listened to her instincts way back at the reunion and refused to have anything to do with him. But it was too late for should haves. Linc O'Grady would haunt her every waking moment for the foreseeable future no matter what she did.

Alice Henderson poked her head into JoAnna's office. "I'm ready to leave unless you need something else," she said.

JoAnna shook her head. "That's fine, Alice. I'll see you tomorrow."

The older woman hesitated for a moment, studying JoAnna's pale face with concern. "Would you like to have a drink with me? I'm a good listener."

"I, uh...I don't think so," JoAnna answered. The slightest bit of sympathy from this motherly woman was all it would take to start her tears flowing again, and her eyes were still sore from the previous night. "But thanks, Alice. Maybe some other time."

"All right. I'll hold you to that," Alice replied with a smile. "See you in the morning."

When she heard the outer office door snap shut behind her assistant, JoAnna pushed her chair back and walked to the window. As she stared out at the rush hour traffic on the street below, a sharp pang of homesickness assaulted her. She wanted fresh air and sunshine and sagebrush. She ached to see the Double R's endless prairie vistas.

"For Pete's sake, Roberts, running away won't solve anything," she muttered in disgust. "The Double R isn't Tara and you're not Scarlett O'Hara."

But the longer she stood there, the more the idea of going home appealed to her. It wouldn't hurt to get some distance between herself and Madison for a while. Alice could take over the office for a few weeks or a few months if it came to that. And it had been years since she'd done any real ranch work. Perhaps it was time to find out just how competent she would be at running the Double R.

The only hassle she could see would be getting JD out of her way. She wasn't up to discussing Linc with her father yet, and she certainly didn't want to spoil his first months of marriage with her problems. But JD and Sally hadn't been able to take a honeymoon yet because he hadn't wanted to leave the ranch until after the first of the year.

Without stopping to consider the matter further, JoAnna marched back to her desk, picked up the phone and dialed her father's number. He answered on the second ring, and after a few minutes of chitchat about the wedding, JoAnna got down to business.

"Did you and Sally go ahead and get your passports for the cruise you talked about taking in January?"

"Yup, got 'em last week," he answered.

"How would you like to go now?"

"You know I can't do that."

"Sally deserves a honeymoon, Dad."

"Well, of course she does, and she'll get one. But it ain't a good time to be gone."

"What if I came home and took care of the ranch for you? Barney's a good hand. I'm sure we can handle everything between the two of us."

"I couldn't ask you to do that, Jodie."

"You didn't. I offered. How about it?"

JoAnna could almost hear the wheels turning in her father's head and braced herself for his next question.

"What about Linc? Will he be coming with you?"

"No. He, uh, left."

"Where'd he go?"

"I don't know, and I don't want to talk about it. I'd just like to come home for a while."

"Oh, hell, Jodie, I'm sorry if Sean and I—"

"I'm not blaming you or Sean O'Grady, Dad. Now what do you say? Are you going to get out of my hair and let me try my hand at being a rancher?"

The silence on the other end of the line lasted so long, JoAnna was afraid he would refuse. But at last, JD's gravelly voice answered. "I'll call the travel agency in Miles City in the morning. How soon can you get here?"

"Oh, by Friday, anyway."

"Sure this is what you want?"

"Yeah. Thanks, Dad."

"I'll call you after I talk to the travel agent."

"All right. Give Sally my love."

The next morning, JD reported that he and Sally could take a cancellation for a three-week cruise to the Caribbean on Friday afternoon. Events moved rapidly after that. Alice was more than willing to manage the employment agency for a while, espe-

cially with the raise JoAnna offered her in return for the increased workload.

JoAnna spent the rest of the week briefing her assistant, in-
terviewing college students to live in her house while she was
gone and doing the thousand and one jobs that always pop up
before an extended trip. She pushed thoughts of Linc aside as
best she could, promising herself there would be plenty of time
to think about him once she got to the ranch.

She finished packing Thursday night. Glancing around the
bedroom to make sure she hadn't forgotten anything, she spied
the heel of Linc's running shoe poking out from under the nightstand. Tears immediately welled up in her eyes. JoAnna cursed
under her breath, then snatched up the offending object and carried it out to the kitchen. Might as well get rid of every last
reminder of the man.

After retrieving a cardboard box and the grocery sack from
the basement, she stuffed Linc's books and Reebok into the
carton. She debated including some kind of a note in the package
while she hunted up Marty Taylor's card and some strapping
tape, but decided against the idea. What could she say, anyway?

I miss you like hell? I love you and I need you? I'm so lonely
and miserable, I can't stand it? Shoot, Linc knew all of that. If
he didn't, he sure as hell ought to.

JoAnna taped the box shut and addressed it, then stuck
Marty's card into the back of her wallet. She doubted she was
pregnant, but she'd hang on to it until she was absolutely certain.
After setting the box beside the front door, she stepped back,
looked at it for a moment and muttered, "Wherever you are,
Linc O'Grady, I hope you're every damn bit as miserable as I
am!"

Marty Taylor rapped on the door of the guest room. "Mail
call, you old cuss," he said.

"I'll get it later," a disgruntled voice replied.

Marty banged on the door with the side of his fist. "Come
on, O'Grady, it's time you came out of there." He waited a
moment. "Suit yourself," he bellowed when there was no reply.
"By the way, your mail's from Wisconsin."

The door flew open before Marty finished taking one step.

Linc staggered out, blinking as if the bright light of the hallway hurt his eyes. "Did you say Wisconsin?"

Shaking his head in dismay, Marty said, "Lord, I've seen corpses look more alive than you."

Linc glared at him for a second, then snatched the package out of Marty's hands. When the strapping tape defied his efforts to rip it open, he cursed violently and stormed back into his room. He set the box on the floor and started pawing through the top dresser drawer.

Marty followed, crossing to open the drapes. The morning sunlight betrayed the depths of his friend's despair. A congealed plate of food, untouched by the looks of it, adorned the top of the television. Crumpled wads of paper littered the desk and surrounded the waste basket. A pyramid of empty beer cans covered the nightstand. The bed looked like a war zone.

Still, the room looked better than Linc. His hair stood up in tufts, as if he'd been trying to pull it out by the handful. His bloodshot eyes had dark circles under them, and his gaunt cheeks and chin looked as if he hadn't shaved in at least a week. His shirt and jeans were so rumpled, he must have slept in them.

Marty walked over to the dresser and propped an elbow on the top. "When the hell are you gonna give in and call her?"

Linc shot him an impatient glance, then opened another drawer. "Have you got a pocket knife? I can't find mine."

Marty dug in his pocket and produced a pile of change, a stick of gum and the requested knife. Linc snatched the knife and, turning his back on his friend, sliced open the box. His hands shaking, he lifted the cardboard flaps.

The air in his lungs rushed out in a disheartened sigh when he saw the shoe and the books. He'd hoped for a letter, a note— some word from JoAnna. But maybe she'd stuck it in one of the books.

Tossing the Reebok over his shoulder without noticing that he'd bounced it off Marty's chest, Linc grabbed the first book by its front cover and shook it hard. When nothing dropped out, he pitched it over his shoulder and reached for the next one and the next, working his way through even his notebooks until the bottom of the box mocked him with its emptiness.

Cursing viciously he picked up the damn thing and hurled it at the opposite wall, toppling the beer can pyramid. As if the noisy clatter had drained the last of his strength, Linc's shoulders sagged and his head fell forward until his chin nearly touched his chest.

Marty pushed a mass of books and papers aside with the toe of his boot and laid a hand on Linc's shoulder. "Call her, man."

Linc gulped, shook his head. "I can't."

"What you can't do is go on like this. She's given you the perfect opening. Call and thank her for sending back your stuff, and—"

A bitter laugh grated out of Linc's throat. "That wasn't an opening. It was her way of getting me out of her life for good. Sort of like taking out the garbage."

"So? Who says you have to stay out?"

Linc's head came up and he looked at his friend with tortured eyes. "You don't understand, Marty."

"Well, how the hell can I, when you won't tell me what happened?" Marty demanded. Then he lowered his voice and coaxed, "Come on, Linc. Maybe I can help."

"Just give me a little more time."

Marty snorted in disgust and resignation. "All right. But you've done enough of this wounded badger bit. Get in that bathroom and clean yourself up. And then you're gonna eat something decent and get outside for a while. Understand?"

Giving him a half-hearted smile, Linc nodded. Marty waded through the mess to the doorway. Turning there, he grinned at his friend. "Better clean this room up while you're at it, pal. My darlin' wife'll nail your hide to the wall if she sees it like this."

When the door closed behind Marty, Linc went into the bathroom and followed orders. He felt decidedly better after a shower, a shave and some clean clothes. Someone, no doubt Marty, had left a couple of trash bags on the bed. Smiling at the thought of petite Janice Taylor nailing his hide to the wall, Linc made the bed and put the bags to good use.

As he tossed the crumpled papers on the desk into the trash, he knocked the receiver off the phone. The dial tone beckoned; his hand hovered in midair. Maybe Marty was right. Had JoAnna sent that package to give him an opening?

Before he could lose his nerve, Linc grabbed the handset and punched out JoAnna's office number. The receptionist wouldn't tell him anything more than that JoAnna wasn't in. She finally put him through to Alice Henderson when he refused to believe her.

Alice greeted him politely and listened to his request, then said, "I'm sorry I can't help you, Linc."

"Did she leave orders not to put my calls through?" he asked quietly, dreading her answer.

"No. She's not here."

"Oh, she's at home?" Linc asked, his spirits lifting. Maybe JoAnna hadn't gone to work because she was just as miserable and upset as he was. "I'll try her there."

"No," Alice said quickly, as if she feared he would hang up. "She's not in Madison."

Linc's hope shriveled like a tomato left on the vine over the winter. "Where is she?"

"She's in Montana, managing her father's ranch." The older woman hesitated a second before adding, "I think she'd love to hear from you, Linc."

"Well, uh, thanks, for the information."

"She calls in every other day. I can give her a message or tell her you phoned, if you like."

"Don't bother, Alice. Nice talking to you."

He put the handset on its cradle with exaggerated care to keep from slamming it down and shattering the woman's eardrum. He balled his hands into fists, and his chest and throat suddenly felt tight. So. He'd been right after all.

He'd barely been gone a week, and JoAnna was already back on her precious damned Double R, no doubt having a grand time with her precious damned father. Well, she could have them both as far as Linc O'Grady was concerned. She wasn't wasting any time getting on with her life. He might just as well do the same.

"Get in there, you mangy varmint," JoAnna muttered to the wall-eyed calf who didn't want any part of the metal corridor in front of him.

The animal balked until she swatted him on the rump. Then he managed to stomp on her toes as he scrambled to follow the calf ahead of him down the passageway leading to the squeeze chute. Cursing under her breath, JoAnna hobbled after another reluctant critter.

Sean O'Grady dropped the lever that pulled in the sides of the chute, forcing the animal inside to hold still. Barney Jenkins, a wiry bandy-legged little man who had worked for JoAnna's father for years, squirted medication up the calf's nostrils with a pistol-grip vaccine gun. The calf bawled loudly in protest, and Sean released him a second later.

"Ya gotta give these little fellas room, Jodie," Sean drawled with a teasing grin.

Since the calves now weighed somewhere between four and five hundred pounds, JoAnna shook her head at him and grinned back, thinking, *Little fellas, my sweet patoot!*

"Why don't you trade places with her a while, Sean?" Barney suggested. "If she's gonna be a rancher, she might as well learn how to do this."

Maintaining the smooth rhythm of the operation, Sean captured the next animal between the squeeze bars and nodded his agreement. He patted JoAnna's shoulder as she passed him. A lump rose in her throat at the paternal gesture, and she wished for the umpteenth time that Linc could see this man who loved him so much as she saw him.

For all his gruffness and occasional overbearing manner, Sean O'Grady was a gentleman. Though she sensed his regret and curiosity over her breakup with his son every time he looked at her, he hadn't pushed her to talk about Linc. He'd been a big help to her over the last two weeks, and she found herself feeling more affection for him with each passing day.

Sean herded the next calf into the chute. JoAnna pushed the lever down, then turned her attention to Barney's patient instructions.

By eleven-thirty most of the vaccinations were finished, and JoAnna went up to the house to put dinner on the table. The men lavishly complimented the roast beef, potatoes and gravy, green beans and apple pie she'd prepared, but even though she'd been working since sunup, she didn't have much of an appetite.

Since the veterinarian was coming to vaccinate the heifers for Bang's disease that afternoon, Sean and Barney refused a second cup of coffee and went back out to prepare for his arrival. JoAnna cleaned the kitchen, then wandered into the living room.

Needing a few more minutes of peace before joining the men, she stood at the picture window and gazed out over the landscape.

There was the prairie, abundant with the craggy buttes and sagebrush she'd longed for in Madison. And though the thermometer outside the window read only thirty-five degrees, the sun was shining. The Double R had survived two weeks of her management, and the tasks JD had outlined in a detailed list for her were progressing on schedule.

She was glad to be home. Though the jobs were often dirty and exhausting, she enjoyed working alongside Barney and the neighbors, who traditionally helped one another with the big seasonal tasks such as branding and shipping cattle. Most of all, JoAnna was glad to know she had what it took to be a rancher.

She felt immense satisfaction at what she had accomplished, but there was still a deep, empty well of loneliness inside her soul that nothing could fill. Not even the Double R.

"It's only been three weeks. You just need more time," she assured herself in a choked whisper. Squaring her shoulders, she turned from the window and marched back out to the corral.

The next morning, JoAnna helped Barney separate the calves from their mothers for weaning. The resulting cacophony of cows and calves bawling themselves hoarse for three solid days set her teeth on edge. A storm system moved into the area, bringing a miserable, freezing rain with it that settled the dust. The moisture was good for the calves' lungs, but it depressed JoAnna even further.

Thanksgiving Day dawned cold, but clear. JoAnna helped Barney feed the calves and chip the ice from the water tanks before trudging back to the house to shower and change clothes. Gaye had invited, well, actually demanded that JoAnna come for dinner to celebrate her reconciliation with Brady.

Though celebrating anything, much less a romantic reconciliation, was about the last thing JoAnna felt like doing at the moment, she couldn't refuse. Besides, she chided herself, rattling around alone in her father's house all day would give her too much time to think about Linc.

Still, she dawdled over her hair and makeup as long as possible, arriving at the Scotts' home in time to help with last-minute dinner preparations. The house was packed with chattering relatives and friends, and JoAnna did her best to enjoy the day. But the congenial family atmosphere only served to make her feel more lonely and isolated.

Every time one of Gaye's big, good-looking brothers put an arm around his wife, she longed to have Linc beside her, putting his arm around her. Whenever Timmy sought her out, or one of the three new babies in the family was passed to an eager aunt or grandma, her arms ached to hold a child of her own—one with dark, glossy hair and heart-melting blue eyes.

And when Gaye and Brady announced over pumpkin pie and coffee that they were getting married again and moving to Seattle after Christmas, love and devotion shining in their eyes, JoAnna's throat closed up and she had to leave the room.

She slipped away as unobtrusively as possible and tiptoed through the kitchen to the glassed-in back porch. Blinking rapidly, she crossed her arms beneath her breasts and looked out over the yard. The denuded trees jerked before a chill Canadian wind. The flower beds were bare and empty, the vegetable plot forsaken. Even the grass looked as dry and dead as she felt inside.

The door to the kitchen opened. Turning, JoAnna saw Gaye step out into the porch, her big green eyes filled with concern. She shut the door behind her, then walked over and put her arm around JoAnna's waist.

"I'm sorry," Gaye said softly. "I should have realized how hard this would be for you."

JoAnna sniffed and gave her a watery smile. "No, I'm sorry. I'm happy for you and Brady. Really."

"I know that, *idjit*," Gaye answered, squeezing JoAnna's waist, "but you wouldn't be human if you didn't feel a little sorry for yourself."

"Yeah, well, that's gotta stop. Dad and Sally will be home next Monday, and I don't want to rain on their parade, either. Go on back inside, Gaye. I'll be fine."

Shaking her head, Gaye indicated a wicker sofa covered with bright floral cushions. "I haven't had a chance to really talk with you all day. Let's sit down for a minute." When they were settled, she asked, "Haven't you had any word from Linc at all?"

JoAnna shrugged. "Alice said he called the office, but he wouldn't leave a message."

"Does he know you're here?"

"Alice told him."

"Oh, JoAnna, call him," Gaye urged. "I'll bet he'd jump at another chance to work things out."

JoAnna shook her head. "Not unless I'm willing to give up everything that's important to me."

"But look at you. You're miserable without him. And what's more important than Linc?"

"Nothing's more important. But I just can't turn my back on my home and family the way he can."

"It doesn't have to be a matter of turning your back on them," Gaye argued. "There's always room to compromise."

"I tried that."

"So, try again."

JoAnna sighed. "There's no point in that, Gaye. We've hurt each other enough. Every time we had an argument, I'd always wonder if he was going to take off again."

"He wouldn't do that."

"How do you know?" JoAnna demanded. "For that matter, how do you know Brady won't take off and leave you and Timmy again?"

"She doesn't know that, JoAnna," a deep male voice answered from the doorway.

JoAnna and Gaye looked up to find Brady crossing the room. He must have come out to the porch when they were too engrossed in their conversation to notice. He sat down in a matching wicker chair opposite them, studying both women with a serious expression.

"Brady," Gaye said hesitantly, casting JoAnna a worried glance, "maybe you should go back in the house."

"No, that's fine," JoAnna replied. "I want to hear what he has to say."

Brady gave JoAnna a warm smile and leaned forward, putting his elbows on his knees, his hands clasped between them. "What I meant was, Gaye can't know I won't take off. But she loves me enough to take the risk."

"From where I'm sitting, that's a mighty big risk, Brady," JoAnna told him honestly.

Brady nodded his understanding, but before he could reply, Gaye said, "There's something I haven't told you about our divorce, JoAnna. Remember when I told you I wasn't blameless?"

"Of course. Go on, Gaye."

Gaye sent Brady a sad smile, then admitted, "Brady never wanted to live here. He only came back to help his dad with the ranch for a few years while his brother was in the service. I knew that when I married him, but I thought I could change his mind about finishing his engineering degree. He wanted Timmy and I to go with him when he went to Seattle, but I wouldn't do it."

"Why not?" JoAnna asked, frowning in confusion.

Gaye hesitated a moment, then answered, her voice flat with regret. "I was too scared to leave Powder River."

"I don't believe that," JoAnna argued. "You spent four years in college in Bozeman, for heaven's sake."

"And they were the loneliest years of my life. Until Brady left me."

"But you've never had any trouble making friends. You were our head cheerleader—"

"JoAnna!" Gaye protested with a laugh. "Would you get real? That was high school. In Powder River I was a medium-sized frog in a tiny pond. But in Bozeman, I was hardly even a tadpole! I was lost without you and my family, and I couldn't wait to come home."

"Why didn't you ever tell me this before?" JoAnna asked.

"Because I was ashamed to admit what a coward I was," Gaye admitted. "You were doing so well in Madison. I...shoot, compared to you, I felt like an idiot."

Remembering how alone and lost she had felt during her college years, JoAnna groaned. Then she gave Gaye an apologetic grin. "I'm sorry you felt that way."

"It wasn't your fault. But don't you see, JoAnna? I let my fear take over. I had this master plan in my mind of how I wanted my life to be, and I couldn't deviate from it. As a result, Timmy and I lost Brady."

"What happens if you really hate Seattle?" JoAnne asked.

"I won't," Gaye answered with conviction. "For one thing,

I'm not going by myself. And for another, I'm going with the expectation of loving it.''

"And if she does hate it," Brady put in with a loving smile at Gaye, "we'll figure something out. We're going to work damn hard at our marriage this time. From what I saw of Linc at your dad's wedding, I think he loves you enough to work damn hard, too.''

JoAnna looked down at her hands. "I wish I could believe that. But I can't take the chance that he's using me to get back at JD and Sean.''

"JoAnna," Gaye scolded impatiently, reaching for her friend's hand, "you know better than that.''

"Just because you and Brady are—''

"No, now you listen to me," Gaye insisted. "I love my family and my home as much as you do, and it's not much easier for me to leave Powder River now than it was three years ago. But even with Timmy and all of my family around me, my life has been damned empty without Brady. Take it from somebody who knows, pal, you won't be happy without Linc, either. And nobody, including your father, will thank you for sacrificing your happiness. The last thing JD needs now is for you to turn yourself into a martyr.''

"Are you quite finished?''

Gaye's eyes filled with tears at JoAnna's icy snarl, and JoAnna immediately felt lower than a worm. Softening her tone, she said, "I'm sorry. I know you're just trying to help.''

"Yeah, well, it doesn't look like I'm helping much," Gaye replied dryly. She accepted a handkerchief from Brady. "I just don't want you to make the same mistake I did. I know what you're going through, and I know it's scary as hell. But life is one big risk after another, hon. Don't throw away your happiness and Linc's because you're afraid to take this one.''

JoAnna hugged her friend and murmured a husky, "I'll think about it." She cleared her throat, then stood and said, "If you'll forgive me for ducking out on the dishes, I think I'd like to go home now.''

It took fifteen minutes to say her goodbyes. JoAnna blew out a sigh of relief as she drove away from the Scotts' house. Her discussion with Gaye and Brady played over and over in her mind like a cassette on auto-reverse all the way back to the ranch. By the time she parked JD's pickup in the garage and entered the house, her emotions were in a turmoil, and she felt a headache coming on.

She took some aspirin, brewed a cup of tea and carried it into the living room. Sitting in her father's recliner as she sipped the hot liquid, JoAnna closed her eyes and willed her body to relax. At first, the house seemed blessedly silent after the hubbub at the Scotts'. But after a few moments, she became aware of the wind's mournful howl against the windows and the hollow sound of the grandfather clock ticking in the den.

Unbidden, a vision of Gaye's earnest face appeared before JoAnna's eyes. "There's always room for compromise," her friend said. "So try again."

"This is different," JoAnna whispered defensively.

She rationalized away Gaye's arguments every way possible. Her friend was blinded by her romantic notions and her own present happiness. Gaye didn't know the depth of Linc's resentment toward his father and JD. Gaye and Brady both had brothers and sisters. They didn't have the obligations JoAnna and Linc carried as only children.

Still, no matter how hard she tried, JoAnna couldn't refute at least one of Gaye's statements. She was miserable without Linc, and she was very much afraid that the rest of her life would be empty as hell without him. But it didn't have to end this way. Did it?

If Linc would agree not to sell the Double R and the Shamrock, she could agree to live around Billings or down in Wyoming or over near Rapid City. Or they could agree to live someplace even farther away for five years and then reevaluate that decision. Perhaps if they had some time to establish themselves as a happily married couple first, Linc wouldn't feel so threatened by being close to their fathers. The possibilities were endless, if only Linc would agree to try again.

Slamming the footrest lever down, JoAnna bolted out of the recliner and into the kitchen. She grabbed her purse from the counter top, yanked out her wallet and fished Marty's card from the back pocket. Her heart pounding with excitement, she dialed the unlisted number Linc had written on the back of the card and held her breath until a voice on the other end of the line said in a soft, southern drawl, "Taylor residence. This is Bobby Taylor speaking."

JoAnna grinned as she pictured Marty's sandy-haired, seven-year-old son. "Hi, Bobby. This is JoAnna Roberts. I visited your family a while back with Linc."

"Oh, yes, ma'am. I remember you. Happy Thanksgiving."

"Same to you. Is Linc there by any chance?"

"Well, uh, not right now. He went to a party or somethin' with Miss Debbie. She's real pretty. Said he'd probably be late when he left."

"Oh," JoAnna answered, feeling like a punctured helium balloon. "I see. Well, thank you, Bobby."

"May I give him a message, Miss JoAnna? Mama says I'm always supposed to ask that."

The message I'd like to give him is not for your tender ears, JoAnna thought grimly. Aloud, she said, "Yes, Bobby. Just tell him the rabbit's alive and well. He'll know what I mean. Can you remember that?"

"I surely can, ma'am. And I'll be sure to tell him. Bye now."

JoAnna hung up the phone, not sure whether she wanted to laugh, scream or cry. Eventually she did a little of all three. But when she finally regained a modicum of control over her emotions, she washed her face, marched into the den and tackled the paperwork that never seemed to get caught up.

There would be no more sleepless nights over Linc O'Grady, she vowed as she got ready for bed four hours later. No more tears, no more what ifs, no more...anything. She would become the best darn rancher in Powder River County. And Linc and his Miss Debbie could just go to hell and stay there.

Chapter Fourteen

"We're home, Jodie!"

At the sound of her father's booming voice, JoAnna dumped the armload of clothes she was carrying on to Sally's old bed and charged back into the main part of the house. She found JD and Sally in the kitchen, their tanned faces beaming with happiness, their hands full of luggage.

"Welcome home!" she cried, so relieved to finally have some company in the big house, her eyes misted with tears.

JD set the suitcases down and held his arms out to her. JoAnna rushed into them, fiercely returning her father's bear hug before giving Sally a hug, as well. She pulled back a moment later, demanding, "Well, tell me all about it. Did you have a good time?"

"Oh, it was fantastic," Sally replied with a smile. "But it's good to be home."

"You can say that again," JD agreed, sniffing the air appreciatively. "Do I smell cinnamon rolls?"

"Baked fresh this morning," JoAnna told him, taking a tote bag from Sally. "Let's get your bags out of the way, and I'll put on a pot of coffee while you unpack."

JD picked up the suitcases and headed for the hallway to the bedrooms. He stopped short at the open door to the apartment Sally had lived in before their marriage and, after glancing inside, turned to JoAnna, his eyebrows raised.

"What's goin' on in there?"

"I'm moving out there so you newlyweds can have more privacy," she answered.

Sally protested. "This is your home, JoAnna. You don't have to do that."

JoAnna gave her new stepmother a wicked grin. "I know I don't. But I don't want to hear any, uh, funny noises in the middle of the night."

Sally blushed and JD snorted with laughter. Inclining his head toward the master suite, he said, "Come on. Let's dump this stuff. I'm starving."

They spent the rest of the day getting JD and Sally resettled and talking about the cruise and what had happened at the ranch during the last three weeks. JoAnna excused herself after dinner and finished moving her things into the apartment. The next morning, she gladly relinquished the kitchen into Sally's capable hands and rode out with her father to check on the stock.

JoAnna was neither surprised nor offended that JD wanted to inspect the ranch; she would have done the same thing in his place. He was lavish with praise for the work she had accomplished, and he obviously enjoyed sharing his knowledge about the land and the animals with her. Life settled into a pleasant routine over the next two weeks, at least for JD and Sally.

Despite her Thanksgiving Day vow to forget about Linc, JoAnna found herself thinking about him more often than she liked to admit. She worked hard every day with her father and relished the close relationship she was developing with him and with Sally. Witnessing their love for each other warmed her heart, and she was delighted to have them home.

And yet, every time they shared a private joke, an intimate glance, an affectionate touch, JoAnna was reminded of how much she missed sharing all of those things with Linc. With each passing day, her appetite dwindled, her sleep became more sporadic and was tortured with erotic dreams, and she felt as if her nerves were being stretched out like barbed wire on a fence.

She found Sally's energetic preparations for Christmas depressing and began spending the evenings in the apartment, reading and watching television. JoAnna hid her anguish behind a cheerful demeanor, but she knew she wasn't always successful judging from the occasional worried glances her father and step-mother gave her when they thought she wasn't looking.

Finally, one night about a week before Christmas, JoAnna went into her apartment after supper and settled in with a blood-curdling horror novel. A sharp rap on the hall door startled her a few minutes later. Sighing, she marked her place and went to answer the summons.

Without waiting for an invitation, JD entered the room and sat down in an overstuffed easy chair. He studied his daughter intently while she closed the door and returned to the loveseat. JoAnna bit back another sigh when she saw the determined glint in his eyes. "What can I do for you, Dad?"

"How long are you plannin' to stay, Jodie?"

"What's the matter?" she asked with a nervous laugh. "Have I worn out my welcome?"

Her father let out a derisive snort and shook his head at her. "You know you're always welcome here. But what about your business in Madison? Shouldn't you be getting back to it?"

JoAnna shrugged. "Alice says everything's fine. But I suppose I'll go back sometime after Christmas. I can stay longer, though, if you need me. In fact, I've been thinking seriously of selling the agency and coming home for good."

JD leaned back against the chair cushion and drummed his fingertips on the armrest. "Why?"

"Why not?" JoAnna retorted. "You've been after me to do just that for years."

"And you've always refused. So why the change in attitude now?"

"It just seemed like as good a time as any. That's all."

"You mean you've been planning to come back all along?"

JoAnna nodded, then briefly told him about her promise to her mother.

JD heard her out, then rubbed one hand down over his face. "Jodie, I understand how you feel about your mother," he said, leaning forward, "but you can forget about that promise. I think she was more concerned that you and I wouldn't make up our differences back then. But we've done that. Haven't we?"

"Yes, we have," JoAnna answered quietly. "But I don't understand your attitude, Dad. Don't you want me to come home and help you run the ranch anymore?"

"Only if it'll make you happy."

JoAnna's chin came up defensively. "Now that you've got Sally, I'll just be in the way. Is that it?"

"No, dammit! That's not it!" He glared at her for a long moment. Then the hard expression in his eyes softened, and he said more gently. "Even if I didn't have Sally, I wouldn't want you to sacrifice your happiness for me or the ranch."

When JoAnna remained silent, he added, "That's what you quarreled with Linc about. Isn't it? Coming back here to live?"

She looked away, muttering, "I don't want to talk about him."

"Well, that's just too dang bad, because we are gonna talk about him," JD replied sternly, moving over to sit beside her. "I've respected your privacy as long as I could, but I can't stand back and watch you suffer like this any more."

"I'm fine."

"Oh, sure ya are." He grasped her forearm and held her wrist up to the light. "The way you're droppin' weight, why, a good gust of wind'll blow ya clear down to Alzada."

JoAnna looked up into his worried eyes, and suddenly tears streamed down her face as if a water pipe had burst. She threw her arms around his neck and sobbed against his chest. He wrapped his arms around her and consoled her as if she were still a child.

When her tears were finally spent, he produced a white handkerchief from his hip pocket, wiped her eyes and made her blow her nose. She hugged him one last time, murmuring, "I love you, Daddy."

He cleared his throat. "I love you too, honey," he said huskily. "And that's why we've gotta get this mess with Linc straightened out. Now tell me what happened."

The story came out slowly at first, then faster and faster until the words and emotions poured out in a rush. At last, JoAnna finished with a gulp. "And so you see, Dad, it's too late to do anything. Linc's already dating someone else."

JD studied her thoughtfully for a long moment before shaking his head at her in disgust. "Now, that's about the biggest pile of bull I ever heard in my life."

JoAnna drew back as if he'd hit her. "Well, gee whiz, Dad. Don't go overboard with your sympathy."

"I don't need to. You're feelin' sorry enough for yourself for both of us and the rest of the county, too. I can't believe I raised such a snivelin' coward."

"A coward! How can you say that?"

Her breasts heaving with indignation, JoAnna started to jump off the loveseat. JD grabbed a belt loop on the waistband of her jeans and hauled her right back down. She turned on him furiously, and he clamped one hand over her mouth.

"You didn't come home to give Sally and me a honeymoon," he said, looking her straight in the eye. "You came here to hide. All that stuff about your promise to Katherine, your duty to me and the ranch, is just a bunch of malarkey, Jodie Marie. It's just one big excuse to keep from committing yourself to Linc."

JoAnna shoved his hand away from her mouth and hissed, "That's not true."

"The hell it's not! You got hurt pretty bad the first time around. And you're still so damn scared he'll hurt you again, you didn't even give him an honest chance."

"You're just saying that so I'll marry him and produce some grandchildren," JoAnna accused.

"I don't need grandchildren," JD informed her bluntly, suddenly starting to smile.

JoAnna eyed that smile suspiciously. "Since when?"

"Since this afternoon." His smile broadened even more. "Sally's pregnant."

JoAnna's mouth dropped open. Laughing, JD reached out and gently tapped her chin. She shut her mouth with a snap, then said quietly, "That's, uh...that's great, Dad."

"You don't sound very happy about it."

JoAnna smiled slightly and shook her head. "It's, uh, just that now I understand why you don't want me to come home."

"Oh? And why is that?"

"Well, obviously, you don't need me anymore."

He grabbed her by the shoulders and gave her a hard shake. "Would you knock it off? I'd like nothing better than for you and Linc to come back here to live. There's plenty of land and plenty of work for everybody. But if he doesn't feel comfortable with that, you've got no business trying to force him into it."

"I didn't—"

"You sure as hell did, Jodie! It sounds to me like you wanted him to guarantee you'd always live happily ever after. You wanted everything all tied up nice and neat beforehand, but marriage doesn't work that way."

"I was just trying to be practical, Dad."

"Honey, you were being completely impractical. When you're married, you never have all your problems solved. And if you do, well, look out, 'cause here comes another one. But you gotta love and trust each other enough to keep trying."

"Oh yeah? I seem to remember you saying that if Linc really loved me, he'd swallow his pride and learn to tolerate you."

"He's already swallowed plenty of pride. He left the rodeo circuit to be with you. And he came to the weddin' and acted civil. Hell, after some of the things I said to him years ago, I'm surprised he was able to do that much."

"It wasn't easy for him," JoAnna said thoughtfully.

"Of course it wasn't. But he did it. And I think if he felt secure about you, he'd eventually come around."

"What do you mean secure?" JoAnna demanded. "I told him I loved him. What more could he want?"

JD looked at her as if he couldn't believe she was such a nitwit. "Jodie, a man's got to know he comes first with his wife. You practically told him to his face that the Double R was more important to you than he was. How do you suppose that made him feel?"

"Well, it didn't take him very long to replace me," she grumbled.

"Baloney! He's just lickin' his wounds. Now be honest for a change, Jodie. Do you love Linc? Really love him?"

"Of course I do!"

"Enough to take him just like he is? Warts and all? Enough to fight for him?"

She raised troubled eyes to his. "I don't know. I'm not even sure how to go about it."

JD climbed to his feet and put his hands on his hips. He looked down at her for a moment before saying, "You'd better start figurin' it out. I don't think you've lost him yet. But by golly, you'd better do something pretty damn quick or you will.''

"What can I do?"

"You'll think of something. Linc's a helluva man, but you're gonna have to decide if you're woman enough to put your love on the line for him.''

With that, JD turned and left the apartment. He walked into the living room, sat down on the sofa beside Sally and put his arm around her.

"How is she?" Sally asked, her forehead pleated with worry.

JD shrugged. "I think she'll be okay now." A second later, he chuckled, then shook his head. "If I know that daughter of mine at all, poor ol' Linc's gonna have his hands full any day now."

"If I'm woman enough," JoAnna seethed, pacing back and forth across the apartment's small living room. "If I'm woman enough!"

How could her father be so unfair? He'd made it sound as if she had been completely in the wrong and Linc had been perfectly justified in leaving her and then taking up with some southern belle floozy. And calling her a sniveling coward and impractical!

She picked up her book and heaved it against the wall. It bounced twice when it hit the carpet. JoAnna stared at it for a long moment, then suddenly her aggression drained away, leaving her hollow-eyed and exhausted. Feeling at least a hundred years old, she flopped down on the loveseat, leaned her head back against the cushion and shut her eyes.

Images of Linc danced beneath her closed lids—Linc roaring out of the chute on that huge bull at the reunion rodeo, waltzing her around the carousel platform at the House on the Rock, posing beside her bed in his blue bikini underwear, loving her with his eyes and his hands and his mouth.

God. She loved him. Wanted him. Needed him. Nothing was more important—not the Double R. Not her father. Not her business in Madison. Without him, nothing had any meaning. How could she have been so blind that she hadn't seen that?

Tears leaked out of her eyes, ran down her temples and into

her ears. *Dammit,* she thought, dashing them away with her fingertips. *JD's right. Gaye's right. I'm a sniveling coward and a worrywart. So what are you going to do about it, Roberts?*

Turning sideways, JoAnna braced her back against the armrest and put her feet up on the cushions. Would Linc be willing to give her another chance? She didn't know, but she'd sure as hell have to dig up some courage somewhere and find out.

She eyed the wall phone in the kitchenette, then quickly shook her head. No, it would be too easy for him to hang up on her. She needed to see him face to face. But was he still in Nashville? There was only one way to find out.

JoAnna swung her feet to the floor and walked into the kitchenette. Dialing from memory, she placed the call. The seconds it took for the phone company's equipment to work seemed like an agonizing hour, but at last, she heard Marty Taylor's voice on the other end of the line.

"Marty, this is JoAnna Roberts," she said, sucking in a deep breath. "I need to find Linc."

Chapter Fifteen

Linc gazed at the autographed photos of Grand Ole Opry stars on the wall opposite their booth with feigned nonchalance while Marty read the last poem. A barmaid wearing a blue-and-white checked western blouse, a skimpy denim skirt and white boots rushed by, giving Linc a harried nod and a smile when he raised two fingers to signal they were ready for another round. He polished off the rest of his Scotch, then looked at his friend expectantly as Marty laid the paper aside.

"Well? What do you think? Any hits in that batch?"

"Only if there's a sudden market for funeral dirges," Marty answered dryly.

"Aw, come on. They're not that bad."

Nodding toward the doorway to the dining room, Marty said, "Let's get something to eat and we'll talk about it."

Scowling, Linc shook his head. "I'm not hungry, and I want to talk now. What's wrong with those poems?"

"Nothing's wrong with them. I'm sure they express exactly what you're feeling. But they're so damn mournful, they make me want to go find a bridge and jump off. I'm tellin' you, Linc, it's time to call JoAnna."

"Would you lay off that?"

Marty banged down his glass in frustration. "Not until you either tell me what happened or start acting like the Linc O'Grady I used to know and like again."

Linc looked away and was grateful for a momentary reprieve before answering when the barmaid delivered fresh drinks. He gave her a generous tip, took a gulp from his glass, then faced his friend again with a disgruntled expression.

"Oh, all right. But it's a long story."

Marty rested his forearms on the table. "I've got plenty of time," he drawled.

Searching for a place to begin, Linc swallowed another mouthful of Scotch. He waited until the fiery liquor settled to a warm glow in his belly, then he started at the very beginning. Marty listened with rapt attention, interrupting only with an occasional question or to order more drinks.

At last, feeling a little drunk and a lot better for having shared his problems with his friend, Linc sighed and said, "And that's it. It's over for good this time."

Marty shook his head in amazement. Then he sat back and let out a whoop of laughter that drew attention from all corners of the crowded bar.

"Shut up, Taylor," Linc snapped. "Geez, you wonder why I didn't want to tell you anything?"

"No, Linc," Marty protested, wiping his eyes as he struggled for a more serious expression. "I'm not laughing at you, buddy."

"Well, what's so damn funny?"

"Doesn't the whole situation strike you as being just a little ironic?"

"No. And it doesn't strike me as amusing, either," Linc answered impatiently. "How much have you had to drink, anyway?"

Marty waved the last question aside. "That's because you're too close to it. But look, you lost JoAnna the first time because of blackmail. And now you've lost her again for the same reason. Only this time, you're the blackmailer."

"What the hell are you talkin' about?"

"You made her choose between you and her dad. If that's not emotional blackmail, I don't know what is."

Linc sat back and crossed his arms over his chest. "You're wrong. I didn't do any such thing."

"Sure you did. I don't blame you for not liking him much, maybe wanting to get back at him. Maybe you're even jealous of him. It doesn't really matter why you did it. But do you honestly believe her dad could bust you two up if you really love each other? Has this guy got horns and a tail or what?"

"Of course not. He's just an old blowhard like my dad. But they can both be a damn big pain in the ass, believe me."

"So? You're a big fella. If you can climb onto those big old bulls, surely you can handle a couple of cantankerous old guys like them."

Linc rubbed his chin thoughtfully. "Well, I don't see you living close to your in-laws, Taylor," he grumbled. "Don't they live in California?"

"If it meant the difference between having Janice or not having her, I'd live right next door to 'em. What you're not understanding here, Linc, is that family ties are a lot more important to women than they are to men. Shoot, my mama says that if it weren't for Janice and the newspapers, she wouldn't have known if I was dead or alive for the last ten years."

"So because of that, I'm supposed to give in and do what JoAnna wants? Even though I don't want to?"

"Did you have a good time with Debbie? Or Arlene? Or Teri?" Marty prodded.

"You know damn well I didn't."

"Why not? They're all pretty and bright. Fun to be with."

"Because they're not JoAnna," Linc muttered under his breath.

"What's that? I couldn't hear you."

"I said," Linc told him with a reluctant grin, "because they're not JoAnna."

"You're damned astute sometimes for a dumb old cowboy," Marty answered with a chuckle.

"I try. But how can JoAnna help but feel awful if I can't get along with her dad?"

"You're underestimating her. She struck me as a pretty sharp lady. If the situation's as bad as you think it might be, she'll be willing to move. And you're forgetting that her dad loves her, too. If he was friendly at the wedding, don't you think he'll at least try to get along with you for her sake?''

"Maybe."

"The thing is, Linc, no matter where you live, you and JoAnna will have to present a united front to the world. Every marriage has its frustrations and irritations. Just don't let her dad or yours be any more than that.''

Linc drummed his fingertips on the tabletop for a moment. Then he asked, ''What if she won't give me another chance? That message she gave Bobby sounded like she was nailing the coffin shut.''

"How much do you love her?''

"What kind of a question is that?''

"Buddy,'' Marty drawled sympathetically, ''you may have to crawl.''

Groaning, Linc covered his face with his hands. Marty slid out of the booth and laid a hand on his friend's shoulder. ''Just tell yourself it takes a big man to admit he was wrong. I've gotta go to the john and call Janice before she sends the cops out lookin' for me. Why don't you order us a hamburger?''

Marty strolled away, whistling under his breath. At the pay phone, he glanced over his shoulder. When he saw Linc talking to the barmaid, he dropped a quarter in the slot, punched out the number of the motel across the street and asked for room 301. The receiver on the other end was picked up before the first ring ended.

"I think he's just about ready,'' Marty said, smiling to himself. ''Why don't you come on over?''

JoAnna stepped through the tavern entrance, blinking rapidly to help her eyes adjust to the dim lighting. She hung her coat on a rack and jumped when someone laid a hand on her shoulder. Turning, she saw it was Marty Taylor and laughed self-consciously. ''You scared me half to death.''

Marty grinned as he eyed her bright red dress and chunky black jewelry. ''You look great, JoAnna.''

"Thanks.'' Her eyes darting around the room, she smoothed down the sides of her skirt. ''Where's Linc?''

Marty gestured with his thumb. "In a booth right around that corner. Don't worry. He'll be glad to see you."

"I hope you're right."

"Hey, I'm always right. Promise me one thing, though."

"What's that?"

"I get to sing at your wedding."

Returning his teasing smile, she reached up and kissed his cheek. "If this works, you've got it."

"Go on now," Marty ordered, taking her by the shoulders and turning her in the right direction. "He's waiting."

JoAnna shot him one last nervous smile, then squared her shoulders and marched into the bar. Her steps slowed as she approached the corner Marty had indicated. Her stomach felt as if it had turned into a rock, and her pulse fluttered erratically. Lord, what if Linc told her to take a hike?

Telling herself this was just another one of life's risks she had to take, she turned the corner. Her heart lurched when she spotted Linc. She paused for a moment, absorbing the sight of him. He looked good. Darn good. Unaware of her scrutiny, he shifted on the bench seat. With his shoulders hunched forward, elbows on the table, the fingers of one hand drumming the Formica, he appeared to be lost in troubled thoughts. If only she could walk over there and put her arms around him...

JoAnna gulped once for courage and approached the table. Praying her voice wouldn't sound as shaky as she felt, she said, "Buy you a drink, Cowboy?"

Linc's hand stilled. His head whipped around. His eyebrows shot up. For an instant before the shock of seeing her wore off, JoAnna thought she saw a flash of pure, undiluted joy in his blue eyes. He glanced at the empty glass in front of him, shook his head, then looked back up at her. But while his mouth stretched into a smile, his eyes took on a wary expression that made JoAnna cringe inside.

"What are you doing here, JoAnna?" he asked quietly.

"I came to see you. Mind if I sit down?"

"Uh, no. Of course not."

JoAnna slid into the booth. Folding her hands in her lap, she racked her brain for something to say that would ease the tension. Unfortunately she felt every bit as rattled as she had that first day she'd seen him at the rodeo. The best she could come up with was, "How've you been?"

"Fine." He twisted in his seat for a better view of the room and said, "Marty's around here somewhere."

JoAnna sighed inwardly. He wasn't going to make this easy for her. She couldn't help feeling disappointed at his attitude, but she supposed she deserved it. "He left, Linc."

Eyes narrowed, he turned back to her. "He knew you were coming?"

"Yes. He told me you'd be here tonight."

Linc's mouth curved into a sardonic smile, but all he said was, "Well, I guess you'll have to eat his hamburger for him."

Though even the thought of food made her feel nauseous, JoAnna nodded.

"Want something to drink?" he asked, beckoning for the barmaid.

JoAnna nodded again. "We need to talk, Linc," she said after they had ordered their drinks.

A waitress from the adjoining restaurant cut off any response Linc might have made. She plunked down two platters heaped with enormous hamburgers and fries. After assuring the waitress that they had everything they needed, Linc turned to JoAnna. "I thought we'd just about said it all back in Madison. Unless, of course, that rabbit croaked after all."

His cool tone brought an urge to dump the contents of her platter in his lap. Instead, JoAnna shook her head. "Nope. He's just fine."

"Then why are you here?"

Her chin came up to a challenging angle. "To be honest, right now, I'm not too sure. I'll be happy to leave if that's what you want."

Linc suddenly felt ashamed of himself for acting like such a jerk when what he really wanted to do was grab JoAnna and kiss her. Lord, she looked beautiful. Seeing her was an exquisite kind of torture. He wanted to believe she'd come to reconcile, but his emotions were still so raw, he was afraid to hope, afraid to hear what she'd come to say.

Each second of silence shredded JoAnna's nerves a little more and a little more, until she simply couldn't stand it any longer. If he had to think that long about whether he wanted her to stay, she'd obviously made a huge mistake. Shoving her plate aside, she started to leave the booth. His hand shot across the table and grabbed her forearm so fast it blurred her vision.

Their gazes locked in a silent battle of wills.

Finally Linc smiled apologetically and said, "No, stay. Please."

JoAnna slowly eased back onto the padded bench. Linc released her arm and followed suit. Pushing his own plate out of the way, he studied her for a moment before saying, "I'm, uh, ready to listen now."

She sipped from her drink to ease the sudden dryness in her mouth and throat, then looked him straight in the eye. "I want to try again. You name the terms."

Maintaining a neutral expression, he asked, "Why?"

"I love you."

Her heart was right there in her eyes for him to see. He wanted to fall on his knees and say a prayer of thanks. He wanted to jump up and let out an ear-shattering yell of happiness, dance around the room and buy drinks for everybody in the bar. He wanted to touch her so badly, his palms and fingers burned. But he had to ask one more question.

"What about JD and the Double R?"

"They still mean a lot to me," she said honestly, "but not half as much as you do." Her chin quivered and her voice dropped to a husky whisper. "Oh, Linc, I've been so miserable. I was wrong, and I'm sorry, and I don't ever want to be without you again. I think that about covers it."

Linc couldn't take the anguished entreaty in her eyes one more second. He reached over and pried her fingers away from the glass she gripped so fiercely. Tugging on her hand until she leaned across the table toward him he met her in the middle and tenderly kissed her lips. "Oh, babe, I've missed you too."

JoAnna pulled back, giving him a misty smile. She closed her eyes a moment later and whispered a heartfelt "Thank God."

He framed her face with his hands. When she looked at him, he confessed, "I was just about ready to come looking for you."

"I was afraid you'd already found someone else. Bobby told me about Miss Debbie."

"Were you jealous?"

"Yup."

"No need to be. She thought I was boring."

"Good."

They sat back and grinned at each other for a while. "What changed your mind, babe?" Linc asked.

Considering his question, JoAnna sipped her gin and tonic. Then she tipped her head to one side and answered, "It was a combination of things. I found out that even when I was in complete charge of the Double R and everything was going fine, I wasn't happy. It didn't mean anything if you weren't there to share it with me."

"What else?" he asked, reaching for her hand.

"Well, I had quite a talk with Gaye and Brady. They pointed out that I was, uh, missing you a lot, and suggested that there were other compromises I could consider. That's really why I called on Thanksgiving. But when Bobby told me about your date, well..."

Linc swore under his breath. "That was one of the rottenest evenings I ever spent! You mean we could have resolved this back then?"

"Maybe. But the final nudge came from my dad." She smiled at the memory. "He called me a sniveling coward."

Linc stiffened at that, giving her a fierce scowl. "He what?"

"Listen, he was on your side," JoAnna protested with a laugh.

As she briefly recounted her discussion with her father, Linc felt a grudging admiration and gratitude growing inside him for JD Roberts.

"He was right, Linc. And so was Gaye," JoAnna concluded. "I was so scared things wouldn't work out between us and so worried about having every little detail in place before committing myself, I lost track of just how much you mean to me. You may have to whack me alongside the head once in a while to remind me not to do that, but I'm going to change, believe me."

"Hey," Linc said with a wry smile, "you weren't the only one who was wrong, you know. I don't think I was really trying to get back at my dad or JD, at least not consciously. But I wanted all of your attention, and I resented it every time you even thought about your dad or the ranch. I didn't want to share you with anybody or anything, and that's not exactly a mature attitude. I won't let my insecurities get the better of me again."

Her heart filled to bursting with happiness, JoAnna leaned across the table and gave him a warm, lingering kiss. Ignoring the interested looks they were getting from the customers nearby, she whispered in his ear, "Wanna go to my room and finish this discussion in private, cowboy?"

The corners of his eyes crinkled, and he chuckled wickedly. "That depends on where you're stayin'. How far is it?"

"Right across the street."

"What are we waitin' for?"

After tossing several bills on to the table, Linc escorted JoAnna through the bar and held her coat for her. They made a dignified exit from the building, then raced across the street like a couple of kids, arriving at her room laughing and out of breath. Once inside, she turned to him, wrapped her arms around his neck and backed him up against the door.

He pulled her to him in a fierce embrace, capturing her eager, parted lips with his own. The tartness of gin and lime lingered on her tongue, but he'd never tasted anything sweeter. Her perfume went to his head more potently than the Scotch he'd been putting away for the last two hours. Her soft, hungry moans made him feel strong as a bull and yet weak in the knees.

At last, he wrenched his mouth away. Gasping for air, he said, "I thought we were supposed to finish our discussion."

JoAnna ran her hands down over his shoulders to the open front of his suit coat. Sliding them inside, she pressed her palms against his thundering heart. She looked up at him with laughing eyes. "Later, O'Grady."

A deep chuckle rumbled out of his throat as he pushed her coat off her shoulders. "I love the way you say that word."

"What word?" she asked, her fingers already busy unbuttoning his shirt.

He unhooked her necklace and shoved it in his pocket, then fumbled with the zipper on the back of her dress. In a second, the dress hit the floor, and she stood before him wearing a lacy black teddy and high heels.

She unbuckled his belt and found the clasp and button at the waistband of his trousers. "What word, Linc?" she asked again, sliding down the zipper.

With a throaty growl, he scooped her up in to his arms and

carried her to the bed. Laying her on the crisp white sheet, he muttered, "Later," and followed her down.

Momentarily satiated, JoAnna rested her head on Linc's shoulder and traced the sculpted lines of his pectoral muscles. He let out a contented sigh, cuddling her closely against his side. She twirled a wiry tuft of hair around the tip of her index finger, tipping her head back to look at his face.

"I've been thinkin', JoAnna," he announced, trapping her tickling fingers against his chest.

"Mmm. Sounds serious," she murmured, dropping a kiss on his collarbone.

Linc rolled onto his side facing her. "I *am* serious. I'm ready to name my terms."

Curling her arm around her head, she gazed lovingly into his eyes. "Fire away."

"I want to stay here in Nashville for Christmas. Just you and me."

"All right."

"I want to get married as soon as possible."

"All right."

He raised a suspicious eyebrow at her. "Don't you want some say in where we're gonna have the wedding and who's gonna come?"

"Nope."

"Why not?"

Propping herself up on one elbow, she cupped the side of his face with her free hand. "Because the only thing that matters is that we're together."

He closed his eyes for a moment. When he opened them again, they were a deep, rich blue and so filled with love and tenderness, JoAnna's breath caught in her chest.

"Okay. Here's my final condition," he said. "After we're married, I want us to live in Powder River for at least a year."

Shaking her head, JoAnna protested, "Linc, you don't have to do that."

"Yes I do, honey."

She started to argue, but he held up his hand to cut her off. JoAnna subsided with a worried frown.

"Much as I hate to admit it," he explained with a reassuring smile for her, "when I think about it logically, it makes a lot of sense for us to live there. I'm not promising we'll stay there forever, but I don't think I'll ever be able to really put the past behind me unless I try it."

"Are you sure?" she asked, not quite daring to believe him yet.

"Yeah. The thing is, I've been intimidated all along by the idea of being around our families. If I was really honest about it, I guess I'd have to admit that deep down, I was more afraid that I couldn't stand up to your dad than I was that you couldn't."

"Shoot, you can handle anything you want to, Linc."

A big grin spread across his face, and he told her what Marty had said about not letting their fathers be anything more than frustrations and irritations.

JoAnna chuckled. "We can always call them old F and I," she said.

Linc threw back his head and laughed. Then he wrapped his arms around JoAnna and rolled them over until he lay on top, bracing his weight with an arm on either side of her. She linked her fingers behind his neck, her eyes shining with joy.

"Well, what's your answer, Roberts?" he demanded with mock gruffness. "Shall we plan a wedding and go home?"

She pulled him down to within kissing distance. "Whenever we're like this, darlin', we *are* home."

Epilogue

Eighteen-month-old Eric Jason Roberts shoveled the last bite of his father's birthday cake into his mouth, then banged his spoon on the high-chair tray. "Mo, Jo!" he demanded.

Holding back a laugh at the determined set to her little half brother's frosting-smeared chin, JoAnna looked at her step-mother. "What do you think?"

Sally brought a damp cloth from the sink of JoAnna's brand new kitchen. "No way, buster," she told Eric firmly, grabbing his sticky right hand.

Twisting his head to escape Sally's scrubbing, the little boy appealed to his father. "Mo, Dad!"

"Aw, Sally," JD coaxed, "one more little piece won't hurt him."

"Yeah, Sal," Sean O'Grady put in with a grin. "Eric's a growin' boy."

Sally put her hands on her hips and, using the same tone she'd used on her son, informed both men, "One more bite of sugar and this kid'll be swinging from the light fixtures."

Hoping to distract Eric's attention, JoAnna struggled to her feet and carried the leftover cake from the table to the work island. Linc passed her with a load of dirty dishes. As he rinsed and stacked them in the dishwasher, he looked over his shoulder and saw JoAnna looking out the bay window at the pond, rubbing the small of her back.

He left the dishes and walked over to her. Putting his arm around her shoulders, he turned her back toward the table. "Come on, honey. You've done enough today. Time to put your feet up."

Sean eyed JoAnna's distended belly for a moment, then nudged JD with his elbow. "Look at how low that baby's ridin'. I'll betcha five bucks she has it tonight."

Shaking his head, JD refused the wager. "I think you're right, Sean."

JoAnna glared at both of them. "Will you two knock it off? I'm not one of your heifers."

Her father and father-in-law exchanged a laughing glance. "Well, shall we go set up that crib?" JD asked Linc.

"It's already up," Linc answered, taking the chair beside JoAnna's.

Freed from the high chair, Eric toddled over to his sister and lifted his chubby arms. "Up, Jo!"

Linc reached down and scooped the little boy on to his lap. "Jo's tired, bud. Will I do for a change?"

Eric nodded vigorously, wrapping his arms around Linc's neck. Sally pulled up a chair and looked around the room with a smile. "You did a great job on this wallpaper," she said, turning to her son-in-law.

"Thanks." He smiled at JoAnna and gave her belly an affectionate pat. "I'm just glad we got moved in before the baby got here."

JoAnna smiled back at him, then sucked in a sharp breath when one of those nagging twinges that had been bothering her since lunchtime traveled from her back around to her navel.

Linc frowned at the funny expression on her face. "What is it?"

She waved his concern aside. "Just another one of those Braxton-Hicks contractions Dr. Shelton told us about."

"Sure?"

Eric leaned over and patted her stomach as Linc had done. "Baby?"

"That's right, honey," she told him, just as another twinge hit her, this one much longer and stronger than the last. When it passed, JoAnna glanced up at Linc with an excited, if somewhat anxious look in her eyes. "That one felt like it meant business," she said, giving him a shaky smile.

Linc handed Eric to Sally and pushed back his chair. "Well, guys," he said to JD and Sean, "it looks like you were right. Time to go to town."

JD and Sean leaped to their feet and stared at JoAnna in consternation for a moment. JD recovered first and charged around the table to his daughter's side. Within seconds, he was barking out orders.

"Sally, call the hospital. Sean, go out and gas up my pickup. It's got better rubber on it than Linc's. Linc, find her suitcase. Oh my God, Jodie, uh, well, you just sit there. Everything'll be all right."

Sally carried Eric with her to the phone. Sean headed for the door. "Jodie'll be more comfortable in my car, JD," he argued.

Linc inhaled a deep breath, then bellowed, "Everybody just hold it a damn minute!"

Everyone froze, looking at him in surprise. JD opened his mouth, but before he could speak, Linc planted himself in front of his father-in-law and poked him in the chest.

"JoAnna is *my* wife. That's *my* baby. And *I'll* take care of them," he said, emphasizing each word with another jab.

Glaring at Linc, JD flushed to the tips of his ears. Linc glared right back until JD sighed and dropped his gaze. When he looked at his son-in-law again, he raised both hands in a placating gesture.

"You're right, son," he admitted. "Sorry I overstepped again." Then he gave Linc a sheepish grin. "But maybe after tonight, you'll understand me a little better."

Linc's fists slowly relaxed. Shaking his head, he clapped a hand on JD's burly shoulder. "You know, Grandpa," he drawled with a reluctant smile, "you could be right about that."

Tension-relieving laughter filled the room, and in a few minutes Linc and JoAnna walked out to their pickup to start the drive to Miles City. JD, Sally, Eric and Sean gathered around the truck for quick goodbye hugs and kisses. Finally, Linc started the engine, and the others stepped out of the way. As he shifted into first gear, the sound of his father's voice came through the open window.

"I'm tellin' you, JD, if it's a boy, they're gonna name him after me."

"Like hell, O'Grady. He'll be Jason Daniel."

JoAnna touched Linc's shoulder, giving him a sympathetic smile. "As soon as the baby's old enough to travel, what do you say we visit Marty and Janice for a few weeks? I think we could both use a little break from old F and I."

Linc shrugged. "Sounds good to me. But would you do me a favor tonight?"

"What's that?"

He took his attention from the road for a moment, his eyes dancing with laughter. "Just do your best to have a girl. Please?"

* * * * *

Stories of love and life, these powerful
novels are tales that you can identify with—
romances with "something special" added
in!

Fall in love with the stories of authors such
as **Nora Roberts, Diana Palmer, Ginna Gray**
and many more of your special favorites—as
well as wonderful new voices!

Special Edition brings you
entertainment for the heart!

SSE-GEN

SILHOUETTE® _Desire_®

Do you want...

Dangerously handsome heroes

Evocative, everlasting love stories

Sizzling and tantalizing sensuality

Incredibly sexy miniseries like **MAN OF THE MONTH**

Red-hot romance

Enticing entertainment that can't be beat!

You'll find all of this, and much *more* each and
every month in **SILHOUETTE DESIRE**. Don't miss these
unforgettable love stories by some of romance's hottest
authors. Silhouette Desire—where your fantasies will
always come true....

DES-GEN

If you've got the time...
We've got the
INTIMATE MOMENTS

Passion. Suspense. Desire. Drama. Enter a world
that's larger than life, where men and women
overcome life's greatest odds for the ultimate prize:
love. Nonstop excitement is closer than you
think...in Silhouette Intimate Moments!

SIM-GEN

Silhouette ROMANCE™

What's a single dad to do when he needs a wife by next Thursday?

Who's a confirmed bachelor to call when he finds a baby on his doorstep?

How does a plain Jane in love with her gorgeous boss get him to notice her?

From classic love stories to romantic comedies to emotional heart tuggers, **Silhouette Romance** offers six irresistible novels every month by some of your favorite authors! Such as...beloved bestsellers **Diana Palmer, Annette Broadrick, Suzanne Carey, Elizabeth August** and **Marie Ferrarella**, to name just a few—and some sure to become favorites!

Fabulous Fathers...Bundles of Joy...Miniseries... Months of blushing brides and convenient weddings... Holiday celebrations... You'll find all this and much more in **Silhouette Romance**—always emotional, always enjoyable, always about love!

SR-GEN